John Esten Cooke

Canolles

The Fortunes of a Partisan of '81

John Esten Cooke

Canolles
The Fortunes of a Partisan of '81

ISBN/EAN: 9783337266929

Printed in Europe, USA, Canada, Australia, Japan

Cover: Foto ©Andreas Hilbeck / pixelio.de

More available books at **www.hansebooks.com**

FORTUNES OF A PARTISAN OF '81

BY JOHN ESTEN COOKE.

DETROIT:

E. B. SMITH & COMPANY.

1877.

CANOLLES:

THE FORTUNES OF A PARTISAN OF '81.

I.

UNDER THE MOON.

On a May evening in the year 1781, just as the sun had disappeared, a man riding a powerful black horse emerged from the great morass known as the "White Oak Swamp" on the right bank of the Chickahominy, in Virginia, and went at a long steady gallop in the direction of James River.

An hour's ride brought him in sight of a large and imposing house. This house, known time out of mind as "Chatsworth," fronted southward toward the river, from which it was separated only by a sloping lawn and a low fence, and a single glance showed that it had once been the residence of a man of great possessions. The facade was long and elegantly decorated, the portico, extending the entire length of the building, was reached by a broad flight of stone steps, and through the trees to the right and rear were seen extensive stables, outhouses and servants' quarters. Over the gateways were armorial devices in stone; the garden fell in terraces, ornamented with edgings of box; the place, it might be seen, had once been splendid. But now all things were going to decay. The sward was overgrown with weeds, the fences were falling, the outhouses and quarters were deserted, and some plaster had fallen from the ceiling of the porch and lay where it fell. Everywhere, in the house, the grounds, the inclosures, were the evidences of poverty and neglect.

The man coming from the White Oak Swamp made a circuit, and halting his horse in a little clump of trees not far from the front of the house, remained for some time looking at it in silence. He was apparently from twenty-five to twenty-eight, rather low in stature, broad-shouldered, and wore a nondescript costume, half that of a civilian, half that of a soldier. There could be little doubt, however, that the latter was his true character. From his holsters protruded a pair of horseman's pistols, and around his waist was buckled a strong leather belt, sustaining a heavy broadsword. His air above all was that of the soldier —cool, resolute and commanding. His face, not unhandsome, but bronzed by sun and wind, had a peculiarly phlegmatic expression—that of a man not likely to be surprised or daunted by anything—but with this phlegm was mingled both pride and melancholy. The motionless figure seemed to suit the scene and the hour. The last flush of sunset had faded in the west; above the tree tops glimmered faintly now a thin crescent moon slowly sailing through diaphanous clouds; the murmur of the great stream came like a lullaby through the deepening gloom, and the walls of Chatsworth looked ghostly in the dim moonlight.

"Well," muttered the horseman, "I have come on an errand which will probably result in nothing; yes, that will be the result. And yet I must hold this interview. I wonder if the fair one will insult me very grossly? Doubtless."

He threw a keen glance around him, as though reconnoitering from habit, and touching his horse with the spur, rode up and dismounted in front of the house. An old horse-rack, leaning from age, stood near, but the man did not tie his horse there. He led the animal to an abandoned outhouse in the rear, where a door stood open, concealed him in the building, and, returning to the front of the house, went up the broad steps and knocked.

A light had just appeared in the apartment to the right, and at the sound made by the falling of the great bronze knocker, a shadow was thrown upon the tarnished lace curtain at one of the windows; the shadow remained stationary for a moment, then it disappeared, then a step was heard in the hall, and a voice said behind the door:

"Who is that?"

"A friend," was the reply of the man.

"What friend?"

"If Miss Talbot will open she will discover," said the man. "An enemy would find little difficulty in forcing an entrance."

There was a short silence. Then, as though the logic of the speaker had produced conviction, the door opened, and the light from the room fell upon the horseman.

"You, sir!" exclaimed the person who had opened
—a young lady—"you here, sir?"

"Myself, madam," said the stranger coolly.

"Your business?"

"To prove myself the friend of Mrs. Talbot and her
nieces."

"Indeed!"

She was about to add something more to this chill
exclamation, but apparently changing her mind turned
her back and swept with a haughty air back into the
room, which was occupied by an elderly lady and a
young girl. The apartment had about it the same air
of past splendor seen in the exterior of the mansion.
The walls were heavily wainscoted in rich paneling,
but the woodwork had warped and shrunk. The cor-
nices were superb, but in many places had fallen.
The marble mantle-piece had cracked from side to side.
The gilding of the portrait frames had nearly disappeared, and the once fine carpet was in rags. Some
old carved-back chairs, an antique center-table on
which burned a single candle in a silver candlestick,
and a rug in holes, were all the furniture.

The elderly lady, who was knitting with tremulous
fingers, wore a frilled cap, a black dress, and a white
handkerchief which passed around her neck was secured by an ancient breastpin in the front. Beyond
these commonplace externals there was nothing to attract in her appearance. The younger persons were
more striking. The one who had admitted the visitor
was about twenty-five—tall, dark-haired, dressed with
what might be called tarnished elegance, but undenia-

bly a beauty. The eyes were dark and penetrating, and the complexion superb; but the fair face was spoiled by an expression of discontent and ill-humor, which had ripened into positive scorn and anger, now as the stranger entered. Her companion was apparently about nineteen, and quite different in appearance; her hair of a rich brown, her eyes blue, her face of a pure oval, and her figure *petite* and slender. Her dress was as simple as her companion's was pretentious, and the bodice, with its long waist and opening at the neck in the fashion called " Marie Stuart," distinctly outlined an exquisitely maidenly figure. In face and form there was an indefinable grace and freshness; the girl had about her that indescribable something sought to be expressed by the word feminine. She seemed made to love and be loved—to confide and be confided in. The brilliant eyes of the elder dazzled and repelled a little — the dove's eyes of the younger drew you. And these opposing characters were seen even in their positions and attitudes. The elder sat with head erect in the full blaze of light, looking coldly straight at the new comer. The younger occupied a low seat nearly in the shadow, near the mantle-piece, her head dropped a little, and she stole from beneath her long lashes a searching glance at the visitor.

He advanced into the centre of the room, bowed, and remained standing.

II.

WHAT TOOK PLACE ON A MAY NIGHT.

The stranger remained thus erect and motionless for some moments, leaning one hand on the center table, and looking thoughtfully around him, especially at the old portraits, whose eyes seemed to fix themselves upon him in the dim light. From this fit of absence he was now aroused abruptly.

"Well, sir?" said the elder young lady, flirting her train around with evident irritation.

The stranger's eyes fell from the portrait, and he looked at her—coolly, but with a lurking expression of satire on his swarthy face.

"You would say, madam, that it is time for me to explain the object of my visit?"

"Yes sir!"

"An unwelcome one, apparently, at least to yourself personally, madam."

"As you please, sir!"

He looked at the young lady with grim interest, and said, coolly:

"My object in visiting Chatsworth this evening, Miss Talbot, is to inform you that this place is no longer safe for unprotected ladies, and to counsel you to leave it."

"You are very good, sir!" was her almost scornful reply, "and where shall we go?"

"To the house of some friend in the upper country."

“ We are unprotected ladies, as you say. How are we to take this journey without an escort?”

She looked straight at him as she spoke, and evidently waited for and anticipated his reply:

“ I am at your service, madam, and that of your aunt and sister, if you desire it.”

The reply came back as suddenly as a blow:

“ I, for one, sir, prefer the tender mercies of the British to placing myself under your protection.”

Again the expression of grim interest came to the stranger’s face; he exhibited no other indication of any feeling whatever.

“ So be it, madam,” he said quietly; “ it is for you to decide in a matter that concerns yourself. The times are troubled. Gen. Phillips is within a few miles of you on his way to Petersburg, and Lord Cornwallis is advancing, and will soon arrive. These gentlemen are gentlemen, but troops are hard to control. The horsemen of Col. Tarleton, especially, are said to be an unruly set. With or without justice they are stigmatized as robbers and marauders; and marauders, permit me to add, madam, are bad visitors for unprotected ladies.”

The elder young lady—who alone took part in the colloquy—had listened to these words with an expression of distain, amounting to insult. At the word marauders however, she suddenly raised her head and fixed a pair of flashing eyes upon the stranger.

“ Marauders, did you say, sir ? Colonel Tarleton a marauder?”

“ His troops at least bear that repute, madam, whether deserved or not.”

"Well, sir," said the lady, with a curl of her beautiful lip, "has it never occurred to you that there are other marauders in this war besides Colonel Tarleton?"

"Doubtless there are such, madam," was the cool reply.

"Persons," continued the lady, flushing with scorn and anger, "persons who are neither Americans nor British, neither friends nor enemies, who prey on all indiscriminately—who, actuated solely by a base love of gold, by a low passion for plunder—"

She paused, panting. All at once the younger sister rose to her feet. Her face, too, was burning and her eyes flashing.

"For shame, sister!" she exclaimed, "to thus return kindness by insult—to meet the offer of friendship with such bitter words, such words as no lady should address to a gentleman!"

The elder turned her head and stared at the speaker with as much astonishment as wrath.

"Indeed, Miss!" she exclaimed with a sort of explosion, "when will you speak again? I am to be lectured and directed in what I am to say by you!"

"I do not lecture you; but you have no right to speak thus. You do not speak for me. You shall know that at least."

Before the astounded elder sister could reply the stranger took three steps forward, raised the hand of the younger to his lips, bowing as he did so, and said in a low voice:

"Thanks, Fanny!"

He then turned to the elder and said, with perfect composure :

"Madam expresses herself so plainly that it is impossible to misunderstand. I at least do not. But I am losing time. My proposition is refused, I see. So be it. I beg to take my leave now, as I have far to ride to-night."

He bowed, exchanged a long look with the younger sister, still erect, flushed and beautiful in her indignation, and slowly left the room. As he disappeared he looked over his shoulder—this time at the old portraits on the wall, especially at that of a very beautiful woman. As he did so, an expression of melancholy tenderness came to his face, and a breath resembling a sigh escaped from his lips.

He went out of the house, walked in the dim light of the crescent moon to the out-building where his horse was concealed, and was about to mount, when the trample of hoofs was heard approaching up the river's bank.

The stranger concealed himself in the outhouse, and looked and listened.

Suddenly a troop of about twenty-five mounted men swarmed into the grounds, and a person evidently in command leaped to the ground, throwing his bridle to one of the men, and knocked at the door. The stranger stole from tree to tree, and had just come in sight of the door, when it was opened, and the light fell on the person who had knocked. He was a young man wearing the uniform of an English lieutenant of cavalry, and a sound like a low scream was heard from the house.

"Do not be alarmed, madam," came in response to the scream, "there is no reason whatever why you should be. I am aware that there are none but ladies here, and only beg that I may rest a moment."

He turned to the troop, ordering "Keep your ranks —let no man stir."

With which words he entered.

The stranger, concealed in the shadow of a large oak, remained motionless for about a minute. Then he seemed to form a sudden resolution. Stealing in the same cautious manner from tree to tree, he gained the rear of the house, silently went to a small porch at the back door, raised a window noiselessly and as silently entered an apartment in rear of that which he had just left.

All his movements had indicated a perfect knowledge of the localities, and he now stole toward the door between the two apartments, through the key-hole of which a long ray entered the dark room.

Placing himself at this key-hole, and alternately applying his eye and his ear, he looked and listened, and what he saw and heard from his place of concealment we shall proceed to describe.

CHAPTER III.

WHAT THE LISTENER OVERHEARD.

The British officer—a young man of about twenty-five, slender, with light hair, a joyous expression, and clad in a rich uniform covered with gold braid—was standing in the middle of the apartment, his plumed hat in his hand.

The ladies had risen and were trembling.

"I beg you will dismiss apprehension of annoyance from myself or my command, madam," he said, in a frank, gay voice, addressing Mrs. Talbot, "and will resume your seats. I am Lieutenant Ferrers, of the British cavalry, and if you have ever heard of me you must have heard that I am not a very dangerous visitor to ladies."

The ladies sat down; the officer remained standing.

"I have the pleasure, I believe, of seeing the family of Colonel Cartaret?"

"No, sir," said the elder of the young ladies, speaking for the rest as in the interview with the stranger.

"Ah, then I was misinformed," returned the smiling young officer. "Is not the name of this estate Chatsworth, the former residence of Colonel Cartaret, who espoused the English side when the present war broke out?"

"Yes, sir," replied the young lady, who had recovered her calmness, and even began to direct the artillery of her beautiful eyes upon the officer, " this is Chatsworth, but——"

" Ah! I understand now. You would say, madam, that you are neither relatives of Col. Cartaret nor sympathizers in his political views."

" We are cousins only."

" And good American sympathizers, doubtless!" came in the same gay tone. " Well, that is natural, and I am far from attributing any fault to you for being such! The fact is unimportant, and I am myself no very savage partisan. Partisan! The word reminds that I am on a little expedition to hunt up one of these same gentry; but now since you are good patriots, ladies, I cannot ask you to assist me."

" To assist you, sir? In what manner?" said the young lady.

" By giving me information. To be plain, madam, I am looking for a certain Capt. Canolles, chief of a band of—well, marauders, I may call them. Can you tell me where I can find this Canolles?" he added, laughing.

Canolles, listening within a few feet of the speaker— for the stranger secreted in the adjoining room was that personage—waited, with a grim smile on his lips, for the young lady's reply. It came promptly.

" He was in this room a quarter of an hour ago."

" In this room?" exclaimed the officer, turning quickly toward the door.

" But it is useless to pursue him. He is miles away by this time."

" He is your friend, perchance?"

" No, indeed!"

" Your enemy ?"

The young lady hesitated. Then she said coldly:

" Everything connected with that person is a subject of perfect indifference to me!"

" Ah! I see, madam. Despite your patriotic views you cannot approve of Capt. Canolles—a mere marauder."

" Who could ? "

" You are right, madam. He is said to fight under no flag, to have no end in view but booty, and even to rob both sides alike."

" That is his reputation."

" A strange character. Who and what is he ?"

" Ask him, sir!" suddenly came from the young sister, and the officer turned quickly, with a smile on his lips.

" Right, right!" he said, " and I hope soon to have an opportunity to address the question to him. To be frank, ladies," he went on in the same gay tone, "Gen. Phillips, in whose command I have the honor of serving, desires particularly to lay his hands on this worthy Canolles. On the General's first expedition up the river one of his sailing vessels was boarded in the night not far from this spot and the crew overpowered before assistance could reach them. Unfortunately the vessel contained a considerable sum to pay off the troops, and this was carried off."

" Doubtless by the person you are in search of," said the tall young lady.

" Yes, madam. The vessel was set on fire, after the crew were turned loose in the boats, and they reported that they had heard the marauder addressed by his men as Capt. Canolles."

Canolles, listening attentively, came near uttering a low laugh.

"A daring affair," the smiling young officer went on, "and perfectly within the rules of honorable warfare, if these men—they are called "Rough Riders," I believe—fought under the American flag. But they had no flag whatever, I am informed. So the General would be extremely glad to have an interview at his headquarters with the Captain."

"In which laudable desire you aim to gratify him, sir!" came from the smiling lips of the elder of the young ladies, who continued to reply to the officer. She had not ceased to direct toward him the same flashing glances—brilliant, provoking, far from hostile—and it was easy to see that the young Briton was more and more struck by her beauty.

"Allow me to admire your penetration, madam!" he went on in his former tone. "The General ardently longs to see this same Canolles, and even has another motive. He is on his way from Brandon to Petersburg—has some more money under convoy—and we naturally have a nervous apprehension that the worthy Canolles will attempt to lay his hands on that also, since booty is his game and the main chance of his object in warfare."

Canolles, looking and listening through the keyhole, lost, suddenly, his expression of grim enjoyment, and bent close, with an ardent light in his eyes. The conversation had evidently assumed a new and far stronger attraction for him.

"There is no danger, I trust," said the lady, "of another such robbery. Gen. Phillips is then on his way to Petersburg? There was such a rumor."

"Oh, it is no secret, madam, and I may inform you of the fact without scruple. Perhaps I was less justifiable in speaking of the gold which the general convoys with him. That was somewhat imprudent."

"Imprudent, sir?"

The officer laughed.

"You may give information of the fact to General Lafayette, who is not far distant, or—"

The officer paused, again laughing.

"Or some one may be concealed here—listening. In that room, for instance."

He pointed to the room in the rear.

"Oh, if that is your only fear, sir, you are at liberty to satisfy yourself."

The officer took two steps toward the door. Canolles, bending close, did not move; but he quietly stole his hand to the hilt of his broadsword.

"Have I your permission to look, madam?" said the young officer. "Pardon me, but war is an unceremonious trade."

"You are perfectly at liberty, sir, although that room has long been unused, and the door, I think, is locked."

"Do you give me your word that no one is concealed there?"

"My word of honor, sir."

2

'The officer came back.

"That is enough, madam. I should be ungallant, indeed, to doubt an assurance issuing from such lips."

A glance of unmistakable admiration accompanied these words, and the person to whom they were addressed bashfully cast down her eyes.

"I may add," said Lieut. Ferrers, "that even if what I have said came to Gen. Lafayette's ears it would prove of no advantage to him. The convoy is strongly guarded, moves with the army, and it would prove utterly impossible to capture it, even if the attempt were made by a *corps d'armee*."

The young officer bowed, put on his hat and added:

"I now beg to take my leave, ladies. The boats in which I crossed will be in danger if I do not return by daylight. I propose to scout toward the swamp in which our Capt. Canolles makes his den, I am informed; and as he moves, it is said, by night on his marches, I may succeed in having an interview with him. Believe me, that another interview—that which I have had the pleasure to hold this evening already—has been highly agreeable"—the look of admiration was repeated—"and I shall always think of Chatsworth with pleasure. Excellent Col. Cartaret! I had the honor to know him—a perfect gentleman, acting from sincere convictions, and dead now in exile. That is sad, but war is always a sad affair. He had a son, he told me, in the American army; he spoke of him with great tenderness. But I must take my leave, ladies. I have not asked you to inform me where I should find our Capt. Canolles, nor what his errand here was this evening. If good fortune serves me I shall cross swords with him to-night."

The young lieutenant then bowed, went out of the room, and was heard ordering " attention!" Then his sabre clanked against the stirrup as he mounted.

He had scarcely left the apartment when Canolles, holding up his long broadsword carefully to avoid being heard, noiselessly retired, passed through the window in the rear, and stealing toward the outhouse in which his horse awaited him, leaned against a tree trunk and saw the British troopers slowly defiling out of the grounds, the dusky figures dimly visible in the faint light of the crescent moon.

When they had disappeared he mounted his black horse, leaped the low fence in rear of the house and set off swiftly in the direction of White Oak Swamp.

CHAPER IV.

IN THE WHITE OAK SWAMP.

"White Oak Swamp" is a great morass extending from a point northeast of Richmond, along the western bank of the Chickahominy to the boundary of Charles City, and nearly to the banks of James River. It is a strange weird tract—the home of the venomous moccasin, and the melancholy whippoorwill, whose cry comes from the far depths like that of some mysterious guardian of the swamp. All here is solemn and depressing. The almost impenetrable thickets bar all advance. The ground is slimy and treacherous. You place your feet upon a prostrate log, and it suddenly turns. You attempt to pass an open space apparently of greensward, and you sink to your waist or your horse to his girth. Tangled vines festoon the trees, from which you are saluted by the unearthly laughter of the owl—tall flags wave their broad blades above the ooze, from which comes the threatening hiss of reptiles. Sad and sorrowful by day, this swamp is strange and menacing at night. To move through it even by day is difficult, to penetrate it by night an utter impossibility, unless to a person familiar with every foot of the path over which he advances.

Canolles reached the edge of the dreary tract, riding at a long gallop, and disappeared in its depths. The moon gave scarcely any light, but he seemed to make his way steadily and surely, picking his path without hesitation, and guided, it seemed, by the north star glittering through the tangled foliage overhead.

He went on thus for about half an hour. Then he emerged on an open space, beyond which a dull-looking entrance of slimy water stretched. He crossed the space, reached the dull expanse, and at a peculiar cry stopped and repeated it. A third cry came; he at once plunged into the water, and in a few moments reached a sort of island of considerable extent, where a group of about twenty men of the most outlandish appearance were gathered around a blaze. In the background were seen a number of half subterranean huts, built of boughs plastered with mud. Near these huts were tethered to the stunted trees as many horses as there were men.

Canolles made a sign to a person who seemed second in command, and, retiring with him, held a rapid consultation. The two then returned, and at a low order from Canolles the men hastened to their horses and mounted. This manœuvre was effected so rapidly that in two minutes the troop was in line; and placing himself at the head of the column, Canolles led the way back over the route by which he had come.

Defiling slowly and silently through the swamp—a band of phantoms apparently in the dim light—the Rough Riders at last reached firm ground; and then, at an order from their captain, who led the way, set forward in an easterly direction at a swift gallop. The hoof strokes of the horses made no noise in the sandy road, and no word was uttered by any one in the troop. In an hour a faint glimmer in front indicated that they

were approaching the banks of the river, and at a movement of the hand from Canolles the men halted.

Canolles then went forward alone, his horse walking
slowly.   He was following the road moving from a well-
known ferry to Chatsworth, and soon discovered that his
calculations were correct.   Lieut. Ferrers must have
landed at this point; and there before Canolles, as he
cautiously drew near the bank, were the large flatboats
in which the British troopers had been ferried across.
A brief reconnoissance showed that only a few men had
been left to guard the boats, and returning silently to
his command, Canolles ordered them to move forward.

In five minutes the few men at the boats had been
captured, and the boats were in possession of the partisan,
who ordered his troops to dismount and embark with
their horses. This was rapidly done—the prisoners
were also placed on board—and the boats then moved
silently from shore, breasting the broad current which
shone in the dim light of the setting moon.

The chances seemed to be that Lieut. Ferrers would
not enjoy his desired interview on this night with Capt.
Canolles, who having the choice presented to him of
crossing sabres on the north bank of James River with
the young Englishman, or going in pursuit of the treasure under convoy of the British troops on the south
bank, unhesitatingly made choice of the latter.

In a few moments the boats, crowded with the dusky
figures of men and horses, were lost in the darkness.
Then the splash of the paddles slowly died away in the
distance, and finally no sound disturbed the silence but
the subdued murmur of the great stream singing its
low song in the calm spring night.

CHAPTER V.

FERRERS ROUSES THE WRONG GAME.

The boats containing Canolles and his horsemen had just disappeared in the darkness, through which glimmered the faint light of the setting moon, when quick shots were heard in the distance above Chatsworth, on the banks of the river; the sound drew nearer; then came shouts, the clash of sabres, the trample of hoofs, and suddenly the shore swarmed with the troops of Lieut. Ferrers, with a force of American cavalry close upon their heels.

The aim of the British troops was evidently to gain their boats. Seeing that they had disappeared the men lost hope, called aloud for quarter, and in spite of every attempt made by Lieut. Ferrers, threw down their arms.

At this spectacle, Ferrers uttered a volley of expletives, and driving his horse with the spur violently through the chaotic mass huddled on the bank, crossed sabres with the leader of the Americans, coming on with long leaps of his horse in front of his men. He was a young man of about twenty-three, and bore the most astonishing resemblance to Canolles, except that his face was fresher and more youthful and his expression gay and impulsive. He wore the uniform of an American lieutenant of cavalry, was plainly an excellent horseman, and meeting Ferrers full tilt crossed sabres, and a hand-to-hand fight ensued. How it would have ended it is difficult to say, as they seemed equally matched. A third person decided the result. This was an American trooper, who seized Ferrers from behind, dragged him from the saddle, and in an instant the young Englishman was beneath the trampling hoofs of the horses, exposed to imminent peril of his life. So great indeed was this peril, that, brave as the young man was, he closed his eyes, when he suddenly felt an arm around him, and he was lifted to his feet. He opened his eyes, looked at the person who had thus rescued him from being trampled to death, and saw that it was the young American officer.

Then this quick dialogue ensued:

"You are in command of this force, sir?" said the American.

"Yes," returned Ferrers.

"Surrender, then. You are overpowered. It is not your fault, for my force is double your own: Order your men to surrender, sir!"

"Surrender! cursed word!" exclaimed the young Englishman with a rueful laugh. But he gave the order, and then shaking himself as though to recover from his stunning, added:

"You are Capt. Canolles?"

"Canolles? No."

"Who then? Your name and rank, that I may at least know whose prisoner I am."

"My name is Henry Cartaret, and I am Lieutenant of the Virginia Light Horse."

"Henry Cartaret!" exclaimed the young Englishman.

"Yes."

" Cartaret, of Chatsworth."

" Once," was the rather sad reply.

" The son of Col. Henry Cartaret, who left Virginia at the beginning of the war?"

" He was my father."

Ferrers seized the young American by the hand and shook it heartily.

" So you are really Harry Cartaret, of whom I have heard your father speak? I knew him well and loved him as much as I respected him, which was a great deal. Glad to make your acquaintance, Harry!—though never was such a devilish introduction!"

The gay youngster rubbed his shoulder, which had been bruised in his fall, and added with his light laugh, which seemed to defy trouble:

" Who would have dreamed of my falling into such a trap to-night!—first the bad luck of meeting a force double my own, and then my boats gone! Who under heaven could have extracted them? I'd have made a stand and got off, my dear Cartaret, but for this cursed ill luck! Well, well, it is the fortune of war. Some good fellow of your party now in our hands will be benefited when I'm exchanged. Then I'll be after you, perhaps, and catch you napping—patience, and shuffle the cards?"

The two young fellows laughed like schoolboys, and half an hour afterward Lieut. Harry Cartaret and Lieut. Tom Ferrers were riding along amicably towards Gen. Lafayette's headquarters, followed by the American troops in charge of the prisoners.

As they passed Chatsworth Ferrers said, with the laugh which nothing seemed able to suppress:

"You were not concealed there to-night?"

"Concealed?"

"Yes, in that room in the rear?"

"What room?"

"And they gave you no warning—did not put you on my track?"

"Who? I had no warning. I met your force by pure accident as I was returning from a scout."

"Oh! well, then, the devil's in it. I am the victim of bad luck, and against bad luck no fellow can fight? But I'm glad they did not betray me—especially that tall one—she's a beauty."

"The tall one?"

"I mean the taller of the two young ladies at Chatsworth."

"Oh! Eleanor Talbot?"

"Do you know her?"

"She is my cousin."

"Well, my dear Harry, you see I knew your father, who liked me too, and I feel like a friend of the family, which makes me unceremonious—well, all I have to say is that you've a devilish handsome cousin!"

"You have seen her?"

"I called this evening, in pursuit of a certain Canolles. By the by, who is Canolles? The ladies seemed acquainted with him."

The laughing face of Harry Cartaret grew sad.

"He is a person about whom there are many and conflicting reports," he said.

" Very well. But suppose we come across him to-night?"

" Come across him ? "

" Yes."

" What then ?"

" He may attack you."

" Attack me ? "

" Why not? He is said to make war on his own responsibility—to fight against both sides and to have no flag but his own."

Cartaret gravely shook his head and replied :

" He will not attack me."

" Are you certain of that ? "

" Perfectly certain."

" And why should he not ? "

" I may tell you some day—I cannot tell you now."

" Oh, pardon me, my dear fellow. I'm afraid I've been indiscreet."

" No indiscretion at all, believe me," returned Cartaret.

" And so I am not to be rescued ! " laughed Ferrers. " I see I must give up all hopes of that dramatic scene ! Think what a farce it would be ! I cross the river to beat up the quarters of the worthy Canolles—you and I meet each other—you take me prisoner—but before you can reach headquarters with your valuable capture, presto ! change ! Canolles appears upon the scene, and rescues from your clutches the very person who came to hunt him ! Ha ! ha ! "

Cartaret laughed in reply, and the young men rode

on side by side in gay talk, with the air rather of old
friends than chance acquaintances.

Meanwhile Canolles crossed the river, formed his
men in column, and was silently advancing through the
darkness toward the camp of Gen. Phillips, on the Petersburg road.   His information was thorough and minute.   A cocked pistol and the promise of a heavy sum
in gold had acted upon one of the men captured with
the boats.   Canolles knew where to find a wagon containing ten thousand pounds sterling, and seemed to
have made up his mind to have it in spite of Gen.
Phillips and his whole army.

CHAPTER VI.

THE SPRING OF 1781.

At the opening of our narrative the curtain had just risen on the great fifth act of the Revolutionary drama.

Beginning at Concord six years before, the war had steadily drifted southward. The thunder of cannon had rolled on from Boston to Long Island, then to the banks of the Delaware, then to the environs of Philadelphia, then to the Carolinas, and now Lord Cornwallis, after marching and counter-marching, advancing and retreating, through the swamps and rice fields, was coming to open the last campaign of the war on the soil of the Old Dominion.

Virginia had been spared in a great measure the ravages of war in her own dominion, but now the heavy hand was to fall upon her in her turn. The conflict on her soil had opened with January, 1781, when Arnold, with about one thousand men, chiefly royalists brought from the north, advanced to Richmond, burned a part of the place, laid waste the surrounding region, and then, hotly pressed by the brave Gen. Nelson, in command of the Virginia militia, had retreated to Portsmouth, where he awaited further orders from his British employers.

His orders came in April, but the British officers, who regarded him with ill-concealed disdain, were spared the mortification of again marching under him as their

commander. Gen. William Phillips was assigned to
lead the English column, which now ascended James
River toward Petersburg. The force sailed up the
river, landed at City Point, at the mouth of the Appomattox, pushed forward to Petersburg, and the place
was attacked and fell into the hands of the British in
spite of hot resistance from the Americans under
Baron Steuben.

Then opened on the party of James River a brief
and animated episode of the war. Arnold was sent to
Osbornes, a village on the river, where he attacked and
destroyed a small American fleet, burning and capturing two thousand hogsheads of tobacco, then a species
of currency. Meanwhile Phillips, whom Arnold
hastened to join, advanced northward to Manchester,
opposite Richmond; attempted to cross; discovered
that Lafayette had arrived on the day before and was
ready to fight him; retired; descended the right bank
of the river to Bermuda Hundred, burning on his way
the thriving town of Warwick, a larger place than
Richmond and an important post, and embarked again
for Portsmouth.

It was on this expedition that an American prisoner
is said to have made his historic response to Gen.
Arnold.

"If the Americans should catch me," asked Arnold,
"what would they do with me?"

"They would bury with military honors the leg
which was wounded at Saratoga," replied the prisoner,
"and hang the remainder of you on a gibbet."

Before reaching Portsmouth, Gen. Phillips was met

by a boat bringing him orders to retrace his steps—Lord Cornwallis was on his march and would form a junction with him at Petersburg.

This was on May the 6th. Three days afterwards, that is to say on May the 9th, Gen. Phillips had re-ascended James River, reached Brandon on the southern shore, landed his troops there, and was rapidly advancing to again seize upon Petersburg, where Lord Cornwallis was daily, almost hourly, expected.

It was now a race between Phillips and Lafayette which should first reach the place. The brave young Frenchman had been assigned by Washington to the command of the American forces in Virginia—had made a forced march of 200 miles to reach Richmond; arrived in time to protect the place, and rightly supposing that the reappearance of Phillips in the upper waters of James River meant Petersburg and the junction with Lord Cornwallis, hastened toward the threatened point to occupy the town and prevent the union there of the English armies.

This brief and rapid summary of the state of things toward the middle of May, 1781, will inform the reader of the surroundings of the various personages of this narrative: Lord Cornwallis advancing steadily from the south in the direction of Petersburg, Gen. Phillips pushing on from Brandon to form a junction with him, and General the Marquis Lafayette hurrying from Richmond as fast as he could drag his cannon in the direction of Petersburg to occupy the town, and with his right hand stretched toward Cornwallis and his left toward Phillips, hold them asunder.

We return now to our narrative, which aims to present rather a series of pictures and portraits than to record historic events.

This was the situation of the pieces on the great chess-board of war when the gay young Englishman, Lieut. Ferrers, crossed James River near " Chatsworth " to scout along the northern bank in the direction of White Oak Swamp, with the object which we have heard him state, and when the worthy Capt. Canolles, chief of Rough Riders, and fighting under no flag but his own, overheard the object which his enemies had in view, declined the challenge, and seizing the boats in which Ferrers had crossed, went on a far more business-like errand to the south bank—which errand, as the reader must have surmised, was to beat up the quarters of Gen. Phillips, and seize upon his ten thousand pounds sterling.

CHAPTER VII.

CANOLLES REAPPEARS.

It was the morning of the 10th of May, 1781—the day after the scene just described.

The long harsh thunder of cannon shook the hills on which the town of Petersburg stood; and the brilliant sunshine flashed back from burnished gun-barrels, bayonets and scarlet uniforms swarming on the wide plateau on the outskirts of the eastern suburb of " Blandford," which, with " Pocahontas " on the north bank, formed the village, town or borough of Petersburg.

Gen. Phillips had distanced his adversary. Knowing how much depended upon the occupation of Petersburg, the English commander had not lost a moment on the march, had pushed forward from Brandon as soon as his troops landed, and late at night had entered Petersburg, just as the vanguard of Lafayette was approaching the spot from the northward.

With the dawn came the roar of cannon. Lafayette had posted his artillery on Archer's Hill, an eminence on the north bank of the river, opposite the town; opened on the English camps in the direction of Blandford, and hour after hour the long roar of the American cannon continued, to which the British guns replied.

Let us now follow the fortunes of one of the chief

personages of this history, whose fate it was to become better acquainted with the English commander than he probably desired to be.

"Bollingbrook" was the handsome, broad-winged, low-pitched mansion of the wealthy McBolling, crowning one of the Blandford hills. In the main apartment of this house, a room of considerable size and furnished with the utmost taste and even luxury, a man of middle age, clad in the undress uniform of a British Major-General, was lying upon a couch, and breathing heavily. Every detail of the personal appearance of this individual indicated pride, and a haughty and unbending disposition. It was not an unattractive face, otherwise; and plainly that of a man of birth and breeding. Thomas Jefferson wrote of him that he was "the proudest man of the proudest nation on earth," and his impression certainly did not belie his character. This was Major-General William Phillips, commander of the English forces in Virginia.

He was plainly the victim of a bilious fever. His face was flushed, his breath came in gasps, and when the rush of the American shell was heard passing over the house, he muttered in hoarse and labored accents:

"Why won't they let me die in peace?"

Opposite the couch sat a tall officer apparently above sixty. His appearance was striking. His face was of a uniform red, and his hair and mustache—he wore no beard or whiskers—was snow-white. His commanding stature, curt and unceremonious bearing, and nonchalant tone of voice, best described by the word grunt, stamped him as a peculiar individual. You might see that Col. Lord Ferrers—for that was the officer's name—cared for nothing or nobody, was a sort of high-bred Diogenes, of a cynical turn, not without a dash of humor, and was an intimate friend of the British commander, for they addressed each other in the most informal manner.

Phillips breathed heavily, and from time to time turned restlessly on his couch.

"Why did I ever come to this wretched country, Ferrers?" he groaned. "I am burnt up with fever contracted in the marshes around that hole, Portsmouth! My pulse seems on fire! I have a presentiment that I shall die of this attack."

"Nonsense!" grunted Lord Ferrers; "but you are right about the country. Never was such a damnable region on the face of the globe!"

"And then to have that man Arnold for my second in command!" continued Phillips, feverishly.

"Cursed traitor! Sold his country—or tried to—for ten thousand pounds—the *canaille!*" returned Ferrers.

"And this *canaille,* as you rightly call him, will be your commander when I die."

"Hope you won't die, Phillips! Arnold command me! I would rather have the devil himself over me."

The English commander breathed heavily.

"And then this last and crowning enemy!—to have my money chest a second time seized under my very nose by this bandit Canolles—the very man who boarded my tender and robbed me before. Was there ever such an insolent or successful affair? Lucky I have one satisfaction. The leader of the gang—Canolles himself—is in my hands, and he shall hang or have a bullet through him before to-morrow."

"Right—highwaymen take the risks—Canolles fights under no flag, I'm told. What were the particulars? I was in the advance, and have heard none of the details."

" I will tell you what took place in a very few words. I had halted the troops within a mile or two of this place—the vanguard having entered and taken possession, as you know—when the detachment guarding the baggage wagon was attacked while asleep in bivouac, the men cut down as they sprang to arms, and the money chest carried off before the alarm was given to the rest of the army. A more daring affair I never heard of; and the leader of the gang—Rough Riders they call themselves—must have proceeded on sure information, obtained I know not how or where."

" Ask him, as you have hold of this same leader. How was he caught ? "

" While fighting with desperation. The money was first hurried off—unluckily it was in a number of small sacks, gold and Bank of England notes—and then Canolles faced about with a part of his command, made charge after charge to cover his retreat—his men all got off—and their leader would no doubt have been as successful, but his horse was shot under him, fell, and before he could extricate his feet from the stirrups in which his spurs had become entangled, he was seized and made prisoner."

" A brave fellow, at least."

"A robber! A common thief! Fighting under no flag!"

"Well, that's ugly—devilish ugly!" grunted Ferrers, "and the rascal must hang, I suppose. The money is clean gone, eh?"

"Every penny! The marauders vanished like so many phantoms in the darkness."

"They were pursued?"

"Of course—and the detachment sent in pursuit came up with them, or rather in sight of them, as they crossed the river."

"You mean the Appomattox?"

"Yes. There was just light enough from the stars to see them swimming their horses in the middle of the stream. They landed near Bermuda Hundred, and no doubt found some means to cross James River to White Oak Swamp, where this Virginia swamp fox kennels with his booty."

"Well," said Ferrers, "of all the cursed, devilish, unlucky *contretemps* that I ever heard of, this is the most diabolical. I was going to send to the paymaster this very morning for my pay—not a penny in my purse—and here all the gold is gone! It is necessary to hang that man, Phillips! No, don't hang him. He's a brave scoundrel. Shoot him like a soldier. Never be harsh on a game highwayman like that!"

"I will consider. First, however, for an interview. I must know, or endeavor to discover, where he obtained his information in regard to the convoy."

"I should like to hear. The fact is, the affair is interesting. This Canolles must be a desperado, indeed, to attack the whole British army with a handful of men. I owe him a personal spite for carrying off my pay, but ——"

"To say nothing of the pay of the troops—they are already grumbling. But I'll have him here before detailing the squad to shoot him."

Gen. Phillips summoned an orderly and directed that Canolles should be brought to headquarters. He then turned to Col. Ferrers, and said:

"By the by, where is your nephew? Was he not sent to scout along the north bank of the James!"

"Yes, to hunt up this same Canolles. They must have crossed each other—while he was after Canolles, Canolles was after us!"

A low laugh curled the white mustache of Ferrers. It was easy to see that his indignation at being robbed of his pay was tempered by grim admiration of the pluck of the robber.

For some moments the artillery fire had begun to slacken, and it now died into silence.

"What is the meaning of that?" said the General, whose feverish face became more and more flushed.

"Our friends yonder seem tired, or their ammunition has given out."

"Summon a staff officer and let us ascertain, Ferrers."

He was saved the trouble. An officer entered at the moment and announced that a flag of truce had just crossed the river in a boat, and that in the boat he had recognized young Lieutenant Ferrers.

"The devil you did!" exclaimed Lord Ferrers.

"So the rascal Tom has been caught, eh? Serves him right."

"Meet the flag," said Gen. Phillips, "and ascertain its object. Do not stand on technical forms—there's nothing to conceal here. Bring the flag to head-quarters. Some courtesy of Lafayette is under this, and no one shall say that William Phillips allowed himself to be surpassed even by a Marquis."

The officer saluted and left the room. At the same moment an orderly entered, touched his hat, and said:

"Here is the prisoner you sent for, General."

"Canolles?"

"Yes, sir."

"Bring him in; let the guard remain outside."

A moment afterwards Canolles was ushered into the apartment.

CHAPTER VIII.

THE EXAMINATION.

Canolles entered with a firm tread, his frame erect, and his whole bearing indicating no emotion whatever.

"The rascal's a soldier, at all events!" muttered Ferrers; "he must have nerve to look like that with a rope around his neck."

Gen. Phillips, with lowering brows, his face growing more and more feverish, said in a husky voice:

"You are the person who attacked my convoy last night?"

"Yes," said Canolles.

"Your name is Canolles?"

"Yes."

"You are an American officer?"

"I might tell you that I am—I should tell a falsehood. I am not."

"You are not an American officer, sir, and do not fight under the American flag?"

"I do not."

"Under what flag then do you fight, in Heaven's name?"

"Under my own."

Gen. Phillips knit his brows, and fixed his eyes sternly upon the cool face—eyes burning with fierce and growing wrath, but not destitute of an expression of respect for the prisoner's courage.

"I need not inform you, sir," he said coldly, "that the words you have just uttered are your own death-warrant."

Canolles slightly inclined his head.

"I know that perfectly well, General."

"And still you have uttered them?"

"Yes. I might say that I fight under the Virginia flag—here it is"—he drew from his breast a small square of silk, on which was painted the Virgin of the Virginia shield, "but such a plea, I am aware, would be absurd in your eyes, since England makes war on the American States, not on the State of Virginia."

"*Diable!*" uttered Ferrers, "a cool hand, if there ever was one!"

And seeing that Gen. Phillips was too faint or too indignant to continue the interrogatory, he said:

"Let me question the prisoner, General—I am really anxious to ascertain his views and theory in making war on his Majesty."

Canolles shook his head.

"I regret not to be able to enlighten you on that point, Colonel."

"You decline to clear up the mystery, then?"

"Yes."

"Humph?" grunted Lord Ferrers, "that's queer. You must have an object."

"I have."

"Which you will die without accomplishing."

"No; it will be accomplished."

"Hey! accomplished? My friend, you are jesting."

"I am in earnest."

Col. Ferrers suddenly rose in his chair, and said:

"That gold you carried off accomplishes, then, your object in making your private war?"

"Precisely, Colonel."

Ferrers turned to Phillips and said:

"General, you hear! Of all the mysteries that ever were heard of!—but there is something under this that I'd like to fathom!"

"Conduct the examination as you think best," said Phillips, breathing heavily, "I am really too ill to take any part in it."

"Very well—and so, my friend," said Ferrers to Canolles, "you have your own ends in view. You have declared war on Great Britain on your private account. This, to say the least, is irregular in a military point of view—and yet you persist in concealing your motive. Why not fight under the Continental flag?"

"I am not a soldier of that army."

"And that is not your flag?"

"I have said that it was not."

"You decline further explanation?"

"Yes, Colonel."

"Then there's no more to say, and I regret to inform you, my friend, that there can be but one course to pursue in your case."

Canolles again inclined his head.

"You regard me as a common highwayman, Colonel," he said; "so be it—I have at least the heart of a soldier, and I speak to a soldier. Your bullets do not frighten me."

"Good—spoken like a man. Gold or no gold—pay or no pay—at least you shall not hang if I can prevent it, but die the death of the cool fellow you are."

A third time Canolles slightly moved his head. His color had never blanched, and his eye retained its steady and unmoved expression.

"A last word," said Lord Ferrers, "as to a matter rather of curious interest than of any importance. You must have obtained the most accurate and reliable information as to the wagon containing the gold last night. Now, curiosity is one of my foibles. I have said that you should die a soldier's not a highwayman's death if I, George Ferrers, have a say in the matter. Well, relieve my curiosity. Who gave you your information in regard to the money chest?"

Canolles looked fixedly at him.

"You are Col. Lord Ferrers?"

"Yes; why do you ask?"

"A relative of Lieut. Ferrers, who was scouting on the north bank of the James River last night?"

"His uncle. But what has all this to do with the attack you made on the convoy and the seizure of the gold, which, I assure you, was a devilish disagreeable occurrence as far as I am concerned, inasmuch as I am therefore deprived of my pay."

A grim smile touched the face of Canolles—these two cool personages, accustomed to laugh under all perils, seemed to understand each other, and might have been suspected of being father and son.

"I ask if you are related to Lieut. Ferrers, for a single reason," said Canolles.

" Why ? "

" The person who gave me the information of the convoy was Lieut. Ferrers."

As Canolles uttered these words the door opened and Lieut. Ferrers entered the apartment.

CHAPTER IX.

THE LIKENESS.

Col. Ferrers, losing sight for the moment of the singular statement of Canolles, greeted his nephew with a satirical laugh and a grunt.

"So you were caught, were you, my young popinjay?" he said. "How did that come about, and what brings you back so soon?"

But Lieut. Ferrers seemed scarcely to hear the words. He was looking with an expression of the utmost astonishment at Canolles.

"Who is this, uncle?" he said.

"The prisoner?"

"Yes."

"Well, this is the gentleman whom you expected in the innocence of your youthful and confiding disposition to catch napping last night in the direction of White Oak Swamp!"

The young man replied by a bewildered look which evidently excited the elder's amusement.

"You went out to shear, and came back shorn, it seems, Monsieur, my nephew, as they say in delightful, devilish Paris! You went to capture Canolles, and were captured yourself."

"And this person—?"

"Is Canolles in person."

"Canolles?"

"The very man, though you seem to doubt it."

"Impossible!"

"Why is it impossible?"

"Capt. Canolles is, or has the reputation of being, a common plunderer. And this man—good Heavens! What an astonishing likeness!"

"A likeness of whom?"

"Of Lieut. Henry Cartaret, who captured me, a son of Col. Henry Cartaret."

"Of my friend Henry Cartaret, of 'Chatsworth?'"

"The very same."

"Humph! That's a queer idea. Henry Cartaret was the soul of honor—his son in the American army must be the same. What has either of them to do with the worthy Capt. Canolles, freebooter?"

"I cannot tell you. But I can assure you that the two men might be taken for each other, though the expression of face is not the same."

"Strange enough! How is that, my friend?" he said to Canolles.

"How reply to an absurdity, Colonel, or account for a mere coincidence?" said the person addressed.

"The voice! It is the very same!" exclaimed Lieut. Ferrers.

Here Gen. Phillips, who seemed suffering greatly, said in a painful voice:

"Pardon me, Colonel, but this interview is too much for my strength. Allow me to abridge it. Lieut. Ferrers will be good enough to report briefly the circumstances of his capture."

The young man saluted, and said:

"I am ashamed to have to inform you, General, that my failure in the expedition I undertook was complete, and, worse still, that my company were either cut down or captured to a man. Permit me to add, in simple justice to myself, that this was the result of bad fortune, rather than of any fault on my part. I crossed James River, as I was directed, left a guard at the boats, stopped for a brief space to obtain information at a house where I was expected to find friends, and had not gone half a dozen miles beyond, moving with extreme caution, when a force at least double my own of American cavalry came in on my rear. I at once wheeled my column and charged them, but found that the force was too heavy to promise much. I therefore cut through toward the boats, pursued by the enemy, and arrived only to find that they had been carried off."

"Aha!" said Lord Ferrers, suddenly glancing at Canolles, "I think I understand who laid hands on your boats. A gentleman of the name of Canolles, or I'm mistaken. Eh, friend?"

Canolles bowed.

"Yes, Colonel. It was I who captured the boats of Lieut. Ferrers."

"Very well; but let us hear the rest. Gen. Phillips is unwell."

"The Americans were commanded by Lieut. Cartaret. I was compelled to surrender and was conducted to Gen. Lafayette's headquarters, who, ascertaining who I was, very readily allowed me to attempt an exchange and even to accompany the flag of truce, which is without in charge of the gentlemen of your staff, General."

"I have no American officer of your rank, Lieutenant. I might exchange this prisoner Canolles for you, but he is not an American officer, and Gen. Lafayette would not accept him. He is even said to attack both sides. You will therefore return with the flag of truce and convey to the gentlemen composing it the purport of my reply. Now, for the rest. Col. Ferrers, you will be good enough to assemble a drumhead court-martial in one hour from this time to try the prisoner here under charges as a spy and marauder, unprotected by the American flag. I do not insist that he shall be hanged—and he is evidently no common robber. If found guilty under the charges, a detail will be made for his execution by shooting. The man is a soldier at least, and shall have a soldier's death."

"Thanks, General," said Canolles.

A movement of the hand indicated that Gen. Phillips wished to be left alone, and the persons present went toward the door.

As Lord Ferrers passed Canolles he said:

"There is one thing that puzzles me still, my worthy friend. You stated—it is a singular statement—that my nephew, Tom Ferrers, gave you information of that convoy."

"Yes," said Canolles.

"I!" exclaimed young Ferrers, who overheard the words.

"Unconsciously, no doubt, sir," said Canolles, with his immovable coolness. "You, no doubt, recall your visit last night to Chatsworth!"

"Certainly, Captain."

"I was near you."

"Near me!"

"In the adjoining room."

Young Ferrers looked deeply mortified, exclaiming:

"And the ladies knew as much?"

"No."

"They were ignorant of your presence?"

"Entirely."

"The eldest, especially? I mean Miss Eleanor Talbot?"

"She was no more aware of the fact than the rest."

"And you overheard——"

"All you said. Let it be a lesson to you, Lieutenant, not to whisper military secrets. Birds of the air may carry the matter, and"—the old grim smile came back—"some desperado or swamp fox like myself may be lurking within earshot of you."

The young man looked earnestly at him.

"Are you really a desperado—a mere plunderer?"

"Do not all men tell you so?" returned Canolles.

"Yes, but—was there ever such a likeness?"

"You would say——"

"To Harry Cartaret, as perfect a gentleman as I ever knew!"

Canolles listened with an impenetrable expression and made no reply.

"I cannot conceive it possible," Ferrers added, "that a man with your face could be a mere bandit, as you are styled. Were you really such, I should hate you for that likeness!"

Canolles looked fixedly at the speaker and said coolly:

"Do not hate a man, Lieutenant, who, in twelve hours, or sooner, will be a corpse. That saddens you, I see—you have a loyal face and a loyal heart, I am sure—but death does not frighten me. When it comes, I will face it unmoved."

Canolles saluted, and was reconducted to prison by the guard, and Tom Ferrers returned with a heavy heart, and a vague sentiment that the supposed marauder was not what he seemed, to the American head-quarters.

An hour afterwards the American cannonade recommenced, and again the crash of shell was heard as they tore through the houses of Blandford.

Bollingbrook finally became so dangerously exposed in the range of the fire that Gen. Phillips, in whose veins the fever burned more and more fiercely, was urged to take refuge in the basement story of the house. He reluctantly consented, and was assisted down the stairs by some of his staff.

As a cannon shot passed, whizzing by the window, he again muttered:

"Why won't they let me die in peace?"

CHAPTER X.

LAFAYETTE AND HIS MINIATURE.

It was the evening of the day on which the scene just described had taken place, and the sun, about to set, threw long shadows over the banks of the Appomattox and the slow moving current.

A handsome marquee, to employ the term then applied to the tents used by superior officers, stood on a knoll not far from the American batteries, which had ceased firing, and the surroundings of the marquee indicated that it was occupied by the commanding officer of the Americans. A finely caparisoned horse was tethered to a bough near, and champed his bit and pawed the ground impatiently; an orderly walked to and fro in front of the tent; and from its summit floated a long streamer.

The light of sunset, plunging through the opening of the tent, fell upon a camp couch covered with a colored blanket, on which lay a fine cocked hat decorated with gold lace, a pair of riding gauntlets reaching nearly to the elbow, and a richly ornamented sword; also on two or three camp stools, and a table containing pen, ink and paper.

The marquee had only one occupant. He was a boyish-looking individual, apparently about twenty-three years of age, with a bright and animated face, brilliant eyes, a long, straight and prominent nose, and a lofty forehead, retreating somewhat, but clearly indicative both of intellect and resolution. He wore the Continental uniform, with heavy buff facings, epaulets, a stiff standing collar and a voluminous white cravat and ruffles; his hair was tied behind with a ribbon; and on his left breast was a decoration—a Maltese cross suspended by a ribbon.

For the moment the officer seemed to have quite lost sight of all his surroundings—to even be unconscious where he was—and his whole attention was plainly given to an object which he held in his hand, and was gazing at with absorbing attention.

This object was a small medallion of gold, set with diamonds, and contained an exquisitely painted miniature. The miniature represented a young girl scarcely "out of her teens," and the face was one of extraordinary beauty and sweetness. The hair was carried back from the white temple in the fashion called *la Pompadour*, adopted at the court of Marie Antoinette, and the beautiful shoulders emerged from a cloud. The head was bent sideways, and looked at you with a winning smile—it was a little duchess of the ancient regime making love to some one with her *beaux yeux*, and her dimples and roses.

Lafayette—for the young officer was Marie Paul Joseph Roche Yves Gilbert Mathias de Lafayette, Marquis and Major-General in the American army— remained motionless, gazing at the picture, and his gay face assumed an expression of exquisite tenderness. He pressed the miniature to his lips, and murmured, "*Chere Anastasie!*"

Then the gallant-looking young fellow burst into a laugh.

"*Horreur!*" he exclaimed, "a man kissing his spouse's picture, and breaking out into exclamations—the exclamations of a garcon sighing with his first love! How absurd! But no—is it so absurd to love one's wife?—and one might pass a quarter of an hour worse than in thinking of Anastasie de Nooilas de la Lafayette where she sleeps yonder across the sea!"

He fell into a fit of musing.

"Is it not strange," he murmured, "that I should be here, and Madame la Marquisé there? But no, it is better!—a name in history is better than the softest arms, I think! And then—to have known his Excellency and been trusted by him—that is better still, is it not, Anastasie?" he said, addressing the picture with a smile on his lips; "better than to hold even you in one's embrace and hear your musical voice."

He pressed his lips once more to the medallion, which seemed to smile at him, replaced it in his breast, where it was secured by a delicate steel chain passed around his neck, and with a sigh turned toward the table on which lay the papers.

He had scarcely begun to peruse the official looking documents which he opened, and in whose bold clear handwriting any one familiar with it might have recognized the writing of Gen. Washington, when the rapid gallop of a horse was heard approaching the marquee, a cavalier with jingling spurs and clattering sabre was heard dismounting, and a strong, bluff voice exclaimed:

" This is Gen. Lafayette's marquee ? "

" Yes, sir," replied the orderly.

" Tell him that his friend Mad Anthony Wayne has come to see him ! "

" Who, sir ? "

" Mad Anthony Wayne ! "

·The orderly was still in a maze at this odd announcement, when he was pushed aside, Lafayette hastened out of the tent, and hurrying with beaming eyes toward the visitor, exclaimed :

" Welcome! Welcome, my dear *Monsieur L'Insense!* The hour is happy that brings you. Come! Come!"

And opening his arms he caught to his breast the soldierly figure of a man clad in the uniform of a Major-General, covered with dust, and glowing with a pleasure apparently equal to that displayed by his host.

CHAPTER XI.

"MAD ANTHONY."

Major-General Anthony Wayne, universally known in the army as "Mad Anthony" for his reckless courage and unfailing gayety, was about thirty-five years of age, tall, vigorous, and with something dashing, off-hand and attractive in every movement of his person and every tone of his voice. When he walked he seemed to move on steel springs; when he spoke he laughed, gesticulated, and never kept still. You could see that this was a strong, tough, headlong military machine, of which the mainsprings were gayety and courage.

"Welcome! welcome!" repeated Lafayette drawing him into his tent. "What news from his Excellency?"

"He is coming—if not now, a little later—and then, my dear Lafayette, look out for thunder!"

"He was well?"

"As strong as iron."

"Heaven be thanked. Do you know, my friend, there is no one, and never was, like his Excellency?"

"Know it? Yes, I know it—both the man and the soldier!" cried Wayne. "You remember what I told him at Stony Point?"

"You said—"

"I said to Washington, 'I'll storm hell, General, if you'll only plan it.'"

"Mad Anthony!—no, brave Anthony! I do not

recall that; but stay!—I recall another thing. In the attack you were shot down and fell on your knees— when you exclaimed 'March on!—carry me into the fort!—for I will die at the head of my column!'"

"My very words!—and you would have said the same, I'll make oath!"

Mad Anthony thereupon threw his hat upon the table and said:

"My command is moving toward the Rappahannock to reinforce you—I left them and rode a hundred miles to confer with you—no mere despatches for me when I can talk face to face! I'll tell you everything, but at present I could eat a wolf—with sour krout sauce like that used in my native country, Pennsylvania."

"Pardon!" exclaimed Lafayette. "My poor head! Why did I forget?"

He gave orders to a servant, the table was promptly spread, and Major-General Wayne devoured everything before him—after which he drew a long breath of satisfaction.

"Now to talk!" he said.

An animated conversation ensued between the friends, relating to the anticipated advance of Cornwallis, the junction between himself and Gen. Phillips, and the probable result of the campaign, of which Wayne seemed to have no doubt. It was a striking spectacle, the interview between these two brave and joyous young soldiers, thoroughly devoted to the cause, never doubting how the great struggle would terminate, and resolved to stake all that they possessed, including life itself, on the ultimate achievement by the American colonies of their national independence.

At last the eyes of Wayne began to drowse; he yawned, then laughed, then yawned again, and, declaring that he must sleep, if only for an hour, lay down on Lafayette's camp couch, and in a few moments was sound asleep.

Scarcely had the long breathing of the bluff soldier indicated that he had entered the land of slumber when a voice was heard without asking for Gen. Lafayette, an officer entered the tent, and Lafayette rising and holding out his hand said, cordially:

" Ah! it is you, my brave Cartaret!"

" Myself, General, and I have come to make an earnest request which I trust you will not refuse me," returned the young lieutenant in a voice of deep emotion.

Lafayette looked intently at Cartaret. He was exceedingly pale, and the deepest sorrow was stamped upon the bloodless cheeks. It was evident that something had occurred to move the young man to the very depths of his being; and as plain, from his erect carriage and resolute bearing, that he had made up his mind to pursue some course which involved peril and required the nerve of a soldier.

" A request," said Lafayette, losing his smiles. "Need I tell you, my dear Cartaret, that I shall grant it if it is possible?"

" You can do so, General."

" Tell me how."

"You sent a flag of truce to-day to the English camp."

"Yes," said Lafayette; "ostensibly to procure an exchange of the young Lieut. Ferrers—really to slacken my cannon fire and husband my ammunition without leading the enemy to suppose that my supply was small."

Cartaret saluted.

"The exchange was not effected, as you know, General."

"It was not effected."

"There were no American officers in the enemy's hands."

"None."

"Except—the officer called Canolles?"

Lafayette shook his head.

"He is not an officer—not even an American soldier. He has no flag—is a plunderer—even plunders us, it is said. An exchange of Lieut. Ferrers for him is impossible, dear Cartaret."

The young man allowed his head to droop upon his breast. His brows were knit, and he preserved for some moments a gloomy silence.

"Yes, yes," he said at length. "I ought to have known that—and I know it—yes! It is useless to speak of such an exchange, General. And yet——"

He stopped, his face glowing, his eyes full of earnest emotion.

Lafayette looked at him fixedly, and it was easy to see that his look was one of strong sympathy and some curiosity.

“ You would say, Lieutenant —— ”

Cartaret did not reply.

“ Speak ! ” said Lafayette.   “ You speak to a friend
as well as to your commander.   What moves you ?
What have you to do with this person Canolles, and
what request have you to make ? ”

“ I have much to do with him,” said Cartaret, in a
low voice.

“ You know him ? ”

“ Well.”

“ And —— ”

“ I have come to tell you plainly why it is not possible for me to reflect calmly that at daylight, probably
to-morrow, the person of whom we are speaking will
die, and to beg, if necessary to entreat, that you will
grant me permission to take a detachment from my
company—men on whom I can count —— ”

“ A detachment !—with what object, Lieutenant ? ”

“ To enter the English lines, cut my way through
whatever I find in my path, and rescue him ! ”

“ Rescue him !   Rescue whom ? ”

“ Canolles,” replied Cartaret.

CHAPTER XII.

FANNY TALBOT.

The sun was about to set on the same evening—that which witnessed the interview between Gen. Wayne and the Marquis de Lafayette. Fanny Talbot, the younger of the sisters presented to the reader at Chatsworth, was walking in the grassy grounds attached to the mansion, along the banks of the river.

The evening was perfectly still. The broad stream, flowing with a musical murmur under the wide boughs of drooping trees, was dotted here and there with the white triangular sails of the little barks of fishermen living on its banks; and this low, sweet murmur seemed to be the lullaby of some fairy Undine of the river, dreamingly saluting with her song the gold of sunset, the stars which began to twinkle in the orange sky, and the rising moon. From the tender grass peeped up myriads of flowers, the sweet, shy children of the spring; the songs of birds were faintly heard as they sank to rest, and a light breeze passed like an almost imperceptible whisper through the delicate May leaves. It was the hour for dreams—for musing on the past or the future—and Fanny Talbot seemed to follow idly those dreams or recollections which make up so much of the pleasures or the pains of human life.

There was something fascinating in the appearance of this young and gracious creature as she wandered slowly along the grassy slope in the quiet evening; in every movement of her person might be discerned the indefinable charm of youth, freshness, and the sweet dawn of emotion slowly broadening into the fuller day. There was even another and more secret charm about her, impossible to describe—that singular attraction of some human beings which escapes analysis, but reveals its presence, like some delicate and exquisite perfume, that sways all hearts, and is a thousand times more powerful in its influence than mere physical beauty.

This subtle charm accompanied **Fanny Talbot** wherever she moved. Just on the threshold of womanhood —the spring bud opening slowly into the summer flower—she seemed to be looking forward to the full development of her being with timid emotion and surprise. But a single glance at the young face showed that her nature was not weak—on the contrary, that her character was strong and resolute. She was, indeed, all woman in her organization—both timid and firm, both pliable and unbending. Under the shy manner you could see this force of character, and felt that if the moment came this girl would be capable of opposing her will with unfaltering nerve to any obstacle in her path. Of her life during the period preceding the moment when she is presented to the reader, we shall say a few words only, leaving the full development of the circumstances shaping her character and laying the foundation of her after fate to future pages of this narrative. She was the daughter of a very distant cousin of Henry Cartaret, of Chatsworth, and on the death of her parents, which occurred during her childhood, had been taken home to

Chatsworth with her elder sister Eleanor, where she had grown to girlhood under the fostering care of the excellent gentleman at the head of this large establishment. As Mr. Cartaret was himself a widower, he had also offered a home in his house to Mrs. Talbot, an aunt of the two girls, one of those estimable old ladies of whom there is little to say except that they are neutral in everything, gliding through life like highly respectable lay figures on wheels—persons in whom you can never find the least fault—whom you respect, and most justly, for the absence in them of bad qualities, and who are entirely uninteresting.

Fanny grew up in the kind, home atmosphere at Chatsworth, and naturally formed an attachment for the playmate who most frequently shared her rambles in search of wild flowers and birds' nests—her cousin, Henry Cartaret. When she was still very young the youth one day quite startled her by the most unexpected of proposals—namely, that she should marry him as soon as he attained his majority. Fanny received this proposition with the air of a startled fawn, colored and promptly refused him. This ill success had a marked effect on the youth. He had been full of the gayest spirits, prone to laugh at everything, to sing snatches of song from pure light-heartedness as he walked or rode, or lolled on the portico, but when Fanny refused him all this disappeared. He became deeply melancholy and lost all his smiles. He seemed to have no power to bear up against his misfortune; and this indeed was the weak place in a character otherwise admirable. Henry Cartaret was kindly, sweet-tempered, of the highest and nicest sense of honor, but he wanted what is called in rough but expressive metaphor "backbone." Everybody loved him, and felt an impulse to—protect him. Now, when the world feels like protecting a man it does not watch his eye for the indication of his will; and Fanny Talbot, following her sure woman's instinct, knew that her playmate was not the person she should marry. Nevertheless, his deep melancholy had its effect. A woman is always a woman, that is to say, unhappiness in others makes her unhappy, and the instinct of her heart is to remove this unhappiness if she can. So Fanny began to sigh as she pondered in her chamber or her solitary walks; to think with pity of poor Harry, who was breaking his heart about her and never smiled now. One day they met in a glade of the woods, about twilight, whither each had gone unknown to the other, and when they returned to Chatsworth, at nightfall, Fanny had yielded to his suit, and promised to marry him.

She had yielded from compassion, not from love, and reflection told her as much. The result was that she, in turn, fell into melancholy. Many times she nearly made up her mind to go to him and tell him that she had mistaken her feelings, and rashly promised what she ought not to perform. But it was impossible. The young man was in the seventh heaven of happiness, and then her word was plighted—plighted! The girl's sense of honor was extremely high. She had given her word—her honor was involved—she must keep her word, not forfeit **her honor, and marry one** whom she now felt she did **not love!**

This account of Fanny and her fortunes in the years preceding the opening of our narrative must suffice for the present. When events took place resulting in the disappearance of Henry Cartaret, **Esq.,** from Chatsworth, the two young ladies and Mrs. Talbot remained at the old homestead with a few aged servants, and in time Henry Cartaret went into the army, where **his** gayety and the courage of his blood made him a favorite. He became lieutenant, enjoyed his life and his grade, and through his days and hours **ran,** like a thread of gold, the thought that Fanny would marry him as soon as the war was over. Such were the relations between the two young **persons** in the month of May, **1781.**

Was this all about Fanny? The reader is probably too experienced a peruser of the works of the **respectable** composers of fiction who swarm in all the **fields of** modern literature **to** suppose any such thing. **The** writer **of** these pages scarcely merits any credit for frankness when he states that there was much more in the life, as in the character, **of Fanny** Talbot than is here recorded. What the romance of her young life was, and whither the current of events was to sweep her—this for the present must **be a** secret known only to her historian. The dramatic interest of his narra**tive, if** it possess **any** interest, demands that he should await the proper moment for recording many additional particulars in relation to Fanny and other **personages;** and **let** us not forget, what seems about to **be** forgotten **at** the present time, **that** this dramatic interest is **a** legitimate and most important element of compositions aiming to delineate the fortunes as well as the characters of men and women. When not forgotten it is denied, and we are told that metaphysical analysis and subtle apothegm are the true material with which the best fiction should be built. Is that so certain? Do not Shakespeare, Fielding, Scott and all the masters tell us stories? The story is the canvas meant to catch the mind and bear along the vessel; in the hold you may stow away, if you choose, the wealth of Ophir and Golconda. So, may it please the gentle reader, as was said in the good old times, this narrative relates the fortunes of Canolles and some other people, aiming to tell not only what manner of human beings they were, but what befell them.

5

CHAPTER XIII.

FANNY AND ELEANOR.

Fanny was still strolling along the banks of the river when she heard a step behind her, and turning her head saw Eleanor.

Miss Eleanor Talbot had never been a person of happy disposition, never good-natured, and more than all, never under any circumstances contented. Undeniably beautiful, and endowed it would appear with the gift of giving those who gazed at her pleasure, she was rarely pleased herself, and, indeed, passed her life in complaining of the "stupid" hours she was forced to pass in the unutterably stupid shades of Chatsworth. Without a taste for reading—that blessed resource of a life spent in retirement—without a fondness for the little home pursuits—petting flowers, the deft use of the needle, music, or other simple and innocent methods of passing her time, Eleanor Talbot found her life drag on, not dance as it should have danced at twenty; and if her heart could have been opened and read, the mainspring of that rather cold machine would have been found to be a persistent longing for wealth, ease, fine dresses, society and admiration. Wanting these, all else was insipid to her—the gold of sunset, the songs of birds, the flow of the quiet river, and all the fairy sounds blown on the winds of May, which month of months had indeed for her no greater charm than the russet and chill November. In a word, Miss Eleanor Talbot was poor and wanted to be rich; unknown and wanted to be pointed at and admired. She vegetated at Chatsworth, that stupid, *stupid* place, and there, beyond, was the great delightful world, where everybody would burn incense, she was sure, before the shrine of her beauty—entitled, she was persuaded, in her inmost being, to have a shrine and incense.

There were some particulars in the past life of this handsome young lady which were a little curious, as we shall show in due time. At present, let us speak of her interview on this evening with Fanny.

She seemed unusually dissatisfied and out of temper —indeed, so much so that the beautiful face had lost all its beauty and grown sour.

"Here you are dawdling, dawdling, dawdling, moping, moping, moping," she said. "For Heaven's sake, stop!"

"I was not moping, Eleanor," said Fanny, quietly. She seemed quite accustomed to her sister's tone.

"Oh! well, I suppose that you mean to say that you enjoy this sort of thing," replied the elder, waving her hand in a decidedly disdainful fashion by way of indicating the surrounding landscape. "For my part, I would just as lieve be a fish and live in water, there— rather."

Fanny made no reply—a circumstance which seemed to excite more ill-humor than ever in her companion. A little irony and disdain were plain in her voice now as she went on. She smiled—it was not a very pleasant smile—and said:

"No doubt your ladyship is far more happily constituted than myself. You enjoy what is stupid, and are satisfied with what is commonplace—from the possession of more intelligence and simpler tastes than other people!"

It was plain that Miss Eleanor Talbot was in one of those amiable moods peculiar to certain persons, when to vent their feelings is a sort of necessity—to "squabble" the greatest of enjoyments. Fanny looked at her quietly as before, and said:

"You know very well, Eleanor, that I claim no superiority to any one in intelligence or taste—I wish you would not taunt me in this manner, and find fault with me on every occasion."

There was a little irritation in her tone as she ended, but it was very slight. Her companion greeted it, slight as it was, with evident pleasure.

"So I am not the only person with a temper!" she exclaimed. "Even the perfect Miss Fanny Talbot has her little weakness in the same direction!"

"I am not out of temper."

"It marvelously resembles it."

"Well, if I am, you make me so, Eleanor. I do not know what it is in you that annoys me when I feel least like being annoyed."

"Indeed, madam! So I am a virago?"

"No, but you worry people. If I were you I would not do so."

Miss Eleanor Talbot made her companion a little mock ironical courtesy.

"Advice from your ladyship is highly valued. I shall attempt to follow it, and—let me see—in what particular should I strive to correct my unhappy disposition? I am fault-finding, dissatisfied, ill-humored—is that all?"

Fanny made no reply.

"And no doubt all these amiable traits were displayed, according to your ladyship's opinion, in the interview last night with that hero of romance, Mr. Canolles."

Fanny fixed her eyes calmly upon her sister, and said:

"Yes, I think they were."

"Oh, indeed!!!"

Three exclamation points alone can convey an adequate idea of the tone of these words.

"You were unjust to him, and I wonder how you could bring yourself to speak so to one with whom—well, to him—in tones so violent—to employ no stronger word."

It was evident that the long-enduring Fanny was becoming irritated for some reason, in her turn. Her face flushed a little and her head rose almost haughtily.

"Oh! indeed! I am violent, to employ no stronger word, am I! Then, Madame the Duchess, to employ the stronger word. Because I spoke plainly to a common robber—a notorious plunderer—I was 'violent!'"

Fanny lost patience and exclaimed:

" Yes, and unlady-like, if you wish me to use the
other word I referred to."

The younger had become nearly as much out of temper now as the elder—the reader must decide upon the
relative demerit attached to each in this highly discreditable proceeding. At the word "unlady-like"
Miss Eleanor Talbot felt, to judge from her expression
of countenance, a strong desire to "box" her companion; but, gentle as Fanny looked on ordinary occasions, there was that now in her face and carriage of
person which did not encourage the idea that she would
submit to such an indignity very quietly. Had you
seen her one hour before, you would have said that the
result would have been an outburst of tears. Looking
at her now, that theory appeared very doubtful indeed.

Miss Eleanor, relinquishing if she had conceived the
design of personal assault, had recourse to the sharper
female weapon.

" Oh, very well, madam ! Very well, indeed ! So I
am a violent, ill-natured, fault-finding, unlady-like ter-
magant ! I am a coarse, wrangling, insulting, ill-bred
and generally objectionable creature ! I am the black
sheep of the household, while Mademoiselle is the meek
and snow-white lamb ! I am only fit to be taunted and
outraged to my very face, and all because I am not
quite as warm an admirer, to employ no stronger word,
as Mademoiselle is, of a low marauder—a person no
better than a thief."

These words evidently broke down Fanny's remainder of self-control. The barrier gave way and the
waters rushed.

"You should be ashamed, Eleanor!—ashamed, I say! Remember—but it is useless to remonstrate with you! I begin to think that there is something heartless in you!"

"At least I am not love-sick, and while engaged to one—"

"Stop!" exclaimed Fanny; "if you drive me too far I will tell you some unwelcome truths."

"Tell them!" was the angry reply.

"No, I will not—let us part from each other. You irritate me beyond expression!"

"Very well, madam; just as you please. But as we have had the pleasure to speak of the honorable Mr. Canolles, I will inform you of what a servant has just reported, that he was captured by the British last night while endeavoring to break into a money chest, and is probably by this time hanging by the neck, as the American flag does not protect such people as himself."

Fanny Talbot turned her head quickly, and all the color faded from her cheeks.

"Is this true?"

"Oh! I see the intelligence is not very agreeable. Yes, it is true. The men who escaped report it."

"Captured?"

"Yes."

"In the hands of the enemy?"

"I do not know," said Miss Eleanor, with a mocking laugh, "whether he is precisely in the hands of the enemy, as you doubtless understand the phrase, or not. He has probably had his neck encircled by a halter long before this."

Fanny turned suddenly. It was wonderful to see what fire flashed from her eyes.

"Do you know what I meant when I said that I would tell you some unwholesome truths if you goaded me further?" she said passionately.

Eleanor actually quailed before the young girl's eyes.

"I meant that it is not a very graceful thing for a lady to speak as you have done both to and of a person whom she would have given her hand to if he would have accepted it!"

Miss Eleanor actually panted with rage, but Fanny went on before she could speak:

"You dare not deny it! You know it to be the truth! You know that your hatred of a gentleman—yes! I say a gentleman—who has never offended you, springs from your bitter resentment at his not responding to your advances, and for this alone. For no other reason—for no wrong he has ever done you—you taunt and insult him when he comes to offer us a friendly service—you speak to him as no lady has the right to speak to any one—and last, worst, *hatefulest* of all, you revel in enjoyment of the thought that he has died a disgraceful death, with a halter around his neck, as a common criminal!"

Miss Eleanor shook with anger, and exclaimed:

"I will make you repent this!"

"You do not frighten me," was the defiant reply, "and you cannot be more ill-natured than you always have been!"

Tears suddenly came to Fanny's eyes. She was evidently thinking of the terrible news.

"Oh, me! it cannot be true. I must——Oh, me!"

She walked hurriedly away. When she had gone a few paces she turned and said to her sister in a low, hopeless tone:

"I am sorry I spoke to you as I did. I did not mean to—you goad me until all that is bad in me is excited, and I say what I regret. What you said of my feeling for him is not true. I do not say that you know it to be untrue. But oh! how could you, Eleanor! how could you at such a moment?—it was cruel, cruel! But I will say nothing more. Captured! dead, perhaps!"

With heaving bosom, and sobs which she could not suppress, Fanny Talbot walked away, her sister standing still and looking after her, and in a few minutes she was lost sight of in the dense foliage of the woods, the gentle May winds whispering in her troubled ears.

CHAPTER XIV.

THE COURAGE OF A GIRL.

" Miss Fanny ! "

The voice came from a clump of bushes within a few feet of the young lady, and she started and turned her head.

" It is only me—Walter," said the voice; and a boy about sixteen pushed aside the boughs and emerged into the open space near the young lady. He was a bright-eyed, gallant-looking young fellow, with a spry and alert bearing, a lithe and active figure, and wore a nondescript dress; around his waist was a leathern belt containing a single pistol.

The boy was the son of a poor schoolmaster of the vicinity named Hayfield, who had recently died—one of those plain, respectable characters formerly having charge of what were called " Old Field Schools " — and was well known to all at Chatsworth. Lured by his love of adventure, Walter Hayfield had, on finding himself an orphan, joined the company of Canolles, and was almost the sole person in the rough band to whom the latter gave his confidence. In return, the youth had conceived for Canolles an enthusiastic admiration and affection; and of the confidential relations existing between them the interview which now took place furnished ample evidence.

" You frightened me," said Fanny, " and I think my

nerves were already shaken. Oh! tell me—tell me all —you know what I mean."

"About the fight and the captain's capture, you mean, Miss Fanny?"

"Yes, yes—is it true?"

The boy shook his head sadly.

"It is true, Miss Fanny. We attacked the British baggage train and had a hard fight. All got off but the captain and myself."

"You?"

"I was captured, too, but escaped in the dark afterwards. I determined to escape at all risks, to do what the captain told me to do."

"What was that, Walter?"

The boy took from an inner pocket of his coat a sealed package.

"The Captain gave me this a week ago. He seemed to have an idea that something unlucky was about to happen to him. In case he was either killed or captured—which he said would amount to the same—I was to deliver this paper to you, Miss Fanny."

Fanny took the paper, opened it, and the boy could see that her hand trembled a little.

Several sheets of paper were covered with writing in a firm, distinct hand, and the young lady ran through them with nervous rapidity. As she read, her face grew alternately red and pale. It was wonderful to see the variety of expressions which chased each other over her countenance as she read. At one time a deep blush covered her cheeks, and her heart throbbed with what seemed to be a delicious confusion, even with a sort of delight. Then a proud light shone in her beautiful eyes, and she murmured some words which her companion could not hear. Then her cheeks suddenly became colorless, and an expression of acute pain contracted her lips, which trembled visibly, and tears ran down her cheeks.

"Ah! it was like him—like him!" she exclaimed, hastily refolding the letter and placing it in her bosom; "and I understand now why he was so anxious for me to have this if any misfortune happened to him! Ah! thank you, thank you, Walter? I would not have failed to receive this letter for worlds—it was so good in you!"

As though mastered by nervous emotions she walked along rapidly, the boy following her, toward the river. Her eyes were fixed on a point toward the west, in the direction of Petersburg.

"Oh! can nothing be done?" she exclaimed. "Can nothing be done to save him? I do not believe that they would be so cruel. Eleanor said it to make me suffer—"

She turned quickly and said:

"Walter!"

"Miss Fanny!"

"Do you believe that—that he is dead?"

The boy, who seemed to have caught some of his companion's emotion, replied:

"They would not shoot him without trying him first, and there has hardly been time for that—the fight was last night."

"But—think!—they fear and hate him! Oh! this terrible thing of fighting without a flag!"

"Bad enough, Miss Fanny; and I have over and over begged the Captain to have one, but he would not."

"Oh! if something could be done! If something could be done! Gen. Phillips is the English commander at Petersburg, is he not?"

"Yes, Miss Fanny."

"What is his character?"

"They say he is a man of high temper, but a gentleman and a man of honor."

"Do they say that?"

"Yes."

The young lady walked on nervously, flushing and trembling.

"Walter," she suddenly said, "do you love Captain Canolles?"

"You know how much, Miss Fanny!"

"Do you care for me?"

"You know I do."

"Will you help me to save him?"

"The Captain?"

"Yes."

"I would go the end of the world and do anything to save him."

"Then tell me how I can get to Petersburg—this very night. I must go—and now; there is not a moment to lose, if it is not already too late!"

The boy looked with deep surprise at his companion, and said:

"You go to Petersburg, Miss Fanny, and to-night! Are you in earnest?"

" Yes, yes—I am in earnest. I have resolved, and whether you help me or not I will go."

The boy shook his head.

" How can you?"

" You must find the means, and go with me. It is this that I meant when I said you must help me. Think! think! Walter! Do not fail me now."

He was mastered by her excitement and began to reflect—his face as flushed as her own.

" It is a desperate attempt, Miss Fanny," he said at length, " but it is not impossible."

" Ah, I knew you would think of a plan. You are as intelligent as you are brave! What is it?"

Thus appealed to, Walter said:

" It is this, Miss Fanny—but where could you go— to what house, even if we reached Petersburg?"

" Do not trouble yourself about that, Walter. I have a dear friend who will be too glad to see me. What is your plan? Make haste. Time is passing—passing!"

The boy at once proceeded to inform the young lady of his plan. This was to cross the river in a boat, procure horses, which he felt sure he would be able to do, and then he and the young lady would set out straight for Petersburg, ride into the British lines if possible unseen, and if they could not enter the town without capture, submit to that. They would represent themselves as residents of the place, recently on a visit to friends in the country, and if this was not sufficient, as a last resource they could inform their captors that they had important information to convey to Gen. Phillips—which would ultimately ensure the interview which the young lady desired with the British General.

"For that is what you wish, is it not, Miss Fanny?" said the youth.

"Yes, yes! and you may say with a clear conscience that I have important information. This here—in this paper!" She placed her hand upon her breast. "Yes, I must see Gen. Phillips at once. And now, Walter, when shall we go?"

Everything was promptly arranged. Fanny was to return to the house, put on the wrapping made necessary by the cool night, and, stealing undiscovered from the house, meet the boy at a spot agreed upon on the river's bank, where he would have the boat in waiting. They would then set out without further delay on their expedition.

Half an hour afterward Fanny, who had hastened back to Chatsworth, stole away, her figure muffled in a cloak and hood, from the mansion; hastened by paths well known to her through the moonlit woods and open fields, and reached the point on the river bank which they had fixed upon. Walter was awaiting her in a small row-boat half hidden beneath the boughs of a large oak, and assisted her into the little craft, which rose and fell upon the surges gleaming in the moonlight.

At the last moment he said:

"Miss Fanny, I am afraid this is a wild affair, and I do not know that I ought to help you to expose yourself to the danger of a night ride through a country which is occupied by the British."

"I must risk the danger, even if it were greater."

"Think—"

"No, Walter, do not let us think, or if we think of anything let it be of the death that is hanging over—one you love. We must not think. There are times, Walter, when desperate expedients must be resorted to. I must do what is in my power to-night, or I should be miserable to the day of my death. Come, come, do not delay. Every moment is precious!"

Her passionate words overcame all the youth's scruples. Taking the oars, he sent the boat with one long, vigorous sweep into the current, and in ten minutes it had disappeared like a waning shadow in the moonlit night.

CHAPTER XV.

THE COURT-MARTIAL.

Our narrative has been obliged to pass from camp to camp—to return, as it were, on its steps, and to relate what occurred in different places nearly at the same moment.

All the scenes described in the pages immediately preceding took place on the afternoon of the 10th of May. One other scene on the same day and almost at the same hour is still necessary to an intelligent comprehension of the events which befell the personages of the drama.

Nearly at the instant when Henry Cartaret requested the Marquis de Lafayette to authorize his night attack for the rescue of Canolles, and when Fanny, with flushed cheeks and heaving bosom, was reading the paper brought to her by Walter, a court-martial consisting of six officers, presided over by the seventh, had assembled in a tent pitched on one of the Blandford hills, near the old church of that name, and in the immediate vicinity of Gen. Phillips' headquarters.

The marquee had no furniture but a common pine table, a few chairs and a camp couch. On the latter was seated, in a careless attitude, Col. Lord Ferrers, the Judge-Advocate.

From time to time Col. Ferrers looked with ill-concealed distaste, even with covert hostility, at the presiding officer of the court-martial, who wore the uniform of a brigadier-general. He was a man of middle age, with a hawk nose, glittering and wary eyes, firm lips, and a defiant expression, such as may be seen on the faces of men conscious that all around them are unfriendly. A slight limp, observable when he moved, seemed to indicate that one of his legs was a false one. His entire personal appearance was striking, but not very pleasant. Such, to the outward eye, was Gen. Benedict Arnold, the unshrinking soldier, but the political Judas of America.

His connection with the court-martial assembled to try Canolles—for that was the object of the court— was of his own choice, and may be explained in a very few words. The wagon containing the gold carried off by the partisans had been under charge of Arnold's division, holding the rear. The disappearance of the treasure, reflecting as it did upon Arnold, had excited his wrath to the utmost, and having met Col. Ferrers, and learned from him that Canolles was to be court-martialed immediately, he had volunteered to preside over the court. To this Col. Ferrers had demurred, saying that it was unprecedented for a general officer to take part in the trial of so obscure a person. But Arnold had insisted, Ferrers had been obliged to yield, and when the court assembled, Gen. Arnold appeared as the presiding officer.

He sat now at the head of a camp table, stiff, cold and unbending. On his dark face seemed written in letters of fire the consciousness that the British officers around him in their inmost hearts despised him.

He raised a paper from the table, and said in a hard and metallic voice:

"Gentlemen of the Board, you will please answer to your names."

The list was then read, beginning with the name of Col. Ferrers, Judge-Advocate, and each man replied "Present" when his name was pronounced.

"You are aware, gentlemen," Arnold then said, "that this Board is assembled to examine into the case of the man Canolles, who robbed the convoy last night of the money for the pay of the troops. The question to be examined will be whether the attack was made by regularly enrolled soldiers of the American army, or by common marauders. Is it your pleasure that the prisoner should now be introduced?"

"Yes," was the reply of Ferrers and the other officers.

"Bring in the man Canolles."

At this order, a sergeant stationed at the door of the tent made a sign to some one without, and a moment afterwards Canolles was ushered into the tent. He advanced with a firm tread, surveying the members of the court one by one, after which his eyes remained intently fixed upon Gen. Arnold.

"Are you the person called Canolles?" said the latter.

"Yes," was the reply.

"Was it you who attacked the convoy last night?"

"Yes."

"Are you or are you not a regularly enrolled

soldier or commissioned officer of the American army, fighting under the American flag?"

"Before replying to that question," replied Canolles, in his unmoved voice, "I desire to address a question in my turn to the President of the Board."

"Ask it," said Arnold.

"Is or is not the President of the Board Brigadier-General Arnold?"

Arnold's eyes suddenly flashed—it might have been supposed that he suspected what was coming.

"The meaning of your question?" he said. "You are arraigned here to be tried, and it is for the court to interrogate you, not for you to interrogate the court."

"Is there a Judge-Advocate present?" said Canolles, coolly.

"Yes," said Ferrers, rising, "I am the Judge-Advocate."

"You represent both the court and the person arraigned," said Canolles. "Is or is not my question a proper one?"

Ferrers grunted, and grumbled out sardonically:

"A devilish mysterious one—don't understand it—but don't see what harm there is in asking it if it is your fancy."

Arnold set his teeth close, and said with suppressed wrath:

"I waive further objection; what is your question?"

"I repeat it," said Canolles. "Is or is not the President of the Board Gen. Benedict Arnold?"

"I am."

"Then I protest against trial by a court over which he presides."

"You protest?"

"Gen. Benedict Arnold is a traitor!"

The words were pronounced clearly and coolly, Canolles fixing his eyes as he spoke intently on the face of the person he addressed. Arnold rose to his feet, pale with rage, and seemed about to rush upon Canolles.

"Insolent wretch!" he exclaimed, "what do you mean by daring to grossly insult the court?"

"I mean," said Canolles, "that Gen. Benedict Arnold attempted to sell his country for £10,000—the exact sum carried off last night by myself, sword in hand—and betrayed a brave young Englishman, John Andre, to his death. The President questions me—I reply. I demand a fair trial—to be tried by a court presided over by an officer and a gentleman."

CHAPTER XVI.

CANOLLES AND ARNOLD.

It is impossible to describe the effect of the words uttered by Canolles on Gen. Arnold and the officers of the court.

"I call on the officers present to protect the dignity of the court from this gross outrage!" gasped Gen. Arnold with positive rage.

Lord Ferrers grinned.

"The fact is," he said, with a gruff sound which was a grunt or a laugh, "the proceeding of the prisoner is highly irregular."

Arnold's brow knit fiercely, and he said:

"Col. Ferrers is moderate in his characterization of this insolence!"

Ferrers uttered the same ambiguous sound.

"I would observe to the court," he said, "that this discussion interrupts the business before it. The protest of the prisoner is a matter of no moment. If the court is ready, I will proceed to interrogate him, and we will hear what he has to say."

Arnold sat down, pale, and suppressing his rage with difficulty, for he saw on the faces of the officers that they secretly sympathized with the defiant protest of Canolles.

"I am content," Arnold said in a low and stern voice, for this man of unfaltering nerve seemed inaccessible to such emotion as would have characterized another, " I am content that the examination of the prisoner shall proceed without further interruption, and to make no reply to his insolent speech—a speech which, if uttered by an officer and a gentleman, should be answered at the sword's point! The examination will proceed."

Ferrers turned to the prisoner and said:

" Well, as that matter is decided, my friend, I advise you to cease this irregular and unpleasant protesting, and answer the questions I ask you, or those asked by the Board—to begin—"

" It is useless," said Canolles calmly. " I will save the court the trouble of interrogating me by making a general statement."

" Exculpating yourself? "

" Condemning myself."

" Stop," said Ferrers, rising and confronting the prisoner. " You are a brave fellow, Canolles, whether you are a marauder or not, and it shall not be said that George Ferrers, acting as Judge-Advocate, allowed an accused to sign his own death-warrant."

Canolles shook his head.

" I have known from the first that I was a dead man, Colonel," he said, " otherwise I should not have acknowledged my true character to Gen. Phillips and yourself. Were I to assert now that I am an American soldier, fighting under the American flag, what would be the difficulty in ascertaining the truth of my statement? You have only to send a flag to Gen. Lafayette, and I inform you now what the reply would be : That the person called Canolles is not an American soldier, nor commissioned officer; that he makes war on his own account; that he cannot be exchanged, and, being outside the pale of military law, must be left to his fate."

A murmur ran through the court, and every eye was fixed upon Canolles.

"The devil!" muttered Ferrers, "there's nothing to reply to that; but of all the cool hands—"

He left the sentence unfinished, and, addressing Canolles, said:

"You are right, friend; there are witnesses enough to prove everything, and the Marquis Lafayette could do nothing for you. I swear I regret it—I respect a man, marauder or no marauder, who faces death as you do. But what infernal idea ever got into your head, inducing you to risk yourself so, fighting under no flag? I am myself an English soldier and prefer my own colors, but a flag carried by a man like George Washington might suit you, I think."

"I do not like the American flag," was the reply of Canolles.

"Humph!—tell me why."

"It is useless, sir—the considerations preventing me from fighting under the American colors are purely personal."

A species of growl and sigh mingled issued from beneath the white mustache of Col. Ferrers, and he knit his brows.

"You will not explain anything, then?" he said. "Reflect; there may be circumstances connected with your refusal to act with the enemies of England which will operate upon the court and affect their decision in your case."

Canolles shook his head.

"There are no such circumstances."

"Give us an opportunity to form our own opinion, at least."

"Useless, Colonel, wholly useless, and certain considerations make it unagreeable to me to enter upon the subject."

Again Ferrers uttered the sound resembling a grunt and a sigh.

"What all this means, Heaven only knows," he growled, "and of all the affairs in which I have been engaged—come! make a clean breast of it, Canolles! I swear you are no mere low-born plunderer—you are a gentleman, born and bred, if I am entitled to form an opinion, and there is something behind all this. Come! don't be a Quixote! Who and what are you really?"

Canolles shook his head.

"I am not a Quixote, and nothing I could tell you could affect your decision."

Ferrers sat down with an expression of furious ill-humor, and Arnold said:

"Is the court ready to consider the case? As the accused acknowledges the charges it is useless to summon witnesses to prove them. There is now but one question for the court to decide—what punishment and form of punishment should be visited on one entering the British lines at night, without a flag, and—"

Canolles turned quickly and fixed his eyes upon Gen. Arnold so abruptly that he paused.

"Is it permitted me to ask the president of the court a question?" he said.

"Yes," said Ferrers, before Arnold could reply. "Yes! The request is a small one for a brave fellow in your position."

"I proceed to ask it," said Canolles, who had never moved his eyes from the face of Gen. Arnold. "The President of the court affirms that the question before the court is the proper punishment and mode of punishment of a man entering the British lines at night without a flag. Is that the shape in which the question is to be propounded?"

"It is," said Arnold.

"It is proposed, therefore, to inflict upon me the death of a spy?"

"Yes."

"Does the President of the court rely on military precedent for that decision?"

"I do."

"What precedent? The execution of Major John Andre?"

Arnold started as if some venomous reptile had bitten him, and in spite of his enormous self-control turned suddenly pale.

"I will make my question plainer," added Canolles, who spoke as coolly as before. "Major John Andre, Adjutant-General of the British army, entered—no, he did not enter, he was betrayed into—the American lines in a manner probably well known to the President and members of this Board. He was arrested, tried, and the verdict of the American court-martial was that Major Andre having entered their lines at night and without a flag, ought to be considered as a spy, and as such was executed by hanging, not by shooting. Is it the precedent in the case of Major Andre that the President of this court relies on in my case, approving it?"

At these words there was a dead silence in the tent—a silence so deep that the measured steps of a sentinel fifty yards distant were distinctly heard.

Gen. Arnold, whose eyes burned like fire in his pale face, was seen twice to attempt to speak; but each time something seemed to rise in his throat and choke him.

"The President of the court does not reply," said Canolles, whose face had assumed an expression of extreme disdain, " then he doubtless means that he approves the death by hanging of John Andre, of the British army. Well, sir, I—a mere robber and marauder, as you take me—I disapprove it. I say that John Andre was not a spy, and according to military law was guilty of nothing unworthy of an officer and a gentleman. I say if expediency required his execution he ought to have been shot like a soldier, not hanged like a felon. I say more, sir, and am glad to have the occasion to say it—that in my opinion the person deserving death was the American officer who betrayed him, as he betrayed his country, for money—Brigadier-General Benedict Arnold. I am a mere freebooter, you say, sir, and you are going to shoot or hang me. Well, I give you my word of honor that I would rather be shot or hanged than to wear the uniform you wear at the price you paid for it."

Arnold seemed ready to start from his seat with fury. His dark face turned white with rage, and it is probable that but for the interposition of Col. Ferrers some scene of actual violence would have ensued. Ferrers gave an order to the guard, Canolles was conducted under guard from the tent, and in the midst of unheard-of agitation the court proceeded to consider the prisoner's case.

There was little hope of mitigating his punishment. The charges were acknowledged—that the prisoner had with hostile intent entered the British lines at night, without uniform, flag or commission; and in spite of the appeals of Lord Ferrers, which were short and full of rude eloquence, the verdict of the court was that the prisoner Canolles ought to suffer death.

"What death?" said Ferrers, in his roughest and harshest accents, glancing at Arnold as he spoke; "because I give the court notice that if any attempt be made to inflict the penalty of hanging, I have Gen. Phillips' promise—his promise as a man of honor, sir—that the form of death shall be shooting; and before I will sign as Judge-Advocate any other decision of this court, I will retire from my official place here, or I will tear up the paper when it is laid before me!"

Arnold, trembling with rage, could only mutter, hoarsely:

"It is for the court to decide."

The vote was taken, and it was decided that the prisoner should be shot to death.

The court then rose, and the verdict was transmitted to Gen. Phillips, lying burnt up with fever at Bolling-brook House, who affixed his trembling signature to it, and appointed sunrise on the next morning as the time of the prisoner's execution.

CHAPTER XVII.

THE NIGHT BEFORE THE EXECUTION.

It was between eleven and twelve o'clock at night. Canolles was seated writing at a table in a room of a small house not far from Blandford Church. This house had been the residence of a citizen of the town who had fled with his family on the approach of the British forces, and had been taken possession of as the quarters of the officer of the guard, and a place of imprisonment for persons arrested by the provost of the army. Canolles had been conducted thither when dismissed from further attendance on the court-martial, and confined in one of the apartments, with a sentinel before his door.

He was now seated, as we have said, at a table upon which burned a single tallow candle, and was busily engaged in writing—pen, ink and paper having been readily supplied him by the officer of the guard, who, himself a soldier, had a soldier's sympathy for a man who faced his fate with the coolness of the prisoner.

A painful interest always attaches to the demeanor and conduct of a human being who is about to find closing upon him the dark door of the tomb, and who knows that it is about to close upon him. That moment is calculated to test the courage of the human heart and try the steadiest nerves. But yesterday free, safe, alive with the fullest life, and now fettered, condemned, with death approaching steadily and surely! At one instant a strong and active man, with every pulse bounding, every muscle obedient to the will, every vein full of warm, red blood, with the sun shining for you, the birds singing, with the laughter of happy children in your ears, and all the abounding charms of various and delightful life your own; and at the next moment, or soon, so soon! to be an inert clod without sense or motion! The nerves are tried at such a time, and a man shows speedily whether he is brave or the opposite.

It was plain that Canolles was a brave man. His face was quite composed, and his hand perfectly firm as he continued to write on steadily. He was still engaged in writing when a step was heard without, a brief colloquy ensued, apparently between the sentinel and some other person, then the door opened and Lord Ferrers came in.

The old *militaire* was as erect and gruff as ever, his tall figure towered as stiffly as was its wont, and his snow-white mustache covered lips as bluff and firm in their expression as before. Looking closer, nevertheless, any one might have seen in the old soldier's eyes an unusual softness—an unmistakable trouble. He looked at Canolles for a moment without speaking, then he advanced rapidly, holding out his hand, and growled:

"Well, comrade, I'm come to see you."

Canolles rose, pressed the hand held out, and said:

"Thanks, my dear Colonel. But I did not require any assurance that your visit was the visit of a friend—of one soldier to another who is about to die."

"You are right," returned Ferrers in his curt voice, each word jerked, as it were, from his lips, "and I take no credit to myself for coming. I can't sleep. This devilish affair of yours keeps me awake. What infernal complication of diabolical circumstances ever got you into this hobble? I'll tell you one thing. If you don't relieve my mind on this subject it will torture me all my life. Good Heavens! Here you are throwing away your chances of life—there may be chances; you are no mere plunderer. What in Heaven's name ever brought you to this wild plan of fighting under no flag?"

Canolles leaned back in his chair, his right arm resting on the table, and seemed, from the absent expression of his eyes and the fingers drumming on the table, to be lost in reflection. Ferrers, seated opposite, looked intently at him, and if the old nobleman's thoughts had been translated into words, these words would probably have been: "What cursed nonsense to say that this man is a low marauder!" Indeed, everything about Canolles, face, figure, bearing—every expression and attitude, however unconscious, indicated high breeding. You might have conceived that this human being had been led to the commission of crime, perhaps—to believe him capable of plundering from mere love of money was impossible.

For some moments Canolles remained sunk in this pensive mood—a species of reverie taking him away from the actual place and time—then he awoke, as it were, and said:

"I must beg you to pardon my ill-breeding, Colonel; I fear I am becoming too much addicted to this bad habit of reverie—but there is scarcely time now to break myself of it," he added with a smile. "I shall never be cured of it!"

Ferrers knit his brows.

"Stop that smiling, comrade," he growled, "and don't make me like you any better than I do! Do you know whom you resemble when you smile in that way?"

"Resemble?"

"Yes."

"Do I resemble any one else?"

"Yes, you do—you are the image, the very picture of Hartley Ferrers."

"Who is Hartley Ferrers?" said Canolles.

Ferrers looked at him for a moment in silence—a look keen and sorrowful.

"I think, sometimes," he said, "that you are Hartley!"

"My dear Colonel," said Canolles, "you have not even told me who the person you refer to is, or was."

"He was my son."

"Your son?"

"Yes," grunted Lord Ferrers, "a poor, impulsive boy—couldn't control him—wild for adventure, new countries and the life of a wanderer. Poor fellow! instead of being contented with home, he went off, shipped on board an outward-bound vessel, and was never heard of afterwards."

"A very sad event, Colonel, and I sincerely sympathize with you in your affliction."

The old *militaire* sighed.

"All the worse as I have no other children, and Lady Ferrers is long since dead. The strange thing is that you so closely resemble my poor Hartley, which will account in some measure for my liking you, comrade. Your resemblance to the poor boy is startling. But it is, of course, a mere coincidence—an accident."

" Of course," replied Canolles.

" And now," said Ferrers, " to come to the object of this visit."

" It has, then, an object other than to soothe the last moments of a brother soldier ? "

" Yes."

" What object, Colonel ? "

" To save you, if I can, from the bullets that will tear you to pieces at sunrise."

Canolles shook his head.

" You cannot save me Colonel," he said with a smile, " unless you have devised some scheme which has never yet occurred to my mind."

" I have devised the scheme—to obtain from you a full statement of the motives inducing you to make war on the British forces in Virginia, without doing so under the protection of the American flag. The devil. Do you suppose that I am an idiot and don't see that something must be under this infernal folly of yours, Canolles ? Do you suppose that you can fool me into the belief that you are a common highwayman, ready to take a purse; or a low thief stealing money from Gen. Phillips' chest for love of the money and nothing else ? If you think so, you are daft, as they say in Scotland. You are a gentleman. I'll swear you are in every

7

sense a man of honor; and now speak, comrade! Tell me what drove you to this cursed blunder, and I'll go tell Phillips."

Again Canolles shook his head. Leaning his right elbow on the table, he rested his temple lightly upon his hand, in an attitude of easy grace, and said:

"My dear Colonel, do you know it is a matter of regret to me that I have made your acquaintance so late? Your sympathy quite moves me, and makes me long to live to know you better. Unfortunately, your plan is useless."

"Useless?"

"It is trouble thrown away. There is nothing in my motives, or in my discarding the protection of the American flag, to alter the decision of the British commander in my case."

"Hang it! let me judge! You acknowledge that you had peculiar reasons."

"Certainly; I have or had my private reasons. I say had, you see. I have pretty well bidden life farewell."

Ferrers repeated obstinately, knitting his brows:

"Let me judge! let me judge!"

"And let me repeat, Colonel, that it is chimerical to indulge any expectation of affecting the action of Gen. Phillips by informing him of my personal motives. It was impossible for him to act otherwise than he has done under the circumstances. Approval of the finding of the court was a necessity. I am perfectly well acquainted with military law, and know what I risked when I attacked your troops last night, without a flag or a commission. Call me what you will—spy, robber, what not—it is immaterial. My punishment is properly death."

Ferrers looked at the man who uttered these cool words with a singular mixture of grief and anger.

"For the last time, Canolles," he said, "what mystery is under all this affair? Once more, I say, there is no deceiving me as to your rank or character. I have lived more than sixty years in this second-rate world, and I've known all sorts of people—hob-nobbed with Dukes and clinked cups with beggars—and I think I know a gentleman when I see one—and you are one, and as brave as steel to boot."

"Thanks, friend, for such you are."

"Your friend? Yes, I am your friend. Do you suppose I don't make up my own opinions? Do you think that infernal traitor and rascal Arnold's opinion of you had any effect on George Ferrers? If you do, you are most damnably mistaken! If anything, his hostility to you raised you in my estimation. I don't call a scoundrel, that tries to sell his country and lets a brave boy like Andre go to his death, a good judge of the character of a gentleman and soldier; and when you told him as much in the court, you delighted me —it was the happiest moment I've passed for years. Yes, I am your friend, and George Ferrers don't make a friend of everybody. If I could save your life, I would not eat or sleep till I had saved it."

"I know that," said Canolles, his soldierly face lit up by a bright smile.

"And you will not aid me," said Ferrers.

"It would be useless to make the attempt. To every man there is an appointed hour, Colonel; he advances to that hour through a hundred battles unharmed, but when the hour has struck he falls. Well, my hour has come. I face the conviction with calmness, because it is in my blood not to shrink, and I do not regret life as much, perhaps, as you suppose. I have lived for a particular object, and that object, I may assure you, is now accomplished, or will be. Had you not captured me I should have disbanded my men very soon, if not at once, and disappeared like a leaf blown on the wind—I should have left Virginia never to return. Well, all is reversed, you see. I fall into your hands—you take my life, which belongs to you—I give it up without a murmur—and so all ends, Colonel!"

Ferrers inflated his chest with air and then abruptly expelled it.

"Canolles," he said, "I'd give a thousand pounds if you had escaped! To hear you talking in this way just before you are shot is enough to make a man cry like a baby. To think that you are to come to your end so suddenly! That you are to die in the flush of youth, health, strength, happiness—"

He stopped with a choking intonation. Canolles smiled.

"Are you perfectly certain that I am happy and will regret life, Colonel?"

"You ought to."

Canolles shook his head with the same sad smile.

"Humph!" grunted Ferrers, attempting to conceal

his emotion under satire, "perhaps it is a matter of indifference to you whether you live or die?"

"To be frank with you, it is."

Ferrers looked keenly at the speaker.

"You have some secret trouble, comrade."

A slight color slowly stole over the face of Canolles, and he said in a low voice:

"Yes."

"Can I do nothing to relieve you of it?"

"Nothing——it is hopeless," was the reply, in the same low voice, accompanied by a heavy sigh.

"Nothing is hopeless," grunted Ferrers.

"This is. The subject depresses me, Colonel. I need all my good spirits, you see, and to speak of this would make me profoundly sorrowful. My life has been an unfortunate one—let us say no more. But you shall know all about it when I am dead."

He pointed to the paper which he had been writing, and added:

"In this and another paper I have stated briefly but clearly the motives actuating me during my career, for the information of two persons. One paper has by this time reached its destination. Of this, which I have just completed, you must take charge, Colonel, and see that it is delivered to the person whose name I shall write upon it. I shall not seal it—you may read it if you desire to do so."

"What!" exclaimed Ferrers, "does that paper lying there upon that table contain your personal history?"

"Yes."

"All about you?"

"All."

"An explanation of your object in making war on England without marching under the American flag?"

"A full explanation."

"Humph! Then as you have no objection to my reading the paper hereafter, I'll read it now."

He extended his hand, as he spoke, toward the paper, but Canolles as quickly interposed his own hand to protect it.

"Let me beg you to delay a little while, friend. You know it will not be long."

"No; let me read it now. Something tells me that the contents of that paper may, if known to me, and in turn to Gen. Phillips, have a vital bearing on your fate."

Canolles replied with a slow, incredulous movement of his head:

"Again I assure you that the idea is chimerical. Gen. Phillips will not, cannot allow anything here written to influence him."

"Then let me read the paper for my own personal satisfaction," exclaimed Ferrers; "you cannot deny a request so slight as that, Canolles, to the man you call friend."

Canolles hesitated.

"It would only lead," he said, "to questions, discussions, further explanations—and all that would simply make me gloomy, without any imaginable advantage, Colonel."

But Col. Ferrers seemed to have obstinately set his mind upon seeing the writing on the paper before the hour of the prisoner's execution.

"I will ask you no questions—there shall be no discussion."

He extended his hand once more toward the paper.

"Come, let me see it!"

Canolles withdrew his own hand, saying as he did so :

"Well, Colonel, as you attach so much importance to reading this, which, after all, you will be at liberty to read in a very few hours, I do not see why I should further oppose your desire. Since I am not unwilling, and even desire, that you should know my history and see that my motives have not been mean or mercenary, why should I refuse your request."

"I may read, then?"

"You are at full liberty to do so, Colonel."

And Canolles leaned back in his seat, pushing the written sheets toward the old soldier, who ardently extended his hand to grasp them.

Before he could do so a sudden and rapid firing was heard in the vicinity of the house, and through the window could be seen quick sheets of flame lighting up the night, and resembling the flash of the fire-fly's light.

Col. Ferrers, with the instinct of the soldier, started to his feet, grasping the hilt of his sword.

"An attack!" he exclaimed.

Suddenly the long roll of the British drum was

heard, and shouts and orders resounded—the troops were evidently being gotten hastily under arms.

"I must go there!" exclaimed Col. Ferrers, losing sight of all else; and in the midst of the firing, which still continued without abatement, he hastily left the apartment.

CHAPTER XVIII.

THE NIGHT ATTACK.

Young Harry Cartaret, at the head of twenty-five picked men, had passed the Appomattox by wading and swimming, and failing to surprise and overpower in silence the picket guards upon the bank of the river had made a sudden and resolute attack on nothing less than the whole British army.

In proceeding to this desperate extremity he had not acted from mere foolhardiness and hair-brained impulse. His plan, as unfolded to Gen. Lafayette, had been wholly different, and by no means uncertain of success. He had ascertained from a thoroughly trained scout belonging to his company, whom he had sent across the river for the purpose, that Canolles was confined in a house situated only a short distance from the banks of the river; and he relied on surprise, not on attack, to rescue the prisoner. The moon would set between ten and eleven, and the young officer then proposed to cross the river in silence, under cover of darkness, steal upon the picket guard of only a few men, capture or overpower them without the use of fire-arms, in order to avoid an alarm—and in the event of success, the rest seemed comparatively easy. The British troops would be apt to rely with confidence on the pickets to alarm them in case of an attack, and so obscure a prisoner as Canolles would not probably be heavily guarded.   Once inside the British line of sentries Cartaret meant to advance to the house, surprise the sentry there, take him prisoner without noise, and then it would not be difficult to pry open the ordinary door and lock confining Canolles, after which the party would return as quietly as they came, or if necessary cut their way back to the river, plunge in and escape.

There were chances that his reckless project would prove fortunate. War largely depends on surprising an enemy; and what an enemy does not suspect generally succeeds. Cartaret relied on the boldness of his plan for success, and on the excellent composition of the detachment he commanded. They were one and all thorough fighters, ready to follow him anywhere; and just as the moon sank and profound darkness settled down, he set out silently, having full permission from Lafayette, and soon reached the banks of the river.

All was still. The subdued murmur of the stream seemed to render the silence still more profound. Cartaret first entered the sluggish current, which gradually grew deeper; it mounted now to the waists of the young man and his followers; then to the shoulders; then they began to swim, quietly holding their arms out of the water.

Advancing thus like a line of shadows, the party gradully drew near the southern bank, and under the guidance of the scout whom he had sent across to gain information, and who now swam beside him, Cartaret made for a little cove overshadowed by drooping boughs, where a landing was silently effected.

Whispered orders were now passed along the line that the men should look to their pistols to ascertain if the powder was wet, but to immediately return them to their belts, and on no account to use them unless by express orders. This was silently done, dry powder replaced the wet in cases where the spray had damped the priming, the arms were replaced, and Cartaret then advanced in front with six men, crouching down and slowly approaching the English picket, who was seen dimly through the darkness slowly pacing to and fro on his beat.

Cartaret waited until his back was turned. Then he sprang upon him, and before he could make any resistance or discharge his musket, seized him and made him prisoner. Not a sound had been heard. So far the expedition was a success. The man, who was quite prostrated by the suddenness of the assault on him, was ordered to keep silent on peril of his life—he exhibited not the remotest desire or intention to disobey the order—and Cartaret at the head of his men, and guided by the scout, advanced rapidly in the direction of the house in which Canolles was confined.

Unfortunately the intended surprise met with an unexpected obstacle. Gen. Phillips was a cautious soldier, and had posted an interior as well as an exterior picket, and on this, consisting of a vidette and a heavy picket guard, Cartaret now suddenly came.

At the very moment when the presence of this guard was ascertained, the guide whispered:

"There is the house, Lieutenant."

He pointed as he spoke through the darkness, and

Cartaret saw against the dull night sky the dim outline of the house occupied by Canolles.

"It is impossible to surprise the picket!" was the low reply of Cartaret, whose heart sank.

" Yes, Lieutenant," said the cool fellow, in the same tone, "but you can attack it!"

"Is there any chance of success? I cannot have my men cut to pieces for nothing."

"Maybe they'll not be cut to pieces. Everything is in a surprise, Lieutenant. The army's asleep. We'll capture or kill the guard in five minutes."

Cartaret still hesitated.

" Do you think the men will follow me?"

" Not a man will fail you."

" Pass the word then for every man to have his arms ready. If the surprise fails, we'll depend on hard fighting and take the chances."

"All right, Lieutenant."

And the order was communicated in a low tone to the men, who, so far from failing their commander, seemed to receive it with enthusiasm.

Cartaret then advanced and was promptly challenged. He made no response, and the discharge of the sentinel's musket came like an echo to the challenge. At this sound the guard suddenly rose, arms in hand, shouts resounded, a rapid firing succeeded, and a determined combat took place in the darkness, lit up only by the quick jets of flame from the muzzles of the guns, seen by Ferrers and Canolles.

All this had occurred in a very few moments. The picket guard, unfortunately for Cartaret, chanced to be composed of excellent material; and, although taken by surprise and unaware of the size of the attacking force, they fought obstinately, thus giving Lord Ferrers time to reach the scene of the encounter.

The old nobleman with drawn sword rushed into the midst of the combatants. The tongues of flame enabled him to take in the whole situation at a glance; and shouting, "Stand fast, men; they are only a squad!" he advanced in front, exposing himself needlessly to the American fire.

In spite of the obstinate resistance of the picket, Cartaret would probably have overpowered them, reached the house and carried off Canolles; but the firing had alarmed the forces, the hill suddenly swarmed with red coats, and by order of Col. Ferrers the assailants were promptly surrounded.

Further fighting was plainly useless on the part of Cartaret—a single glance assured him of that—and he gave the order to his men to save themselves. A number of them succeeded in doing so in the darkness, and Cartaret, with half a dozen of his best men, covered their retreat, fighting step by step as they retired.

CHAPTER XIX.

TO WHOM CANOLLES HAD WRITTEN.

It soon became obvious that Cartaret would not be able to effect his retreat. Suddenly a ring of red coats closed around him.

"Surrender!" cried a voice—that of Col. Ferrers—and the glare of torches hastily kindled at a camp-fire near lit up the figure of the old *militaire*, sword in hand, six feet from the young American and his few men.

"Surrender! To whom?" was the reply.

"To me, Colonel Ferrers—that is to say, unless you prefer being cut to pieces!"

As he spoke, the old nobleman lowered his sword and burst into a grim laugh.

"Cartaret, or the devil take me!" he exclaimed. "Saw you once before—the image of a friend of mine. So you came over to capture the army, eh?"

"Not precisely, Colonel—I surrender, of course."

"A night attack with a company, within a stone's throw of headquarters! What a farce! But that's your lookout."

"Yes."

"And I've no fault to find. George Ferrers in his time has amused himself in something like the same way."

Cartaret took his sword by the blade and presented

the hilt to Ferrers.   The old soldier looked at him with the same grim humor, and grunted:

"What's that for?"

"I surrender my sword."

"I don't want your sword.   Keep it."

He turned and gave an order—the troops were directed to return to their quarters with the prisoners, except Cartaret, and then taking the young man familiarly by the arm, Lord Ferrers said:

"Come on, my young friend.   Phillips will wish to ascertain from you what led you to make this crazy attack, and as the poor fellow is sick, you ought to gratify him."

Cartaret replied gloomily:

"I have no objection to inform Gen. Phillips or you, Colonel, what my object was."

"Well, tell me."

"I came to rescue a prisoner in your hands!"

"What prisoner?"

"His name is Canolles."

"Canolles!   You came over to rescue Canolles?"

"Yes."

"Humph!—wonders will never cease!   What on earth have you to do with Canolles?   You take an interest in him?"

"A deep interest."

"Why?"

"It is my secret, or rather his own."

"A devilish strange fellow, on my honor—this Canolles!   There is no end of mystery about him, and he seems to make friends of everybody. The fact is a curious one, as he's merely a highway robber."

"I assure you, Colonel," exclaimed Cartaret, "that he is nothing of the sort."

"Not a robber?"

"No more than you or I!"

"Humph!—well, you don't call him a man of honor and a regular soldier?"

"He is a man of the nicest honor—whether a regular soldier or not depends on technical definition."

"He fights without a flag."

"True."

"Then he is a marauder, unless peculiar circumstances control his action."

"Such peculiar circumstances exist."

"What are they?"

Cartaret shook his head.

"I have informed you, Colonel, that the origin of my deep interest—more than deep interest—in the person calling himself Capt. Canolles was his secret, not mine, since he wishes it to be preserved intact. I now say as much of the motives actuating him, to which you have referred."

"Well," exclaimed Ferrers, "I, too, take a deep interest in Canolles. And one reason is that he is like a son of mine roving about somewhere, if he's not dead."

The words were uttered in a low, deep tone. Cartaret looked at the speaker quickly, but made no reply.

"I think sometimes," added Ferrers, in the same deep tone, "that Canolles is that son."

Cartaret was silent in the same strange manner.
Then he said slowly, and with the air of one who
means every word he utters to make its impression and
engrave itself on the memory:

" Col. Ferrers, you have lived long enough to know
that the most improbable things are often true, have
you not? "

" I have."

" Do you think it impossible that Capt. Canolles is
your son ? "

The young man could feel a slight tremor run through
the old soldier's arm. For some moments he was
silent. Then he muttered :

" No—nothing is impossible—but this is—"

Suddenly he clutched the young man's arm and
dragged him in a direction nearly at right angles to
that in which they had been moving.

" Where are you conducting me, Colonel? " said
Cartaret.

" To prison."

" Then we are not to visit Gen. Phillips ? "

" No."

" Why not?"

" For the simple reason that I don't want you to talk
with him."

" Not talk with him ? "

" Or tell him what brought you over the river to-
night."

" Your reason ? "

" A sound one," grunted the old soldier. " Phillips
is a passionate fellow naturally, and is burnt up with

fever, too.   If you tell him you attacked his troops to rescue Canolles, he'll fall into a rage, and the last chance for the prisoner will be lost."

"Are there any chances?"

"I'm afraid not one, but if there are, I'll not prejudice them.   Come along!   I'll take you to the house where he is a prisoner."

"And I shall see him!" exclaimed the young man in an ardent tone.

"Why not?" growled Ferrers.   "Yes, you shall see him!   And I mean myself to see him, too.   I've seen and had a talk with him already to-night."

"Indeed!"

"A long talk; but I must see him again—something takes me back."

"What is that?"

"To find out who and what he is.   He declined telling me by word of mouth, but had explained everything in a paper that he had written.   I was to deliver this paper to somebody—the name was not yet written upon it—after reading it myself; and Canolles had just consented that I should read it to-night when you began your small display of fire-works yonder and interrupted us.   But come in!   In fifteen minutes from this time there'll be no longer any secret in this affair."

They had reached the house; and raising his head Lord Ferrers saw that the light was still burning in the chamber of Canolles.

Passing the sentinel, who saluted, Ferrers said to Cartaret:

"Oblige me by shutting yourself up for half an hour

in that room on the left, where you will find a camp couch if you are tired. I will then return, and you shall have the interview you wish with your friend."

He then crossed the passage, entered the room occupied by Canolles, closed the door, and peered through the dim light of the tallow candle, which was sputtering and nearly out.

Canolles had his right arm on the table, with the hand doubled up, and his forehead rested easily on the hand. The attitude was that of thought or of sleep. As Lord Ferrers drew nearer he saw that the hand rested upon the paper written by Canolles, which had been folded and addressed to the person for whom it was intended.

"Comrade!" said Ferrers.

Canolles did not move, and the old soldier, who was now at his side, could hear his long, tranquil breathing. The man who was to be shot at sunrise was sleeping as sweetly as an infant.

An expression of singular softness came to the face of Ferrers. The stern brows relaxed, and something resembling tears shone in his eye.

"Poor fellow! brave fellow!" he murmured. "I knew he would be cool to the last. But the paper! the paper!"

He bent down and attempted to draw it from beneath the closed hand of Canolles. The sleeper stirred, his regular breathing ceased, and the hand seemed to close down more heavily on the paper.

"I'll wake him if I try to get it away from him!" muttered Ferrers, and I swear I would not wake him

at such a time as this for ten thousand pounds sterling!
No, no, old George Ferrers! remember this is a soldier
like yourself—and he'll be dead at sunrise!   Sleep on,
comrade—forget your troubles—take your rest—but
there's no harm in my looking to see what name is on
that letter, as I'm to convey it to the person you intend
it for."

He stooped down, slightly moved the hand which the
touch told him was quite calm and composed, like face
and forehead, and looked by the last glimmer of the
tallow candle at the address.   This address was:

" Lieutenant Henry Cartaret,
       Army of the Marquis de Lafayette."

CHAPTER XX.

AT " BOLLINGBROOK."

It was nearly sunrise. The fresh and balmy air of the May morning sweeping across the Blandford hills entered the open windows of an apartment in the " Bollingbrook House," and gently fanned the feverish forehead of a man leaning languidly back in an easy chair and looking out upon the beautiful landscape.

Gen. Phillips had risen half an hour before, slowly made his toilet without assistance—donning an undress uniform—and while all in the house were still asleep had repaired to the drawing-room—the apartment which we have entered once before—and here, lying rather than sitting in his easy chair by the open window, he seemed to indulge in a mood of sorrowful musing.

The landscape upon which his eyes were fixed was singularly lovely. Immediately in front was Blandford Church, even then nearly half a century old, with its ivy-covered walls and grassy knoll glimmering with white tombstones. To the right and left were the tents of the army. Beyond a belt of forest formed a foreground to ranges of hills whose outlines fell gradually away toward the south; and the scattered houses of the triple villages, Blandford, Petersburg and Pocahontas, the quiet, lazy-looking river, the budding leaves, the early flowers and bird songs, and the perfume of dawn

—these made up an exquisite picture, and exerted an influence evidently sweet and soothing to the sick soldier, who, free for the moment from the cares of command, seemed to be carried back to other scenes, perhaps to earlier and happier years.

It was a proud and martial face—the face of General William Phillips—but it had now grown soft; and a certain wistful, longing expression had come to the eyes ordinarily stern and rather cold. In his face there was none of the ill-humor which had characterized it during his interview with Col. Ferrers. A sad smile, even, came at certain moments to his lips, and looking toward the old Blandford church, he murmured:

"Life is, after all, a strange affair at best—what the next hour will bring forth remains still a mystery."

He stopped, mused, then added:

"I have a presentiment that I shall die here, and if I should I shall doubtless be buried yonder near that old church. Am I looking now at my own grave?"

He mused again for some moments in silence; then he murmured:

"Well, well—what matters it? I should have chosen to die, if I had had the power to choose, on the field, in harness—the death of a soldier. Instead, I die from a fever in my bed—for I feel that I shall die; still, all is the same."

The songs of the birds flitting from tree to tree filled up the pause which followed, and seemed to soothe the weary-looking man. There was something inexpressibly sweet in the gay warbling, and the red birds passed from tree to tree like balls of animated fire.

The orioles seemed wild with joy at the coming of spring; the blue birds poured forth an incessant flood of rejoiceful notes; and, sweeter than all, from the topmost spray of an elm in the Bollingbrook grounds, an "English mocking-bird"* filled the air with what seemed a concert from every feathered songster of the fields and forests.

The feverish forehead of the soldier drooped; his eyes assumed a dreamy and almost tender expression; he seemed to have gone back to his youth—perhaps to some early love—and was a boy again, when suddenly a drum rolled, jarring harsh and ominous on the morning air.

At the sound Gen. Phillips rose suddenly in his chair, and turned his head with the air of a man who is listening. Again the drum rolled and he uttered a sigh.

"I had quite forgotten," he murmured, "that poor fellow is to be shot at sunrise, and yonder is the red flush that precedes his death."

Again his head drooped.

"Strange!" he muttered, "strange human life! To-day, a living, breathing man; to-morrow—nothing. Yesterday, this partisan—Canolles—was free, strong, full of hope and the sense of enjoyment, and in ten minutes from this time, by order of a worm like myself—the worm calling himself William Phillips—he will pass from earth riddled by musket balls. And then, in turn, comes the fate of the person who sends

---

* Why called the "English" mocking-bird I do not know, as the bird is found nowhere except in America. The prefix "English" is, however, common in Virginia, and seems meant to indicate the best species of singers.

him to his death! He dies the death of a soldier, and is more fortunate than I am : for I shall die burned up by this fever—this terrible fever!"

Again the roll of the drum was heard, and on the slope of the hill in front might be seen the detail of men drawn up and ready to perform their melancholy duty. The red flush in the east gradually deepened, and the sun was near his rising.

"Poor fellow!" murmured Phillips, "after all, he is to be pitied rather than blamed. Who knows? It was doubtless the result of bad training. He was not surrounded by the sweet amenities, perhaps, of home, but thrown with rough, coarse characters, who warped his life and brought him to these evil courses. And yet this man seemed no common plunderer. He even had about him the indefinable something indicating the gentleman. Well, well, I cannot take account of that. My duty must be performed. A court-martial tries and finds him guilty—he is condemned to death— I am forced to approve the sentence of the court. There is, there can be, no hope whatever for him."

The door behind the speaker opened, and an orderly put his head in.

"The guard with two prisoners, sir," he said. "I told them you could not see them, but one is a young lady, who is crying and says she must see you."

"Crying?"

"Yes, sir."

The face of Gen. Phillips darkened.

"No outrage, I trust. By Heaven! if there is, the

perpetrator shall swing by the neck, be he man or officer."

"I don't think it's that, sir," was the orderly's reply. "The young lady says she has important information to give you."

"Important information?"

"Yes, sir."

"Who is the other prisoner?"

"A young man, sir—rather a boy."

"Place a chair for the young lady—that arm chair—and admit both the prisoners."

A few moments afterwards Fanny Talbot and Walter Hayfield were introduced into the apartment.

CHAPTER XXI.

THE INTERVIEW.

As Fanny entered, Gen. Phillips rose and made a
courtly inclination.   A single glance had told him that
the young girl was a lady entitled to all the respect he
could pay her.

"Be good enough to take a seat, madam," he said,
pointing to the arm chair, which the orderly had drawn
forward in obedience to his directions.

"Oh! no, sir! no, no! I cannot sit down," exclaimed
Fanny, whose eyes streamed with tears.   "There is
not a moment to lose!   I must speak, and speak
quickly!"

Gen. Phillips fixed a penetrating look upon the
young lady and said:

"I will hear with pleasure what you desire to say,
madam.   May I ask with whom I have the honor of
conversing?"

"My name is Fanny Talbot, sir, and I have come to
beseech you to spare the life of Capt. Canolles?"

At these words the face of Gen. Phillips lost its mild
expression and grew cold.   It was plain that he had
misapprehended the object of the young lady's visit.
The orderly informed him that she was crying, and had
come to communicate important information, from
which he had concluded that she had either some complaint to make or some intelligence to give him.   It

now became obvious that her aim was to plead with him in behalf of Canolles—to work, if possible, upon his feelings by entreaties and tears—and knowing that there was no possible ground for pardoning the prisoner, he shrunk from being subjected, in his weak and feverish condition, to an interview as trying as it would be fruitless.

"I pray you will be seated, Miss Talbot," he said, coldly; "or that you will permit me to resume my own seat. I am ill and must sit down."

He sank back in his chair and added:

"You subject me to unnecessary pain by this interview, Miss Talbot. I am not aware of the relations you sustain toward the prisoner Canolles; but, even if he were your brother—the nearest and dearest person to you in the world—I regret to be obliged to inform you that it is impossible for me to interpose in his case."

Fanny sank down in her chair and covered her face with her hands, sobbing bitterly and apparently unable to command her voice sufficiently to speak.

Gen. Phillips looked at her with an expression of sincere pity.

"If I could spare the life of this person, Miss Talbot," he said, "I give you my word of honor I would do so—I would have done so without your interposition. But this is impossible. I am not only a man—I am an official. The prisoner has forfeited his life by his own act. He has had a fair trial. He has acknowledged the truth of the charges against him. A court strongly desirous of sparing him, if possible—

for there never was apparently a braver man—has been compelled to condemn him, in accordance with the laws of war. I have been compelled to approve the sentence of the court or fail in my duty. I am therefore powerless, whatever distress you may feel at the prisoner's fate."

Fanny rose, removing her hands from her wet face, and exclaimed:

"But if there is something that you do not know! —if the prisoner is not the common plunderer you think him!—if he is a gentleman!—as true and noble as any human being that ever lived!—if his object in attacking the convoy was to accomplish an end which all persons must respect him for wishing to accomplish—"

The poor girl stopped, choked by tears, and Gen. Phillips pushed back his chair, gazing at her with the utmost astonishment.

"Miss Talbot!" he exclaimed, "you must have lost your reason under the pressure of distress. The prisoner a gentleman!—true and noble!—his object one that ought to be respected! Surely you are unaware of what you are saying."

"Oh! no! no!—every word I say is true."

"Impossible!"

Her face suddenly flushed with joy.

"But if I prove what I say!—if I show you that the prisoner's motives were not only unselfish, but noble, then you will pardon him, will you not? Oh! Gen. Phillips, people say that you are a man of the highest honor—that this principle guides you in all things;

and I appeal to it now—your authority here is above all—"

"But the meaning of all this, Miss Talbot," interposed Gen. Phillips, with feverish emotion, "the meaning! Speak quickly; the hour is at hand for the prisoner's execution! If you have proof of what you allege in his favor, it behooves you to produce it promptly. You say justly that my authority is controlling, as the head of the army. Yes; but I, in turn, am controlled by the laws of war. I can stay the execution of the prisoner if it seems proper for me to do so; but I must have some valid reason; and, you will pardon me, Miss Talbot, for adding that I do not feel at liberty to base such official interposition upon the mere oral statement of any person."

"I have better proof than my own words!" exclaimed Fanny; "written proof!"

The trembling fingers of the young lady were inserted in the opening of her dress in front, laced after the fashion of the times, with cord over a chemisette.

"Written proof, Miss Talbot!" said Gen. Phillips. "Ah! that is what I ask! I ask nothing better than to be able, consistently with my duty, to save the life you plead for! Marauder or not, Canolles is a brave soldier! The proof—the proof, Miss Talbot!"

Fanny made no reply. She stood as motionless as if she had suddenly been turned to stone. The hand she had placed in her bosom remained there. Her eyes were fixed. Her face was as white as snow.

"The proof, the proof, madam!" repeated Gen. Phillips; "and I must again call your attention, Miss

Talbot, to the fact that time is passing—the prisoner's fate hangs in the balance! In ten minutes it will be too late."

Fanny did not reply. She was fumbling in the bosom of her dress, and trembling.

" I—I—it was here," she murmured in a low voice, "in my bosom. I thought it was safe—but—but—in the darkness, while riding fast—I have lost it!"

As she uttered these words her eyes closed, her slender figure wavered as a flower wavers when the wind strikes it, and but for Gen. Phillips, who started up and supported her, she would have fallen fainting to the floor.

CHAPTER XXII.

AT SUNRISE.

A military execution is one of the saddest incidents attending war. It depresses· the most careless, and appals the bravest, for there is something brutal and repulsive in the whole proceeding calculated to revolt the most hardened spectator. Death in action is one thing—to be shot to death by a file of soldiers is another. In combat the pulse is hot; the smoke, the uproar, the smell of gunpowder fires the blood—a man falls then as a soldier, and dies the death of a soldier. Shot to death by sentence of court-martial, he dies like a hunted animal run down and knocked on the head. His life is coldly extinguished by human beings who have no ill-feeling toward him, who perhaps pity him. He is the victim of an army regulation. He is not killed in open fight, man against man; he is quietly put to death by a detail of infantry who fire on him at the word, see him fall, and then march back to their quarters to breakfast, while others dig a grave and place the corpse in it, and the whole affair is forgotten. Of the brutal thing called war, the most brutal feature is the military execution.

Canolles faced his fate, repulsive as it was, with unshrinking nerves. It is not without reason that the world respects courage in a man, since the trait is one which gives human nature a certain superiority and mastership over fate itself. The man who can look death in the face without the tremor of a nerve is greater than what is opposed to him—and Canolles had this courage to meet his fate with a steady eye.

We left him asleep in his prison with Col. Ferrers looking at him; and this tranquil slumber continued unbroken throughout the rest of the night. Ferrers would neither wake him himself nor allow any other person to do so. Giving express orders to this effect to the guard, and informing Cartaret that his interview with the prisoner should take place toward dawn, he returned to his quarters, directed his orderly to wake him in two hours, and stretching himself on a camp couch fell asleep.

Ferrers had resolved to ascertain the contents of the paper written by Canolles as soon as he woke, for which there would be ample time; and then, if there were any circumstances connected with the attack on the convoy calculated to change the light in which the court had viewed it, he meant to repair immediately to the quarters of Gen. Phillips, apply for a reprieve, and thus afford Canolles another chance for his life.

Such was the plan formed by Col. Ferrers. Unfortunately he lost sight of the fact that his orderly might be as drowsy as himself. This proved to be the fact. The man nodded on his post, gradually his head sank, and in a quarter of an hour he was asleep.

Two, three, four hours passed—day came—the east began to redden—and Col. Ferrers still slept on. The camp stirred—officers moved to and fro—the stifled hum of the forces came on the morning air, and still the old *militaire*, overcome by loss of rest in the earlier hours of the night, continued to sleep as tranquilly as the man whom he had ordered to wake him.

Suddenly the roll of a drum was heard, and Col. Ferrers rose hastily to his feet, rubbing his eyes, and looking around him.

All at once the truth flashed upon him. He had overslept himself, and the orderly had failed in his duty!

The face of the old soldier flushed with passion, and rushing upon the man, who was just awake, he bestowed upon him a kick so violent that it literally hurled him out of the tent. This was succeeded by a volley of oaths and curses, which seemed to relieve in some measure the soldier's indignation, and then hastening from the tent he went rapidly in the direction of the house where Canolles had been confined.

Passing the sentinel quickly he hastened into the apartment where he had left the prisoner. It was vacant. Canolles was nowhere to be seen; but on the table lay the packet addressed to "Lieut. Henry Cartaret," Canolles having added the words, "Deliver this to Col. Lord Ferrers when I am dead."

The heart of the old *militaire* died within him. While he was sleeping day had come; Canolles was to be shot at sunrise; he had already been conducted to the place of execution, and a single glance through the window showed him the disk of the sun slowly rising above the summit of the forest trees toward the east.

Seizing the packet and thrusting it into his breast, he rushed from the room and on past the sentinel.

"They have gone with the prisoner Canolles?" he cried to the soldier.

"Yes, sir," was the reply.

"How long?"

"About a quarter of an hour, sir."

. "And—the other officer captured last night—did he and Canolles meet?"

"No, sir; had your orders not to disturb the prisoner, sir."

Col. Ferrers hastened, almost running toward the spot, nearly a quarter of a mile distant, where a group and the gleam of gun barrels indicated the locality of the approaching tragedy. His face burned like fire behind the snow-white mustache; his breast heaved with emotion and the unwonted exertion. Grasping tightly the paper left by Canolles he hurried on, vainly endeavoring to attract the attention of the men comprising the fatal group.

Habituated to such spectacles, and familiar with the details of military executions, Lord Ferrers could follow every manœuvre and calculate the possibility of his reaching the spot before the order to fire was given by the officer commanding the detachment. This seemed now utterly impossible. The sun had risen above the forest in full majesty, and the detachment which had been detailed for the execution of the prisoner were evidently awaiting the order of the officer in command to perform their melancholy duty.

Canolles stood facing them, with his hands unbound and his head bare. The former favor he owed to the soldierly sympathy of the young officer who had been detailed to superintend the execution.. The officer had made his appearance at the quarters occupied by the prisoner a little after dawn, and had found him awake, and folding the sheets of the paper which he had written.

"Good morning, Lieutenant," said Canolles, courteously addressing the young Englishman by the title which his uniform indicated. "I see you have come for me."

"Yes, Captain—I am sorry to say it."

"The duty is not agreeable to you I see very well, Lieutenant; but we cannot pass through this world without being called upon to perform at times what is repulsive. You are a soldier, sir, hence you lament the necessity of giving the order to your men to fire on a brother soldier, marauder though he be."

"I do not believe you are a marauder, sir," said the young officer with some emotion; "I was within earshot during your trial, and am willing to pledge my honor that you are a gentleman."

"Thanks," was the reply of Canolles. "Sympathy is grateful to a man when he is surrounded by enemies and about to die."

"You have as many friends as enemies in the British army."

"But I die all the same," said Canolles in the same calm voice. "Well, it is the fortune of war. I have played and lost, and will stand the forfeit. A last favor now—it is slight."

"I will grant it if I can, with all my heart."

"I hoped to see a friend this morning before sunrise—Lord Ferrers. We were conversing last night when the American attack took place—a mere skirmish, no doubt—and he was forced to leave me. I expected him to return—he was doubtless unable to do so. I was sure, however, that I would see him this morning, as I think I have his friendly sympathy, and he is anxious to ascertain the contents of this paper."

"Of that paper?"

"Yes, what is written here interests him, or will. There is now no time. Oblige me by seeing that the paper is delivered to him after my death. I have made, as you will see, an endorsement upon it requesting as much."

"Oh, yes! I will deliver it! Do not fear, Captain!" exclaimed the young officer, nearly giving way to sympathetic emotion.

"Thanks once more, Lieutenant; and now I am ready. A last favor—I shall make no attempt to escape on the way to the ground—leave my hands free. I am a soldier, not a malefactor."

"Your wish is granted, Captain."

"And now I am at your orders, sir."

The young Englishman turned toward the door, so much moved that he lost sight of the paper, which remained lying upon the table. Canolles followed him, the guard was put in motion, and the melancholy party proceeded to the place of execution.

They soon reached it, and the men were drawn up in line. Canolles turned and looked toward the east. The red flush indicated that the sun was about to rise.

"My time is short," said the partisan. "Give me a moment, Lieutenant, to say my last prayer. I die a Christian as well as a soldier. I believe with all my heart and soul in our Lord and Saviour Jesus Christ."

He clasped his hands, closed his eyes, and his head drooped; for a few moments his lips were seen moving. He then raised his head, and standing straight as an arrow, fixed his eyes immovably on the detachment.

"Oblige me by inspecting the arms, Lieutenant," he said, "I wish to die at the first discharge."

Nearly blinded by tears the young officer obeyed, inspecting and returning the muskets, one by one. He then took his post on the right of the detachment. Canolles was standing ten or fifteen paces in front.

"Are you ready, Captain?" faltered the young Englishman.

"Ready!" was the reply in the resolute tone of the soldier.

The English officer turned away his head as though to hide from his eyes the terrible spectacle of a human being torn to pieces by bullets, and hurled back, drenched with blood.

"Present!" he muttered.

The soldiers presented.

"Take aim!"

The gleaming barrels fell like a single weapon, and were directed at the prisoner's heart.

"Fire!" trembled on the officer's lips, when a shout was heard behind him, and turning his head he saw Lord Ferrers hastening toward him with violent gesticulation.

“Hold!” shouted Lord Ferrers, and he was seen pointing in the direction of the quarters of Gen. Phillips, about four hundred yards distant.

In front of Bollingbrook House was seen a confused group of men and horses, and in the midst of them a young girl waving a paper. She seemed about to rush with it toward the place of execution, but it was snatched from her hand, one of the men leaped on horseback, and a moment afterward was seen approaching at headlong speed, digging the spurs into his horse at every bound, and waving the paper above his head.

“Ground arms!” cried the young officer to the file of men, and hastening toward the horseman he seized the paper and tore it open.

It contained these words, in the handwriting of Gen. Phillips:

“ Arrest the execution of the prisoner Canolles, who is reprieved until further orders.   PHILLIPS.”

“ Thank God!” cried the young man, and he hurried to Canolles and grasped his hand.

“ You are reprieved, Captain!” he said.

“ And a devilish close graze it was!” exclaimed a panting voice behind the officer. “ Well, Lieutenant, there is no further use for this file of men, I suppose?”

“ None whatever, Colonel.”

And ordering a corporal to march the detachment back to their quarters, the officer said to Canolles:

“ Take my arm, Captain. I am afraid you will have to go back to prison; but you are safe. I never knew a reprieved man to suffer!”

“ Faith! here’s another arm at your service, Canolles,”

said Lord Ferrers. "I meant to offer it to you on your way to this spot, only I reached the prison too late."

Canolles seemed to sustain his sudden good fortune as coolly as he had faced approaching death.

"Ah!" he said. "So you were at the prison, Colonel, after I left it?"

"Yes."

"You saw the paper addressed to you?"

"Yes, here it is."

Canolles extended his hand and took it.

"Since I am not dead, Colonel," he said, "I must resume possession, for the present, of this paper."

"Humph!"

"The reprieve, short as it may be, materially alters things. But be content—I shall probably be shot soon, and then the paper will reach you."

The Colonel muttered some ill-humored words, adding:

"I wonder what induced Phillips to grant the reprieve? I think I saw a woman yonder, but may I be shot if I know who she can be!"

It was indeed Fanny, who had succeeded in moving Gen. Phillips. Reviving from her fainting fit, she had poured forth, with passionate sobs and tears what the lost paper had contained, and doubtless the agony of her tones and the spectacle of the beautiful face contracted with anguish had a fuller effect than the perusal of the paper could possibly have had.

She was still speaking when Gen. Phillips went to the table, fortunately containing pen, ink and paper, and hastily wrote the reprieve, after which he called an orderly.

"Your friend is reprieved until further orders, Miss Talbot. I can grant you so much, consistently with my duty, after listening to your very singular statement."

Fanny seized the paper, exclaiming: "Oh! thank you! bless you, Gen. Phillips!" and rushed out of the room.

"Follow this young lady," said Phillips to the orderly. "Take that paper, and ride at full speed to the place where Canolles is about to be shot. Lose no time; make signals as you ride; deliver it to the officer; it is a reprieve!"

What followed we have seen. As the door closed on the orderly, Gen. Phillips sank back faintly in his chair.

"Well," he murmured, "if I die, as I think I shall very soon, one of my last official acts has been to grant mercy to a poor fellow-creature—and I in turn may have mercy perhaps granted to me! What a strange and moving story! Well, something told me from the first that this man Canolles was no common plunderer —and I feel that what that poor girl stated is true. Poor girl! How devoted in her! how superior women are to men in this noble trait of unswerving devotion!"

He rose and went to the window, through which he saw the arrival of the orderly and the delivery of the paper.

"He is saved!" he said. "When I am gone his fate will be decided by others."

CHAPTER XXIII.

THE DEATH OF PHILLIPS.

Gen. Phillips had been only too accurate in forecasting his fate. The scenes which have been described took place during the day and night of the tenth and on the morning of the eleventh of May.

On the thirteenth of May, while the American forces, under the Marquis de Lafayette still confronted the British army in Petersburg, Gen. William Phillips, "the proudest man in the proudest nation upon earth," breathed his last in the Bollingbrook House from the effects of bilious fever.

He was buried, as he anticipated and probably desired, in the graveyard attached to the ivy-clad old Blandford church. The ceremonies were imposing. Mourning insignia were seen everywhere, the bands played the Dead March, and the army, with reversed arms, followed the hearse, containing the remains of their commander, warmly beloved, in spite of his hot temper and pride, for his many excellent qualities of heart.

The long cortege wound up the Blandford hill, the coffin was removed from the hearse by Lord Ferrers and the other pall-bearers, and lowered slowly to its last resting place. The sublime burial service of the Episcopal Church was then read by an army chaplain—a sudden volley of fire-arms rolled above the grave in honor of the dead soldier—and an hour afterward a mound of green turf, under the shadow of the Blandford walls, alone indicated the spot where Gen. William Phillips was sleeping his last sleep.

The command of the army devolved upon Gen. Arnold, as next in rank, until the arrival of Lord Cornwallis, who was on his march from the South in the direction of Petersburg.

CHAPTER XXIV.

THE SEQUEL.

We shall now, before passing to other scenes of the narrative, relate the sequel of events occurring at Petersburg in this month of May, 1781.

The elevation, by the death of Gen. Phillips, of Gen. Arnold to the supreme command of the British forces at Petersburg, aroused in Lord Ferrers, and the officers almost without exception, a sentiment of the deepest indignation and even disgust. The feeling in the army, as afterwards in London, in reference to Arnold, was general and unmistakable. Compelled to carry out the stipulations made between him and Sir Henry Clinton—a certain grade of rank and a certain amount of money for the surrender of West Point—the English government had given him the rank and paid the money, but there all had ended. The officers of the army were obliged to salute the uniform he wore and obey his orders, but they were not obliged to personally associate with him, and absolutely refused to do so. He was despised by them as a turncoat and traitor to his colors, and the idea now of being subject to the orders of such a person was revolting. Lord Ferrers especially, who had never made any secret of his own profound contempt for Arnold, expressed in the most public places and with utter carelessness his sentiments.

"The fellow's a malefactor!" he growled. "What

the devil does the War Office mean by putting a jail-
bird in command over British officers and gentlemen?
————— ————— ————— ————— —————!"

We regret that respect for the proprieties and a fear
of shocking the reader prevents us from recording the
expressions indicated by the space here left blank.
Such a salvo of oaths, resembling a broadside of cannon, generally concluded the observations of Col. Ferrers on the subject of Gen. Arnold, and other officers
indulged in denunciations as bitter, if not as eloquent
and striking.

The officers, headed by Col. Ferrers, were in this
state of mind in regard to Arnold, when it suddenly
became known that an order had just been issued re-
versing the reprieve of Canolles by Gen. Phillips, and
directing that the sentence of the court-martial condemning him to death should be executed in twenty-
four hours.

When he received this information Col. Ferrers repaired to the quarters of Gen. Arnold, remained shut
up alone for an hour with that officer, and those who
were within hearing knew from the loud and angry
voices that a tempestuous interview was taking place.
The details of this interview were known to no persons
but those who took part in it; but it was afterwards
discovered that Lord Ferrers had protested indignantly
against the death of Canolles; had nearly advanced to
the point of a personal defiance of Gen. Arnold; and
had left the apartment in a rage, muttering curses, and
expressing his opinion of Arnold in a voice loud
enough to be heard by every one in his vicinity.

An hour afterwards Gen. Arnold was called upon to undergo a second interview, though of a different character.

Fanny Talbot, accompanied by Walter, who had been permitted to go free, had repaired to the house of the friend whom she had mentioned, Miss Lucy Maurice, the daughter of a gentleman of the town, and had here remained without seeking an interview with Canolles, but employed every means of interesting those around her in his case. She had been visited daily by Lieut. Henry Cartaret, who had succeeded in procuring his release on parole—the object of Col. Ferrers, who effected his release, being to exchange him for Lieut. Tom Ferrers, a prisoner, as the reader will recall, in the hands of the Americans. Harry, who had promptly visited Canolles in his prison, now joined his exertions to those of Fanny to procure the pardon of the partisan, and like Fanny was shocked by the sudden intelligence that Canolles would be shot on the next morning.

The interview which Gen. Arnold was now called upon to pass through, immediately after that with Col. Ferrers, was with Fanny.

The young lady remained pleading with the British commander for more than two hours. The colloquy with Ferrers had been loud and angry—this one was full of sobs and tears on Fanny's part, to which Gen. Arnold made only cold and brief replies. It was plain that he would no more yield to the entreaties and tears of Miss Talbot than to the indignant protest of Col. Ferrers. The truth was that the denunciation of himself by Canolles during the session of the court-martial had violently enraged Gen. Arnold, and he was not a man to forgive a person who had so bitterly insulted him. Every word uttered by the partisan rankled in his memory—his fury had settled down into a cold resolution to wreak revenge upon him—and finding the occasion unexpectedly present itself, he seized it, allowing no prayer to move him.

The result was that all Fanny's entreaties were unheeded. They even aroused in him a sullen animosity. He would send the man who had publicly insulted him to his death, if only to announce his defiance to the officers of the army, with whose sentiments towards himself he was perfectly familiar. As to this girl—the sweetheart, perhaps, of the prisoner—she should not even see him again. The result of the interview, therefore, was melancholy—it had better have never taken place. When she left him, he said briefly to the officer of the guard:

"Send that young woman out of the lines of this army under guard—in an hour—and tell her that I order her not to return."

And two hours afterwards poor Fanny, mounted upon the horse which she had ridden on her entrance into Petersburg, was outside the lines, making her way with bitter sobs and tears, and pitied by the very soldiers who had escorted her, to Chatsworth.

On the same night Lord Ferrers returned to the quarters of Gen. Arnold and presented him with a petition signed by nearly every officer in the army, asking that Canolles might be reprieved until Lord

Cornwallis had an opportunity to decide upon his case. Arnold received the paper stiffly and in silence, informing Lord Ferrers coldly that he would consider it and return it in an hour with his endorsement. To this Lord Ferrers had nothing to say; he returned to his quarters, and in an hour the petition was brought back to him by an orderly. The endorsement on it was as follows:

"Returned disapproved. The prisoner Canolles was tried by court-martial and condemned to death as a marauder. As I see no reason to disapprove the action of the court, it is hereby approved, and the prisoner Canolles will be executed at sunrise to-morrow.

"B. ARNOLD, Brigadier-General."

Col. Ferrers, on perusing this endorsement, fell into such a rage that he nearly burst an artery. He repaired to Canolles' prison and had a long private interview with him that night, promising to return at daylight.

When he approached the door of the house, just as the first gray of dawn touched the dampness, he was surprised to observe that no sentinel was posted in front of it.

A step further brought him to the gateway of the inclosure. He opened it—suddenly his foot struck against something, and looking down he saw that it was the body of a man, evidently the sentinel on post. He seemed to have been stunned, probably by a blow from the butt of a musket on the back of the head, as his hair was bloody and his breathing indicated that he was not dead.

Lord Ferrers walked slowly into the house, a grim smile curling his white mustache.

"Glad of it," he muttered. "Canolles is safe, and

his Excellency Gen. Benedict Arnold will probably have a fit!"

The old *militaire* wound up with a positive chuckle, and went straight to the room occupied by Canolles. It was vacant, but he saw by the dim light struggling through the window that a paper was lying upon the table. He took it up, held it to the light and read:

"For Colonel Lord Ferrers:

"I shall not be here, my dear Colonel, in all probability, to receive the visit which your brave heart made you promise. I am free, or soon shall be. A youth of my command, called Walter Hayfield, has just surprised the sentinel, stunning him with a blow from his own musket, and opened my prison door.

"As the moment is critical, and the alarm may be given, I must deny myself the pleasure of writing more.

"I have not left the paper containing a statement of my motives and an account of myself, since it was to be delivered to you only when I was dead. As it is possible that I may escape, I must retain it for the present, even from one to whom I owe more than I can express. "CANOLLES."

Col. Ferrers uttered a loud laugh, and his snowy mustache again curled toward his eyes with enjoyment. "Well, of all the cool fellows!" he exclaimed. "How is it possible not to admire a man like that?"

All at once the house swarmed with the guard, who had just discovered the escape of the prisoner.

At their head, half-dressed only, was the officer of the night, the young lieutenant who had exhibited so much sympathy for Canolles when conducted to his execution.

"What is the matter? What has occurred?" he exclaimed, rubbing his eyes. "You here, my Lord?"

"Yes."

"Something has happened?"

" Certainly something has happened, Lieutenant—
Canolles has given Arnold the slip!"

He leaned over and took the young fellow's arm,
exclaiming, with another laugh :

" And I wouldn't have him recaptured for a thousand
pounds!"

10

PART II.

CHAPTER I.

Under the moonlight of a summer night, two girls, in the grounds of Chatsworth, were holding one of those private and confidential interviews dear to the hearts of maidens in their bloom.

The theater of war had suddenly been shifted from the south side to the heart of the Commonwealth of Virginia. Reaching Petersburg soon after the death of Phillips, Lord Cornwallis had assumed command of all the British forces, crossed James River, advanced upon Lafayette, who retired before him toward the Rappahannock, and penetrated the interior, with the sword in one hand and the torch in the other.

A brief and fiery episode of the long conflict followed—fiery in every sense, since Col. Tarleton, the revengeful chief of the English cavalry, defeated by Morgan at the Cowpens, made the hot weather hotter still by setting fire to mills, barns and private dwellings—proceeding, it appeared, upon the theory that war meant war on the unarmed as well as the armed, on non-combatants as on enemies sword in hand. Old men were arrested, negro servants carried off, cattle killed, the throats of suckling colts cut, hen-houses rifled and the whole region laid waste. Wherever Col. Tarleton moved he left behind him blood, tears, mourning, and the prospect of starvation for the poor women and children, flying from their homes in flames.

A hasty dash at Charlottesville, whence the Legislature escaped; a fruitless attempt to seize Gov. Jefferson at Monticello—then news came that Lafayette was marching to give the English battle, and Lord Cornwallis, apparently so anxious to prevent the boy Lafayette from escaping him, fell back rather ingloriously towards the lowlands, pursued by his young opponent.

Such was the condition of things when our narrative resumes its course, and its personages reappear upon the scene.

The summer night at Chatsworth was exquisite. Twilight was just deepening into dark, but a full-orbed moon, soaring through light clouds, poured a flood of dreamy splendor on the field, the forests and the river.

At the foot of the Chatsworth grounds, and immediately upon the banks of the stream, was a mass of rock nearly covered by that exquisitely delicate species of Virginia moss resembling emerald velvet; and overshadowing this rock was a solitary pine, which had thrust itself through a cleft, and expanding slowly with the passing years, now towered aloft, the deep green tassels of its crown bending over the water. In these tassels of the great tree the river breeze seemed always whispering, and the low memorial murmur prompted to those dreams which spring from memory. From the rear or land side a narrow pathway ran around to the river front, gradually ascending; and here, near the summit, and just beneath the stump of the pine, was an indentation forming a seat entirely hidden from an observer on the lawn above. From this romantic retreat, on spring, or summer, or autumn days, you looked out on the river, with its white sails hovering like waterfowl with outspread wings upon the current, on the far misty headlands opposite, and the blue sky drooping down on the far line of forests. At the hour when we visit it now all this was only dimly visible, but there was an added charm. The great moon had thrown across the breast of the stream a long pathway of light, and as the river breeze gently agitated the current this pathway broke into silver ripples, over which the feet of fairies might have danced—a bridge of beams conducting them to some midnight revelry to which "the horns of Elfland faintly blowing" summoned them!

The hiding place in the "Moss Rock," for so the spot was called, was occupied, however, on this night of summer, by two maidens incontestably of mundane flesh and blood—most attractive if not fanciful or poetic beings, with slender but by no means aerial figures, faces not at all misty in the morn, but blooming like the blush rose, and white arms, which the summer evening had induced them to divest of all covering.

One of them—Fanny Talbot—presented a strong contrast to her companion, apparently of about the same age as herself. Fanny, with her large, mild eyes, full of that dove-like softness which we have described; and her bearing as composed, was the precise opposite, indeed, of the other—Lucy Maurice, the friend with whom she had stayed in Petersburg when she had gone thither intent on saving Canolles. Lucy was brunette, tall, with black eyes, raven hair, and white teeth, sparkling with perpetual smiles. In the brilliant eyes, flashing with the spirit of fun, the rosy cheeks and the red lips, never compressed or drawn down with prim reserve, you read the very soul of mirth, health, and that buoyant life which seems to defy melancholy, and make its possessor as happy in the dark days as in the bright—ready, if the sun will not shine, to supply from within a sunshine of its own.

Miss Lucy Maurice had wound her arm, maiden fashion, around the waist of Fanny—the two heads leaned back side by side against the rock—brown and raven curls entangled, and this was the dialogue which ensued between the young ladies.

CHAPTER II.

WHAT LED MISS LUCY MAURICE TO VISIT MISS FANNY TALBOT.

But perchance the reader does not wholly relish this unceremonious manner of introducing a new personage without an explanation of her presence. This explanation is simple.

When Fanny went on her brave expedition to Petersburg, she sought refuge there, as we have seen, with a friend of hers, the daughter of a gentleman of the town. She and Lucy Maurice were old and dear friends, having been schoolmates in the place; and the warm-hearted Lucy, without making any indiscreet inquiries in regard to Fanny's motives, had assisted her in every manner in her power, quietly deferring to the future that myriad of questions which burned upon her pretty lips. This silence was the result of delicacy and a fear of increasing the evident pain and agitation of her friend. When Lieut. Harry Cartaret, however, made his appearance as a prisoner on parole, and she formed his acquaintance, it appeared to Miss Lucy that her reticence was no longer necessary, and she desired the young soldier to inform her who the person called Canolles really was, since Fanny's interest in a mere freebooter was incredible. To this plain question Harry Cartaret had made an evasive reply, looking very gloomy. But gradually his gloom was dissipated by the brilliant light of Lucy Maurice's eyes, and it soon became plain to that astute young lady that she was making a conquest of the youthful son of Mars— an idea which evidently had never in the least entered Lieut. Harry's mind.

Had Miss Lucy indeed known that this handsome young fellow was engaged to be married to Fanny, such was her loyalty and affection for her friend that she would have walked over burning ploughshares before she would have flirted with him—would have turned her back abruptly on her new admirer. Of the relations between Fanny and Harry Cartaret she was, however, perfectly ignorant. Then, having in the dull war days very little to amuse her, and delighted to show the young British officers, whom she treated with immense disdain, how very different and more charming she could be when a rebel admirer appeared, Miss Maurice suddenly deployed all her feminine artillery; her bright eyes shot forth smiles full of fascinating preference; she paraded herself side by side with Harry on the front porch of her father's house at twilight, as the young British warriors clanked by in gallant uniforms and with envious glances, and in every manner strove to say to those jealous youths, "How stupid you seem to me, and how I detest you! Here beside me, playing with the rose I gave him, and whispering to me, is a person I prefer a thousand times to you!"

It was delightful to tell the young British dandies this without speaking to them, and Miss Lucy keenly enjoyed the ceremony, even proceeding so far as to deliberately repair at dewy eve to the grassy grounds around the old Blandford church, much frequented by romantic British youths, and there, leaning with confiding sweetness on the arm of Harry, stroll slowly in the pleasant evening with her eyes cast down, a modest color in her cheeks, and pressing to her lips with bashful confusion a rosebud—gave no doubt, the observant youths concluded, of her love for the devilish confounded rebel fellow let out on parole!

These feminine humming birds will act thus; but sometimes they hover too close to the flowers, and the leaves suddenly close and hold them. Lucy began to be interested in Harry Cartaret—without being aware of it. She had flirted with him for her amusement and to wreak her spite upon the young *militaires*, her enemies, but gradually her feelings became engaged, and she grew far less demonstrative. There were now no more *tete-a-tetes* upon the porch with sweet side glances from sweet eyes; no more promenades around Blandford, and wicked, languishing tones and stolen looks— Miss Lucy Maurice became bashful in reality, and the change had a stronger influence than ever on her admirer. It was plain that Harry Cartaret had fallen in love with Miss Lucy Maurice, and that he was conscious of it now—a consciousness which did not, however, seem to afford him much enjoyment. He grew moody, yielded to fits of gloom, and would sit for a long time without speaking in the presence of Lucy, who was nearly as silent as himself.

He was engaged to Fanny Talbot, and he was in love with Lucy Maurice. There was the source, of course, of poor Harry's gloom. It was not his fault, he argued with himself—he had never meant in the least to fall in love with the pretty face beside him— he had simply opened his eyes one morning to find that she had made him a hopeless captive—and yonder, at Chatsworth, was his betrothed awaiting him; for Fanny, the reader will remember, had been sent out of the British lines by Gen. Arnold.

Poor Harry brooded over this unfortunate state of things, and felt that he was not acting like a gentleman in the least. But his passion remained unchanged. What was he to do? he asked himself. Tell Fanny frankly that his love had changed? Impossible! That appeared to him in the light of absolute dishonor, and dishonor must never attach to the name of Cartaret! Keep his troth with Fanny? His heart sank at the thought. How marry one when his heart was wholly given to another? In whatever direction he turned all was perplexity and misery, and it was with something like relief that the young fellow heard one morning that he had been exchanged for Tom Ferrers, and was at liberty to return to the American camp. He had a last interview with Lucy—the most silent, awkward and constrained interview on the part of both—then with some muttered words, and a sudden blush, he bowed over her hand, touched it slightly with his lips, and left her—left a maiden who proceeded to run up- stairs to her chamber, throw herself on her bed and burst out crying.

Then Miss Lucy Maurice, drying her eyes, proceeded to mope and render her affectionate family uneasy in

reference to her health. What could have produced
so sudden a change in her? each asked the other. The
heat? Or was Petersburg so dull and humdrum now
since my Lord Cornwallis and all his followers had
marched away that it oppressed her? Yes, doubtless
these were the explanations of the young lady's depression; the heat and dullness of the town. So it was
suggested that she should have change of air. It was
utterly shocking that so healthy a damsel should rise
from breakfast without having swallowed a mouthful!
and the suggestion took the practical form, "Go and
make a visit to Fanny Talbot, at Chatsworth, where
the river breezes will bring back your appetite for
breakfast!"

Lucy indifferently acquiesced; her father escorted
her to Chatsworth, where Fanny met her with the
warmest affection, Miss Eleanor with great politeness,
and Mrs. Talbot with that subdued interest which she
bestowed equally upon every occurrence; and then
Miss Lucy proceeded, most unexpectedly and against
all romantic rules, really to get back her appetite.
Youth, like truth, is mighty and will prevail. At
eighteen the stomach—if we may use that inelegant
term, for which, nevertheless, there is no more elegant
substitute—is a great foe of romance. Youth demands
food, and food produces health, and health produces
"feeling well," and feeling well produces cheerfulness,
and cheerfulness that enjoyment of life resulting in
smiles and roses. So Lucy grew rosy, and smiled now
as gaily as ever, and she and Fanny deported themselves very much like two school-girls on a holiday.

Fanny had courageously thought and fought down her own feeling of depression, and had recovered all the brave tranquillity of her calm, brave character. She and Lucy had avoided with sedulous care any allusion to their more private and personal matters, while indulging upon all else with perfect unreserve; and such was the state of affairs, when rambling out on that summer night by moonlight, the young ladies ascended the narrow pathway and ensconced themselves in the hiding place under the great pine on the Moss Rock.

CHAPTER III.

AT THE " MOSS-ROCK."

" Who is Canolles? I might as well tell you, Fan, that I have been burning—yes, burning!—to ask that question for a whole month, and unless it is agreeable to you to contemplate the spectacle of your friend suddenly bursting and expiring from pent-up curiosity you will extremely oblige by relieving her feelings, as it were unlacing her corsage, and allowing her to get a little breath."

This from Miss Lucy Maurice, and then quick laughter from Fanny.

"Do you know one compliment I have always paid you, Lucy?"

"I do not. I know I have paid you one thousand—behind your back."

" I am sure you have. Well, the especial one I have paid you is believing that you have no curiosity."

" Me!" screamed Miss Maurice, with doubtful grammatical correctness. "Good gracious! If there is any one dear delightful vice I have in the purest perfection it is curiosity!"

" I do not believe that."

" It is perfectly true."

" But why do you care to know who Capt. Canolles is, Lucy, and why do you suppose that I can tell you, if there is anything to tell?"

“ You will please not play the female diplomat with me, Miss Talbot, and attempt to throw dust in my eyes. ‘ Why do I suppose that you can tell me ?’ Because you rode through the British lines at night to save his life, and saved it.”

Fanny blushed a little and then laughed to hide what seemed some confusion.

“ Well,” she said, “ of course it would be absurd in me, Lucy, to say that I do not take an interest in—that is—know Capt. Canolles ——”

“ I think it would !” said the vivacious Lucy, with frank laughter.

“ Know him, that is,” continued Fanny, “ better than some other people. Yes, Lucy, I am acquainted with him and have a sincere friendship for him; but you must let me add, dear, that I cannot tell you anything more than this.”

“ ‘ Dear’ ! oh! yes! You are growing suddenly affectionate. You are ‘ dear’-ing me now ! I’ll be your ‘ darling ’ next, when I’m to be shut up and silenced.”

“ You are my darling, now,” said Fanny, with her charming smile, and quietly turning her head so that her cheek lightly touched that of Lucy, after which brief and flitting exhibition of feminine fondness she resumed her dignity by withdrawing the cheek.

“ Oh! very well. Here we are billing and cooing like two ring-doves in love with each other,” exclaimed Lucy, “ and I suppose if one of the stronger vessels of the masculine sex were to see us his lordly nose would turn up in scorn of such lackadaisical proceedings !

Men never believe that women care anything for each other, and as to their kisses, they declare that we always kiss just before we begin to scratch each other."

"We at least have never yet scratched each other, Lucy."

"And I trust we are not going to begin on the present occasion. But—shall I be frank, Fan?"

"Yes."

"I feel a violent desire to scratch you now! You know I am dying with curiosity. I have attempted to express my feelings by that lovely figure of a corsage that is too tight to let one breathe—and you will tell me nothing."

"Lucy, dear," said Fanny, repeating the obnoxious form of address, "I would tell you everything I know about Capt. Canolles, as he calls himself—and by one of the strangest chances in the world I know everything connected with him—but I cannot. He wishes to remain to all but a few persons only what he appears to be, for the present at least; and to reveal his secret even to you would not be honorable in me. You see I am speaking candidly and seriously. I do not attempt to conceal from you—I cannot—that Capt. Canolles is not the person he seems to be. Who and what he is I have no right to say, darling."

"There it is at last! I knew it was coming. 'Darling!' Very well. I see, Fan, there is no more to say. Keep your secret. Only one other question."

"Ask it, and if I can answer it I will."

Miss Lucy looked her companion full in the eye.

11

"My question is going to be indiscreet."

"I am sure it will not be."

"Well, you shall form your own opinion, and you must tell your 'dear darling' this at least. Is Capt. Canolles——I am almost afraid!"

"Go on!"

"Is Capt. Canolles—that is, does he—are there—that is to say—any peculiar relations existing between —yourself and that gentleman?"

"None in the world!" Fanny replied emphatically, with the same blush.

"Well, I am glad to hear that. I've no doubt your friend is a gallant fellow—everybody says so—but you should marry some staid and respectable squire, with a big mansion-house, not a wandering soldier, who carries his house on his back—that is, in a roll behind his saddle."

Fanny, recovering her calmness, greeted these words with a smile:

"Will you follow your own advice?"

"I?—I have no intention of marrying."

"You say that a little sadly, Lucy. I hope you have not gone, like the dear imprudent thing you are, and lost your heart to anybody?"

It was Lucy's turn to blush, which she proceeded to do, not with the moderation of her friend, but in the most vivacious and unmistakable manner. In fact, Miss Lucy Maurice turned crimson, and vainly essayed to laugh.

"Of course not. How absurd I should be."

"You have seen no one then to fancy?"

"No one whatever."

Fanny remained silent for some moments; then she said quietly:

"Do you know an idle thought occurred to me?"

"What idle thought?"

"You will certainly laugh, but the fancy came. Shall I tell you what it was?"

"Certainly."

"I have a cousin in the army."

"Indeed! And pray what is the meaning of that sudden and apparently irrelevant statement, madam?"

"A cousin who is an acquaintance of yours."

"Of mine!"

A quiet flush followed; it was plain that Miss Lucy Maurice began to understand what was coming.

"A cousin whose name is Henry Cartaret—whose acquaintance you made, you remember, at Petersburg."

"Yes—I believe I did see him—once or twice."

"Why, Lucy! you know you saw him more than once or twice before I was sent from the town!"

"I did not count the number of times," was the reply, in a tone of affected indifference.

"Well, to speak plainly, I thought, perhaps, that you and Harry might take a fancy to each other."

"What an idea!"

"The idea is not so absurd. He is very brave and handsome, and somebody else is very pretty, as well as otherwise attractive."

"Call me 'dear,' now, and 'darling,' do."

"I would like to call you cousin—and you would be my cousin if you were married to Harry."

"Well, I am sorry to say that we shall never be more closely related than we are at present, my dear," said Miss Lucy, in a tone of decided pique. "Lieut. Cartaret and myself are merely acquaintances, and to set at rest forever, Fan, any suspicions you may have upon any such subject, I beg to inform you that there are no private or personal relations of any description whatever existing between myself and your cousin, the lieutenant."

"I am sorry."

"As you are so very great an admirer of his, and so ardently desire that my happiness should be consummated in the manner you intimate—which you evidently think would be the result—why not set your own ladyship's cap for his lieutenantship?—this paragon whom you desire for your friend?"

Fanny made no reply. The color slowly mounted to her face. She was evidently hesitating.

"You have not answered me!" said Lucy.

Fanny still hesitated. Then she said:

"Lucy, I should have told you something about myself before this time."

"Something about yourself?"

"You are my oldest and dearest friend, Lucy, and you and I should have no secrets from each other."

"Certainly we should not; but what in the world do you mean, Fan?"

"I mean ——"

The young lady again hesitated.

"You mean ——. For Heaven's sake relieve my suspense. You mean ——"

"I am engaged to be married to my cousin, Henry Cartaret."

CHAPTER IV.

SHOWING THAT IT IS HIGHLY IMPRUDENT FOR YOUNG LADIES TO TALK IN THEIR SLEEP.

A silence so deep that the whispers of the great pine sounded positively loud followed Fanny's announcement that she was engaged to Harry Cartaret. Lucy did not speak, but her friend felt the heart against her arm beat more rapidly.

"What is the matter, Lucy?" she said, "something seems to agitate you."

"Agitate me! Not in the least!" was the low response, accompanied by a short laugh. "What in the world makes you think so?"

"I can feel your heart beating, and you are positively blushing."

"What a fancy! So you are engaged to Lieutenant Cartaret?"

"Yes."

"Since how long?"

"Two or three years."

"And—and—the engagement is not particularly agreeable, I suppose; a very natural conclusion, you must allow, Fanny, as you seem desirous of bestowing your *fiancee* upon your friend!"

Fanny hesitated.

"A natural conclusion, I must confess," she said at length.

"What other could I possibly come to?"

Lucy again attempted a light laugh, only half succeeding, and added:

"When a lady is engaged to a gentleman the theory commonly accepted is that she proposes to espouse him. If, instead of proposing to espouse him, she is anxious to dispose of her interest in the beloved one, or the one who ought to be beloved, to another person, we are at liberty to form a conjecture at least that she repents of her contract and would like to terminate confidential relations with the dear object!"

Fanny sighed and said:

"Years alter things so in this world, dear. I was almost a child when I became engaged to Harry."

"And the woman would like to select for herself, not merely ratify the child's selection."

"I do not care to select anybody."

"You do not?"

"Indeed, no."

"On your word of honor, Fan?"

"On my word of honor."

Lucy Maurice's pretty face assumed a rather wicked expression.

"I only asked," she said innocently, "since something had made me suppose that Miss Fanny Talbot had— But I must not tell tales."

"Tell tales?"

"I dreamed—perhaps it was only a dream—"

"You dreamed!"

"That is to say, Fan, it was you who dreamed."

" Your words are a puzzle to me, dear.   Please tell me plainly what you mean."

" Shall I? "

" Yes, yes! "

" You will not be put out with me? "

" Certainly not."

"Even if I appear in the light of an eavesdropper ? "

" An eavesdropper—you ! "

" Or something of the sort at least."

"It is impossible that you could ever act in such a character, Lucy.   You are the very last person in the world I should ever suspect of such a proceeding."

" And yet I have been guilty of it," was the reply.

"I do not believe a word you say.   You listened ? overheard ?   Where did you listen, and when; and what was it you overheard persuading you that I had any—well, preference for any one ? "

" I will tell you, as I see that you are bursting with curiosity, my dear," Miss Lucy responded, with another laugh, "and, in order that my explanation may have that deep interest which attaches to the pretty pictures in the romancy, I will first describe the scene of the incident which I purpose to relate, beginning in the true style of romance.   Shall I ? "

" Lucy, there is some wickedness under all this," said Fanny, smiling.   " I never saw that expression upon your face—that wicked smile—unless you were about to sacrifice some one to your fondness for teasing."

" Very well ; but allow me to proceed."

" I shall try not to interrupt you."

Assuming a grave expression, or attempting to do so, Miss Lucy Maurice continued:

"Once upon a time there were two young ladies living in an ancient manor house—I believe it was in England—but having always labored under a disgraceful weakness in reference to localities, the points of the compass and topography in general, I am unable to be precisely accurate upon the point in question. The name of the house I am able to say, however, was 'Chatsworth,' and to this hospitable abode one of the young ladies above described had come on a visit to the other above described. I deceive myself. I have not described them. Let me proceed to do so in a few brief pages, in order that a distinct idea may be formed of the personages who are the heroines of the deeply interesting incident about to be related."

Miss Maurice laughed, *sotto voce*, and went on:

"Fancy two young creatures of eighteen, the one called Fanny, the other Lucy—the former a dear, sweet, languishing, romantic maiden, with the softest and dearest eyes, and so lovely that all loved her; the latter a wicked, heartless creature, dark, spiteful, fond of making all around her miserable—"

"What an absurd caricature of both your heroines!" said Fanny, smiling.

"Oh, no! quite accurate!—perfectly accurate, I assure you!"

"Very well, Miss; but the incident."

"The incident? Do you imagine, Miss Talbot, that I am so ignorant of the rules of the great art of

romance writing as to rush into my subject in such an
abrupt manner as you suggest?   I have just said that
I propose dedicating a few brief pages to the portraits
of my heroines."

"Let me imagine them."

"Impossible—where would be the fair authoress if
she thus cut short her narrative and wasted her material?   Do you wish me to take refuge in thrilling metaphysical analysis, superbly superior to incident and—
interest?   Have you read 'Sir Charles Grandison?'
If not, go peruse that sweet romance and see how many
words Mr. Richardson manages to employ, keeping the
reader in delightful suspense as he proceeds, which I
think, however, is better, after all, than the metaphysical analysis."

Fanny shook her head and Lucy went on:

"Well, as your ladyship is impatient, I will spare
you the rest, and rush to my *denouement* by saying that
on a beautiful summer night—it was the month of
June, the moon was—but fill up the picture! Enough,
that the two maidens had retired to rest in one chamber and one bed—not in two chambers and one bed,
observe, my dear!"

"Go on! go on! Lucy.   You are incorrigible!"

"Had retired to bed, as I said before I was interrupted," continued the incorrigible one, "and was
sound asleep, when suddenly—suddenly—"

"What?"

"When suddenly—what do you think?   That a
musical instrument was heard without, in the dreamy
moonlight, and a rich deep voice was heard to accom-

pany it in a madrigal? No! guess again. Was it a rope ladder thrown aloft in order that one of the maidens might elope with the lover in whose face her cruel parents had slammed the front door? No! guess again. What was it that occurred so suddenly? You observe I use the term suddenly."

"Yes, I observe it since you have used it, you foolish girl, nearly half a dozen times. I shall not guess at all. What was this sudden incident?"

"Well, one of the maidens suddenly—awoke!"

"And was that all? A romantic incident, in truth!"

"Not astounding, I confess, but confess in your turn that my manner of prefacing the incident excited your curiosity to ascertain the sequel."

"Which is quite unworthy of such an elaborate introduction."

"True, but observe that I am following the established rules of romance-writing."

"Please forget them and come to the point. One of the maidens awoke—a bat flew into the room, perhaps—"

"No! no! In that case I—that is, she—would have died with fright."

"So the one who woke was the dark beauty?"

"Yes. It was probably a whippoorwill crying from a tree near the house which aroused her; at all events she rose in bed and gazed around her with startled eyes."

"Why not say sleepy eyes?"

"Sleepy is prosaic and unworthy of romantic use.

Startled! startled is the word; with startled eyes! And there, strange to say, plain before her in the moonlight, so clearly outlined in the brilliant beams pouring through the tall window of the chamber, decorated with rich carvings, and old furniture, through long mysterious shadows—so clearly outlined, I say, that the eye took in without difficulty every detail connected with the figure—there before her was—was—can you imagine what she saw?"

"Not possibly!"

"There before her in the moonlight was—her companion, sound asleep."

"Pshaw!" exclaimed Fanny. "Luce and goose rhyme pat, and to the purpose!"

"Very well; if that is the manner in which my efforts to interest are to be treated, I shall not further trouble your ladyship or relate the incident."

"There is, then, a real incident?"

"Certainly there is, or was."

"If you will tell me what it was I will strive to listen in silence."

"Very well. I am not unforgiving—to proceed to the incident. There before the maiden who had waked up was the maiden who was asleep, and I assure you she was a beauty. Do not let me yield to the raptures of description, but simply observe that she was lying with one white arm placed gracefully beneath her head, her beautiful brown curls tucked carelessly about her snowy forehead, and her lips just parted, showing the pearls beneath—orient pearls in vivid contrast to the rich carnations of the pouting lips, and the sweet blush-roses blooming in the maiden cheeks."

"Lucy," said Miss Fanny, "of all the geese I have ever—"

"You said you'd not interrupt me, Miss, and your word is broken. But to terminate this narrative. The maiden was asleep, as I have previously related, and her sleep was tranquil at first. As her companion, however, gazed at her, her features contracted, and an expression of pain and terror passed over them, effacing all their tranquillity. Then she began to murmur some broken words—she uttered a name—"

"Ah!" said Fanny, in a low tone—"a name?"

"The maiden's words were—uttered in a piteous voice—"

"What were they?" said Fanny, in the same low tone.

"Oh, no! no!—do not take his life! Hartley! Hartley! I shall die if you die—since reading that paper!"

Fanny's head sank until her face was entirely concealed in shadow.

"Did I say that?" she murmured.

"Yes, Fan," was the reply of her friend in a serious and earnest tone; and now, dear, you must forgive me for even seeming to have wished to overhear what you muttered in sleep. I could not avoid hearing what you said, and have not the least desire to have you explain anything. Forgive my thoughtless jest about your interest in some one—in some one bearing the name you uttered."

"The name?" came from Fanny, in the same voice.

"The name of Hartley."

Fanny was silent for a long time. She then said in a low, earnest tone :

"I have nothing in the world to forgive, Lucy, dear, and it would be very unjust indeed to find fault with you for simply hearing. Some of these days you shall know all about everything, and—the person whose name escaped me that night. I cannot tell you now, for reasons you shall know fully some day, perhaps very soon. Does that reconcile you to your friend's concealment?"

"A hundred times, Fan!" exclaimed the impulsive Lucy, bestowing an earnest kiss upon the other's cheek; "and now, as it is getting late, let us stop talking and go home."

Fanny arose, and they were about to descend the narrow pathway leading around the Moss Rock, down to the grass of the lawn, when the tramp of hoofs was heard coming down the bank of the river.

They started and listened. There were no troops in this region, though Lord Cornwallis was known to be on his retreat near Richmond. In war times, however, the unknown is always the suspicious, since it may be the dangerous, and the two girls hastily descended the rock, reached the lawn, and ran, arm in arm—two flitting phantoms of the moonlight night—toward the house.

Before they could reach it, the trample of hoofs was near at hand, dark figures emerged from the forest, and a troop of about twenty men, evidently from their uniform English cavalry, rode into the ground.

CHAPTER V.

THE PAYMENT.

In order that the reader may form an intelligent conception of the scene which now took place at Chatsworth and in its vicinity, it will be necessary to return to the preceding night and relate some occurrences at and near the then small town of Richmond.

Just as night had fallen two persons were holding an interview in a small house on the slope of what was and still is called "Shockoe Hill," and from the papers lying upon the table before them it was plain that the interview was one of business.

One of these persons was a gray-haired merchant of the place, a quiet-looking old gentleman, clad in black, who leaned back in his arm-chair and gazed at his companion with a smile of evident satisfaction.

This companion was our friend Capt. Canolles, clad in his ordinary dress, half military, half civilian. Around his waist was a belt containing a brace of pistols, but no broadsword, and his hat and gloves lay upon a chair beside two canvas bags plethoric apparently with coin.

The countenance of Canolles wore its habitual expression of calmness, or perhaps phlegm would be the more appropriate word. The dark eyes of the soldier were fixed upon the old merchant with a thoughtful air, and he had evidently been speaking whilst the other listened.   For the moment there was silence in the apartment—only through the open door was heard a subdued murmur of voices, apparently those of two persons seated on the steps leading to the front door of the small house, overshadowed by the boughs of an elm—two persons who seemed to be conversing confidentially under the friendly stars of the summer night, and with the murmur mingled from time to time the quick sound of a horse impatiently pawing.

"Well," said the old merchant, "all is then arranged, Captain, and nothing remains but to execute the paper."

"Nothing, my dear Mr. Atwell," was the reply of Canolles.

"Before finishing our business, however, Captain," continued the old man, with a smile, " may I beg you to afford me information in a private matter?"

" A private matter?"

"I would ask of you some particulars in reference to your young friend, Walter Hayfield."

" Ah! in reference to Walter?"

The merchant nodded.

"I have peculiar reasons for ascertaining his character, origin, and any other details you may be pleased to give."

"I will inform you with great pleasure.   He is the son of a very estimable gentleman with whom I was very well acquainted—Mr. Hayfield, of Charles City—at one time the owner of a very good estate, which he lost by generous living, and afterwards a teacher.   He was greatly esteemed, and Walter is the counterpart of his father—a young man of the highest character and a great favorite with me."

"I am glad to hear that, Captain. An old man of business like myself is disposed to consider nothing so reliable as the voucher on such occasions of a gentleman of your character. It is not flattery to you to say, Captain, that when you tell me a thing I require no more, and know that it is so."

Canolles inclined his head and replied:

"I am truly pleased to find, Mr. Atwell, that a tolerably thorough acquaintance with each other during a number of years has impressed you with the same good opinion of myself that I most certainly entertain for you. But is it indiscreet in me to inquire why you are so anxious to know Walter's character? Do you propose to offer the youngster a place in your counting-house—turning the youthful *militaire* into a clerk?"

"Perhaps," said the old merchant, smilingly.

Canolles shook his head.

"I do not think he will accept an offer even so advantageous, but do not know."

"Suppose I were to propose to him in time to become my partner and successor?"

Canolles looked at the speaker with some astonishment and said:

"I confess you puzzle me greatly, Mr. Atwell. You have not informed me of the source of this interest in Walter—at which, however, I must add, I am greatly pleased, since my own interest in him is warm."

The merchant, with the same smile on his lips

12

slowly pointed through the door through which came the low voices.

"Listen, Captain," he said.

"Ah!" was the reply, "I really think I begin to understand little Miss Annie."

"Yes," said the old merchant, smiling, "Annie and Walter have fallen in love with each other, like the two foolish young people they are, and I made up my mind twenty years ago, my dear Capt. Canolles, never to thwart another love affair, as the phrase is, unless under a solemn obligation of duty. I say another— you are an old friend, and I will explain the word. I had a very dear daughter, who placed her affections upon a poor but estimable youth. In my narrow-mindedness I refused my consent to their union, and, I fear, worried the poor child into marriage with a richer suiter. The marriage was a wretched one, and my dear girl soon died, and from that moment I resolved never again to interfere on such occasions, save in the event of utter unworthiness in a suitor."

"And you are right, Mr. Atwell. A father is justi-fiable in opposing a daughter's marriage with an un-worthy person who will make her miserable by his vices or his neglect. Simple want of money, where there is good character and energy, should not prove an insuperable bar."

"I fully agree with you."

"So you have resolved not to oppose Walter's union with Miss Annie?"

"I shall favor it since hearing from your lips so high a character of him. And I am not acting, perhaps, so generously as you imagine. I am seventy-two, and must soon pass away. Annie is my only child now, and would be left without a protector. If she marries Walter, I shall take him as a partner. He will succeed to the business when the war and my life end, both which will, I think, occur very soon—and I shall sleep in peace."

"The most rational of plans, Mr. Atwell," said Canolles, "and I assure you the information of your intention quite delights me. Well, as Walter's affairs are all arranged now, and I have business to-night, oblige me by terminating our own affairs. I will proceed to count the sum I have brought you to discharge the remainder of the obligation."

As he spoke, Canolles opened the canvas bags and emptied their contents upon the table. The merchant pushed back the chair. The spectacle was dazzling. Before him lay a pile of guineas and Bank of England notes, evidently amounting to many thousands of pounds sterling; and the bright gold coin sparkled in the light of the lamp swinging above.

"Be kind enough to inform me of the exact amount still due, Mr. Atwell," said Canolles. "We may then calculate the interest, and the residue still owed you may be paid."

The old merchant hesitated, then he smiled.

"That is a magnificent sight," he said, pointing to the coin and bank notes, "in the eyes at least of a merchant, necessarily intent, you know, Captain, all his life upon gain."

"I do not believe," returned Canolles, with the same

smile, "that you have spent your life with any such exclusive object, Mr. Atwell. You have the repute of possessing a large fortune—well, I am perfectly certain that, to employ the common phrase, 'there is not a dirty shilling in the whole.'"

Mr. Atwell exhibited unmistakable gratification as he listened to these words, and said:

"That is my proudest boast, Captain; and now," he smiled, "in return for your fine compliment, I shall charge you no interest."

"I cannot accept such a renunciation," was the reply.

"The present premium on coin will prove a full substitute."

"No; oblige me by computing the interest."

"Then it shall be on the lowest terms."

With which the merchant took a pen, made the calculation, and handed the slip of paper containing it—for he was far too prudent and economical to use a whole sheet—to Canolles.

"Ten thousand two hundred pounds seven shillings and sixpence," the partisan read aloud.

"Precisely, Captain."

"You place the rate of interest at nearly nothing."

The old merchant shook his head obstinately.

"I will not accept one penny more," he said; "either that or the naked ten thousand pounds."

"So be it," said Canolles; "I see that I cannot overcome you, my old friend."

He proceeded to count out ten thousand two hundred pounds seven shillings and sixpence, first exhausting the gold, and then continuing with the Bank of England notes—several of the latter being left. The merchant carefully placed the sum in an old escritoire, double-locked it, returned to his seat, took up a legal-looking document, and, affixing his signature to it, handed it to Canolles, who wrote some lines upon it, folded and sealed it, and then placed it in his breast.

"That part of my plan is accomplished," he muttered, rising. "Now to finish and get away from Virginia."

"You will not leave us to-night, Captain," said Mr. Atwell.

"I must, my good friend; I have business which demands my attention. But before I go I propose to make you a present."

"A present?"

Canolles went out of the house, passed the two indistinct figures on the front steps, lost beneath the shadow of the elm, and, going to his horse, tethered near, unstrapped something from the saddle and returned to the apartment.

"You are a good Virginian, are you not, Mr. Atwell?"

"I believe there is no better living."

You must have heard with indignation of the outrages committed by Col. Tarleton, who marched through Richmond yesterday on his retreat.

"With bitter indignation, Captain."

"Would you like to possess a slight memorial of the worthy Colonel, whose proceedings, I must say, I approve of no more than yourself?"

" A memorial ? "

Canolles unfolded the bundle in his hand, unstrapped from his saddle.

" There is Col. Tarleton's uniform coat," he said, " no doubt his very best, and reserved for gala occasions."

" Indeed ! " exclaimed Mr. Atwell, gazing at the fine garment, which was heavily decorated, well-nigh covered, indeed, with gold lace. " This is really Tarleton's coat, Captain ? "

" Yes.   Should you doubt it you have only to look."

He took from the pocket of the coat a gold snuff-box, upon the lid of which was cut the name " Banastre Tarleton," and a paper which he unfolded and held up before the merchant.

" See, this is a special order signed by Lord Cornwallis and addressed to Lieut-Col. Tarleton."

" What a prize ! Did you capture the coat, Captain ? " exclaimed the delighted merchant.

" Yes, two days ago.   I, too, have a spite against the Colonel for his cruelties in Virginia—in Virginia, I say, inasmuch as I do not consider that I have anything to do with outrages elsewhere—and I attacked him on his way down, killed some of his troopers and captured this coat from his headquarters."

" Indeed, I shall preserve it, Captain, as a treasure."

Canolles held out his hand, and calling, " To horse, Walter ! bid the fair Miss Annie good-night ! " went, after shaking hands with the old merchant, toward the door.

" Captain ! Captain ! " the latter cried.

Canolles turned his head.

" You have left this," said the merchant, pointing to the bank notes lying on the table, " at least five hundred pounds."

" I really have no use for it," was the reply of Canolles; " put it away, my old friend, to purchase a wedding gift for little Miss Annie when she is the bride of Walter Hayfield, to whom I owe my life."

With these words Canolles saluted the merchant, then the young lady as he passed her, and mounted. Walter followed—a low sound, very much resembling a kiss, issuing from the shadow of the elm as he did so—and then the two horsemen, who had turned the heads of their animals eastward, disappeared in the night.

CHAPTER VI.

IN WHICH CANOLLES INFORMS WALTER THAT HAVING AC-
COMPLISHED HIS AIM HE IS ABOUT TO LEAVE VIRGINIA
FOREVER.

It was a bright starlight night, and the air was perfectly still as Canolles and Walter rode out of Richmond, eastward, in the direction of the Chickahominy.

The partisan seemed to be lost in thought, and went
on in silence, his rein lying upon his horse's neck—his
chin resting on his breast. Walter, reflecting the
mood of his chief, rode beside him without speaking,
and they went on thus for half an hour over the sandy
road, which gave back no sound—two phantom horsemen, one would have said, moving to some rendezvous
in the shades of the White Oak Swamp, which they
were approaching. A yellow light in the east, just
touching the summits of the pines, indicated that the
moon would soon rise toward her noon, and no sound
whatever disturbed the stillness but the faint complaint
of the whippoorwill.

At length Canolles raised his head, and turning to
his companion said in the quiet tone habitual with him :

" Walter, you were talking to-night with your friend
Miss Annie, were you not?"

The blush on the boy's face was plain in the starlight.

" Yes, Captain."

" A charming little lady; let me compliment you on your choice."

Walter blushed more violently than before, but made no reply.

" Your affairs are no secret from me," continued Canolles, now in a tone of unwonted softness, " and the proof is that Mr. Atwell and myself discussed them in our interview this evening."

" You and Mr. Atwell, Captain ?"

"Yes—why not ? Is there anything so strange in the fact? and can you suppose me indifferent to the welfare of one who saved my life at the risk of his own, as you did at Petersburg ?"

" Oh, that was nothing, Captain. If there had been a thousand times more risk it would have been my place to run it, after all your kindness."

" Thanks, Walter ! The kind feeling you speak of was in response to your own personal regard for me. The fact remains that but for you I should not be riding here to-night, but sleeping in the Blandford cemetery, or near it. Let us leave that and come to business. Mr. Atwell consents to your union with his daughter, and designs to make you his partner first, then his successor."

Walter thrilled with delight, and seemed too much overcome to speak.

" All was arranged to-night, after Mr. Atwell had ascertained from me such particulars relating to yourself as a prudent father has the right to know where there is a question of bestowing a daughter's hand upon a suitor."

"Oh! thank you! thank you, Captain! You say enough to make me understand that it is to you that I am indebted for my happiness!"

"This union will then make you happy, will it, Walter?" said Canolles in the tone of a father, addressing a son whom he loves.

"Happier than I can tell you, Captain; for—why should I not say it?—for I love Annie better than my life!"

"That is not a very strong expression in your case, Walter," was the partisan's smiling response. "I have seen you risk your life so bravely that you must use some other phrase."

"And Mr. Atwell really consents?"

"Yes, indeed. So you see your partisan career will soon end, and my young hawk will be transformed into a quiet domestic bird, with a dame partlet, and perhaps a brood of young chickens to look after."

Walter colored, looking both delighted and sad.

"There is only one thing," he said, "to trouble me."

"What is that?"

"I cannot bear the thought of leaving you, Captain."

Canolles shook his head.

"You could scarcely go with me, where I am going."

"Where are you going?"

"I shall soon disband the Rough Riders and leave Virginia."

"Leave Virginia?"

"Forever."

Walter discerned in the tone of this single word the deepest sadness, and exclaimed:

" Leave Virginia—and forever!   Something troubles you, Captain!   What is it?"

Canolles did not reply.

" And disband the men—not one of whom but would die for you, rough fellows as they are?"

" Still we must part.   My end is accomplished.   I should have disbanded them before this time—soon after the attack on the British convoy below Petersburg —but for one thing—I mean the outrages of Col. Tarleton.   I wished to take a little private vengeance on that gentleman before I went."

Canolles paused, then went on :

" Listen, Walter," he said.   " There are some things connected with my life which I have not spoken of even to one to whom I am as much attached as I am to you, nor can I speak of them now.   Every man has at some time some peculiar object in view, toward which he is impelled by peculiar considerations or feelings; and such an object has decided my own career.   As I have informed you, my aim is now fully reached; nothing detains me in Virginia, my first and last love— she will soon be freed from her invaders, for the war is near its end—and I shall go."

" You do not go cheerfully," was the boy's low reply; " your voice is so sorrowful.   Tell me what troubles you, Captain !—is it—is it—"

The boy stopped.

" Finish your sentence, Walter."

" You will not be angry !"

" Have I ever been angry with you?"

" I scarce ever saw you angry with anybody."

"Then speak.   You would ask me—"

"If your trouble is connected with—with—the young lady I gave that paper to—Miss Fanny Talbot?"

Canolles, turning his head a little from the boy, made no reply.

"For if you think," exclaimed Walter impulsively, "that—that—she is not a friend—more than a friend to you—you are greatly, very greatly mistaken."

"Mistaken!   Greatly mistaken!   Your meaning, Walter?"

"She loves you!—loves you with her whole heart, Captain!"

Canolles turned a little pale, and replied:

"What a fancy!—unless you mean that she has a friend's regard for me—no more."

"Remember her brave ride!"

"That is a great deal—and nothing.   I should have expected such a thing from her, and was not surprised. But 'more than a friend,' do you say?   That is absurd."

"It is true, Captain, and if you will listen, I will tell you why I know what I say is true."

Walter proceeded to inform Canolles of his interview with Fanny on the evening when he delivered the paper, repeating her expressions and describing her emotion.   Canolles listened, with the same slight pallor, but said nothing until Walter terminated his narrative.   Then he slowly shook his head and replied:

"All that is mere fancy, Walter; and now let us end this talk, which can lead to nothing.   Your unfounded surmise, even if true, could have no effect in inducing me to remain in Virginia.   In a few days I shall leave the country. The enemy are retiring from Virginia, and I have no longer any business here. Perhaps I shall strike one more blow at the excellent Col. Tarleton. We know each other personally, as we were face to face when I attacked him above Richmond and drove him half-dressed from his tent. I confess I should like to signalize my departure from Virginia by either capturing him or making him feel the weight of my hand before I go. I may have the opportunity, since he is not far off from us now."

"He is on this side of the Chickahominy, Captain," exclaimed Walter with ardor, and his young blood suddenly excited by the prospect of an attack.

"Good! then we'll look him up, Walter; but first I must——"

"Halt!" exclaimed a voice from the front; "who goes there?"

"Friends," replied Canolles; "and as I recognize your voice, Harry, it is unnecessary that I should halt."

"Hartley!" exclaimed the voice.

"In person," returned Canolles, continuing to advance, followed by Walter.

Fifty yards in advance a horseman was posted in the road, with a detachment of mounted men near.

"You, Hartley?" said the dusky horseman. "What good fortune! I wished of all things to see you to-night!"

And spurring forward the young lieutenant grasped the hand of Canolles, whom he seemed almost ready to clasp in his arms.

CHAPTER VII.

CANOLLES AND HARRY CARTARET.

Walter Hayfield had checked his horse a few paces distant from the two horsemen, and now heard them exchange a few words which he could not distinguish. Then Harry Cartaret turned his horse, rode back to his company, gave an order to one of his officers, and then again joined Canolles.

"Wait here for me, Walter," said the latter to his companion, "I wish to say a few words to Lieut. Cartaret—then we will ride on."

The two men turned into a field, where a group of seven pine trees rose like dusky phantoms in the moonlight, which now began to glimmer above the trees, and halting beneath the pines, dismounted.

"You say you wished to see me to-night, Harry," said Canolles. "Well, that is curious, as I was in pursuit of you when you halted me."

"Oh! yes! yes, Hartley! My dear Hartley!" exclaimed the young man. "I wished—longed, I should say—to see you, and tell you how much I love you—how noble you are in my eyes."

Canolles fixed a penetrating glance upon his companion—a glance full of surprise and inquiry.

"Ah!" he said quietly, "you have a warm heart, Harry. It is unnecessary to tell me that, or let me see it. I know very well that you love me—marauder as I am; and you know my affection for you is as great."

"You are not a marauder! You are a Chevalier Bayard!—a thousand times nobler than the noblest human being I have ever met!"

Canolles looked at his companion in the same surprised manner.

"Thank you, Harry," he said. "I do not recognize your good sense, but I do your warm heart."

"My good sense more than all."

"What do you mean?"

"I know you at last, Hartley!"

"At last?"

"All your grand self-sacrificing affection for me—an affection I can never repay while I live, but will never consent to profit by!"

Canolles was plainly in a maze, and his penetrating eyes demanded an explanation.

"So you wished to see me to-night. For what purpose?" he said.

"To tell you that I have come into possession of something belonging to you, which should at least be returned to you."

"What is that, Harry?"

"This paper."

He put his hand into his breast and drew out a small package.

"Before returning it, let me tell you how I came into possession of it. When the enemy returned from Petersburg I was detached by Gen. Lafayette to cross the Appomattox and harass their rear. I did so, following them down toward City Point, and chancing to stop at the small house of a plain countryman by the roadside, in order to gain information, observed an open paper lying upon his table."

"Ah!" said Canolles, "some order accidentally dropped by the enemy?"

"That was my conjecture, and I seized the paper, asking the countryman where he had obtained it, or if the enemy had left it. He replied that he had found it lying in a wood road near—a sort of bridle path leading by a short cut toward Petersburg—and thinking it might prove of some value brought it home."

"Naturally; but he ascertained speedily what the paper contained?"

"Not at all. He could not read."

"Oh! I see. But as you, my dear Harry, are somewhat more accomplished, you proceeded to decipher the document."

"Yes," said Harry, in a low tone.

"And this mysterious document——but, one thing puzzles me."

"What is that?"

"Why you should have begun by saying that you wished to return this paper to me, as my property."

"To you—or another person."

"Another person?"

"Yes."

"What person? and what can be your meaning, dear Harry? You puzzle me enormously. What under Heaven have I to do with a paper picked up by chance on the roadside between Petersburg and City Point?"

Harry Cartaret had unfolded the paper and now held

it out toward Canolles, who took it and looked keenly at it.

The moon had just risen above the trees and fell with a flood of light upon the paper. It was that which Canolles had directed Walter to deliver to Fanny Talbot, and which she had dropped from her bosom on her night ride to Petersburg.

13

CHAPTER VIII.

THE COMMISSION.

Canolles had scarcely read three lines of the paper in his own handwriting, when the hand holding it fell at his side and his head slowly drooped until it rested upon his breast. He was leaning against the trunk of one of the seven pines, and the moonlight fell clearly upon both his own figure and that of Harry Cartaret.

The resemblance between the two was more extraordinary than ever. Canolles seemed to have lost something of the brown, almost swarthy tint of his face—possibly from his close confinement in Petersburg—and Harry was burned darker by the summer sun. Their resemblance to each other was thus almost perfect, and but for their different uniforms they would scarcely have been recognized one from the other.

Canolles, as we have said, had let the hand holding the paper fall at his side, and for some moments his eyes remained fixed upon the ground. He then raised his head and looked at his companion.

"Did you read this, Harry?"

"Yes," was the low reply.

"All?"

"Yes."

"I am sorry," was the grave reply of Canolles.

"I know I had no right to do so," said the young man, with a quick color in his cheeks. "I am not given to reading papers not addressed to myself; but remember, Hartley, how I found this—that I thought it would prove an army order, dropped by the enemy. I therefore looked at it, read ten lines, read on, could not cease reading, and did not stop until I had come to the last line and your signature. Blame me if you will—say that it was a want of good breeding—yes!—but you cannot make me regret that I read that paper, for it has shown me who is the noblest man in this world, and made me love him more even than I did before!"

He spoke impulsively, and tears came to his eyes.

Canolles looked at him with the same soft glance—even a softer one than that bestowed upon Walter Hayfield. A sigh escaped him and he said:

"It is truly unfortunate that you ever found this paper, which I surely never intended you to see. How it was lost by—the person to whom it is addressed—unless dropped on her ride—I cannot divine. But that inquiry is now idle. The mischief is done. The ultimate result, however, will be the same."

"No!" exclaimed Harry Cartaret, "it must not be the same! I will never consent!"

He rested one arm on the shoulder of Canolles, then embracing him, as it were, and looking at him with moist eyes through which shone a smile, said:

"*Noblesse oblige*, Hartley! It is impossible for one of the Cartarets to act otherwise than as a Cartaret! People say I am not very brilliant in intellect, I believe. At least I know what is imposed upon me by the name I bear!"

"No one acquainted with you ever doubted that, Harry. Men carry their natures on their faces. I for one know an honest man or a scoundrel as soon as I see him. The rascal's face says, 'I am a rascal!' the gentleman's, 'I am a gentleman!' To cease my moralizing. You have no choice here. It is I who impose your action upon you."

"Never, never."

"In the more important particulars it is already imposed."

"The more important? Yes! I understand—and I have no reply to make to that. Yes, there I am fettered; as to the other—I swear, Hartley, that rather than——"

"Swear not at all!" was the reply of Canolles, with a smile almost tender on his lips. "Let the future decide your action, Harry, be it what it may—and now let us forget all this."

"But——"

"Let us say no more about it, Harry. You love me and I love you. We go different ways, but I think we shall love each other to the end. Not another word now—let the American lieutenant of cavalry and the Virginia marauder part in peace!"

"You are no longer a marauder—if you ever were one!" was the reply of the young man, who seemed to feel the uselessness of further remonstrance, at least for the present, on the subject of discussion.

"I am not a marauder, do you say, Harry?"

The young man drew a second paper from his pocket and presented it to Canolles.

"What's that?" he asked.

"Your commission as captain of Partisan Rangers, from the Governor of Virginia."

"Ah! you have put yourself to the trouble of procuring that?"

"Yes, your non-commissioned fighting has already exposed you to imminent danger of death, Hartley, and might again without this paper. I applied to Governor Jefferson long ago for this commission, but he informed me that he had scruples against making out such a commission, unless it was proposed to have it approved and countersigned by the Continental authorities."

"And you rightly supposed that I would accept no such commission!" exclaimed Canolles.

"I knew you would not!"

"I should not have accepted it if his Excellency Governor Jefferson had begged me to do so on his knees!"

Henry Cartaret sighed, as though the reply of his companion caused him deep regret; but it was equally plain that he knew all argument would be thrown away.

"I therefore informed Mr. Jefferson," he continued, "that I feared there were obstacles in the way of your acceptance of the commission if granting it were coupled with the conditions mentioned by him, and no longer pressed the application."

"Right! But here is the paper."

"If you look at it you will perceive that it bears the signature of, not Mr. Jefferson, but of Thomas Nelson,

Governor of Virginia—a **brave man, and** a noble **title,** **which, I** predict, he will render nobler."

"**I know him very well, and I assent to your predic- tion."**

"**He has been** Governor, as you are aware, since the **first of June,** and no sooner had I **renewed my** application than **Gov.** Nelson exclaimed: 'Commission him! Yes, I will **commission** him, and without **if or but or** asking **leave of** anything! I am Governor of **Virginia,** and I commission a Virginian to fight **the** battles **of** Virginia.' **He** then had **the commission** made **out,** signed it, delivered it to me—and **here it is."**

Canolles took the **paper, placed it in his breast, and said :**

"**I take this paper as a** Virginian ready to fight the battles **of** Virginia. **You** see I use the words of that brave soldier and statesman. The **war** is near its end —I may strike again **only** once, but **I will** strike **with this paper on my person** beside the Virginia **flag I** carry."

With these words Canolles **mounted his horse; his companion** imitated him, and **they rode** back to the highway, where, at a sign from the partisan, Walter joined them—he and Harry exchanging **a grasp of the hand,** evidently as old friends.

" And now, Harry, pass me through your picket—I **must go below," said Canolles,** pointing **toward James River.**

Harry Cartaret did so, the dusky **horsemen dividing to** allow them to pass, **and fifty yards further they parted with a** close grasp of **the hand.**

" I had forgotten," said Canolles, turning back.

" Forgotten ?"

" Keep this paper for me in safety, for the present, Harry."

He gave him the sealed document which he had received from **Mr. Atwell** in return for the **ten** thousand pounds.

" What is the paper?" asked the young lieutenant.

" You shall read and see," was the reply of **Canolles,** "only I attach **a** single condition to your doing **so.**"

" What condition ?"

" That you shall only do so one month from this time. If I am dead in the meanwhile it will be different. You may then **read** the paper at once."

The two **men** exchanged another pressure of the **hand and rode** in opposite directions, Canolles and Walter penetrating deeper and deeper into **the thicket, which soon swallowed the** two horsemen in its moon**lit** depths.

CHAPTER IX.

A RECONNOISSANCE RECONNOITERED.

The partisan and his companion had ridden a mile or two, and were pursuing a road which gradually obliqued in a southern direction—it was what is called to-day the " Charles City Road "—when they all at once became aware that other persons beside themselves were abroad.

A muffled noise of hoofs was heard in front, and Canolles checked his horse and listened.

The sound did not grow louder—indeed, it gradually became fainter. There was no doubt that the horsemen—apparently a considerable party—were moving in the same direction as the partisan and Walter.

" Well, I think some of our friends of the other faction are on an expedition to-night," said Canolles; " in all probability on a reconnoissance. The right flank is the flank to guard—that accounts for Harry's being where we found him—and these gentlemen are riding toward James River, either to plunder the farms of horses or find if there is any American force in this direction."

He dismounted, and stooping down examined the road, leading his horse by the bridle and glancing keenly from side to side.

" A squadron at least," he said at length, " the hoof-marks amount to that. What do you say, Walter ?"

"I think about fifty, Captain."

"My own estimate. Well, let us try and find out who they are, and discover what they are after."

Canolles mounted, touched his horse with his spur and set forward at a gallop, knowing well that the noise made on the march by fifty men—the clash of sabres against stirrups, and the smiting of hoofs—would completely drown the sound of his own and Walter's gallop on the sandy road.

They went on thus for about half a mile, the noise growing gradually louder; and then a dusky mass was seen in front moving slowly, evidently at a walk, over the white road against which the figures were clearly defined in the moonlight.

When he was within two hundred yards of the party Canolles stopped and seemed to reflect.

"We might join the column as stragglers, Walter," he said. "Nobody would be the wiser as the road is so narrow yonder that the shade of the pines makes all dark—but that does not answer my purpose."

"Your purpose, Captain?"

"I am anxious to know who these people are, where they are going, and what their object is."

"Yes, Captain."

"Well, joining the column as one of them would not tell me much, I could ask no questions, and private soldiers know nothing. I will go around."

"Around?"

"To the front, and try to find out what I wish to know. You ought to be enough of a partisan, Walter," he added, observing a puzzled expression on the countenance of the boy, "to understand what plan I mean to pursue."

"I am ashamed to say I do not, Captain."

"Well, come with me, my boy, and take a little lesson—it may be useful to you."

With these words Canolles wheeled to the left, and penetrated the morass for about a quarter of a mile. He then turned to the right again, made his way with the skill of an experienced night rider through the almost impenetrable thickets, and gradually obliquing toward the road over which the column was passing, soon came within sound of voices.

"Listen," he said to Walter, taking no pains to suppress the tones of his voice.

"Unless I am mistaken we are opposite the head of the column, and the voices we hear are those of the officers commanding, and riding in front."

"Yes, Captain!" exclaimed Walter, now highly excited, and even delighted.

"If we can manage to keep near enough to these worthies, we may, perhaps, hear what they have to say, and discover who they are, too."

As Canolles spoke, the moon, which had been obscured for some moments by a cloud, sailed out in full majesty above the fringe of the pines, and the bright light fell upon two British officers, whose figures were distinctly visible to Canolles and Walter through an opening in the thicket.

One of these officers was the tall, stiff, commanding, white-mustache, ruddy-faced Col. Ferrers. The other, who rode on his left, and was nearer to the partisans, was a young man apparently from twenty-five to twenty-eight, short of stature, swarthy, with a thick-set person and muscular limbs, and wore the uniform of a Lieutenant-Colonel of cavalry of the British army.

"That is my especial personal friend, Col. Tarleton," said Canolles. "Lord Ferrers you know, Walter. But where are they going?"

Despite every effort made by the partisan he could not hear what the two officers were saying to each other—which, indeed, amounted to very little. They spoke only at intervals, and then in low tones.

Canolles checked his horse, making a sign to Walter.

"The undergrowth is too thick to go nearer," he said, quietly, "we should be seen, and shot or captured if we tried to force our way through the thicket, as the noise would be heard. Now, I do not wish either to be killed or captured at present."

"Nor I, Captain! and for the same reason you do not."

"What reason?"

"You are going to attack them!"

"I attack them?" said Canolles, laughing. "Why, they are two or three to one, if all my men were even here."

"Which makes it all the more agreeable to you, Captain. Don't try to deceive me as to your intentions!"

Canolles smiled this time, and said:

"Well, let us halt here and count them, if possible, as they pass. There is the head of the column, fifty paces behind the officers. Make your own count,

Walter, and I will make mine, and then we will com-
pare them."

Holding his rein carelessly in his left hand, and raising his right hand with the forefinger extended, Canolles moved the finger after the fashion of a shepherd
counting his sheep, and Walter imitated him. When
the last man had defiled by, the partisan turned his
head and said:

"Well, how many, Walter?"

"Fifty-two, Captain."

"Good."

"What was your count?"

"Fifty-two."

Having uttered these words Canolles made his companion a sign, wheeled to the left, and apparently dis-
missing from his mind all further interest in the reconnoitering party, penetrated the densest part of the
Swamp.

Anybody, however, who had been in the vicinity of
the British bivouac toward dawn, and followed them
afterwards as they continued their march southward
about sunrise, would have been aware, from slight
noises in the Swamp, that some person or persons,
moving stealthily, had the British squadron in view,
and were tracking it step by step as it advanced.

CHAPTER X.

IN WHICH A PROFANE ACQUAINTANCE OF THE READER RE-APPEARS UPON THE SCENE.

The events just related occurred, as the reader has been informed, on the night preceding that on which Miss Fanny Talbot and Miss Lucy Maurice held the interview at the picturesque "Moss Rock," in the Chatsworth grounds, an interview which was interrupted in the manner we have described—that is to say, by the tramp of approaching horsemen, and then the appearance of a body of British troopers swarming on the grassy lawn.

The two young ladies, indulging a natural feminine terror, were running to seek shelter in the house, when one of two officers riding in front of the column—a short, swarthy and thick-set young man in a colonel's uniform—suddenly struck spur to his horse, crying:

"Halt!"

The horse started forward under the spur, but all at once was arrested and rose up on his haunches.

The officer, whose eyes were fixed upon the young ladies, turned his head furiously to ascertain the meaning of this incident.

It was occasioned by a very simple circumstance.

The white-mustached Colonel Ferrers — our old acquaintance of Petersburg—who rode beside him, had caught his bridle, and abruptly arrested the further progress of the animal.

The young officer gave way to rage.

"Your meaning, Lord Ferrers!" he exclaimed, knitting his brow and scowling at Ferrers, who quietly released his hold upon the bridle; "your meaning in this very extraordinary proceeding!"

"My meaning, eh?"

"Yes, sir!"

"Damme!" was the reply of Lord Ferrers, in a gruff voice, indicating great indifference at his companion's anger; "I mean, my worthy Colonel Tarleton, that I am in command here, and that it is not my habit to ride over the fair sex, or allow them to be ridden over —damme!"

Tarleton—for the young officer was that well-known personage—looked furious, but evidently knew his companion too well to reply. He saluted stiffly, reining in his horse, and Lord Ferrers advanced in front of him, bowing to the trembling girls as he did so.

"Good evening, young ladies," he said gruffly, "will you be good enough to inform me what the name of this house is, as all the houses in Virginia have names, I'm told, and this is a devilish fine one—beg pardon!"

"Chatsworth, sir," said Fanny, who had recovered from her fright.

"Chatsworth? Once the residence of Mr. Henry Cartaret?"

"Yes, sir."

"Humph! I thought it was somewhere in this vicinity. Might have known it from the advice of a certain gentleman, that we had better move in this direction—a rascal here behind me—eh, Tom?"

The rascal in question—Lieut. Ferrers—rode forward, saluting the young ladies as he did so.

"So," said Lord Ferrers, "this is Chatsworth, is it, where you spent the evening once, eh? and the rest of the same night in the American camp?"

"Exactly, sir," was the laughing response of Lieut. Tom Ferrers, "and I assure you I should like to repeat the evening, though not the rest of the night."

"Very well—do as you choose; but it's devilish risky, I can tell you."

"I'll risk it, sir."

"But not without permission from *les belles chatelaines*, I can tell you! No forcing your society on ladies while I'm about. I'm going to halt here for half an hour to rest the horses, but no man or officer enters this house without my permission; and what's more, if there is any damage done to the grounds or property, I'll arrest the officer, or mount the man on a wooden horse without stirrups—damme!"

Having made this announcement in a tone distinctly heard by everybody, Lord Ferrers turned to the girls, saluted in the same brief fashion, and said:

"Is it agreeable to you, young ladies, that I should go in and rest, with two or three of my officers? If unagreeable to you, say so, and there'll be an end of it."

"Of course, sir," was the reply of Fanny; and Lord Ferrers, turning to Tom, said:

"Lieut. Ferrers, you will march the troop to that

opening yonder in the woods beyond the grounds, order the men to dismount, but not to picket the horses, and see that no damage is done to fences or any other property."

"Yes, sir."

"I will hold you responsible. After seeing that my orders are obeyed, you may leave your subordinate in charge and come to the house here, if you fancy. I am going in with Col. Tarleton."

"Yes, sir."

"Will you go in, Colonel?"

Tarleton rather stiffly assented, and, leaving their horses in charge of an orderly, while Lieut. Tom Ferrers marched off the men, the two officers followed the young ladies into the Chatsworth house.

CHAPTER XI.

IN WHICH COL. TARLETON LAYS HIS HAND UPON HIS SWORD.

It was in the highest degree entertaining to observe the effect produced by the entrance of the stately old Lord Ferrers and the short athlete Col. Tarleton in their rich uniforms on the excellent Mrs. Talbot. That aged lady, sitting with her knitting in her hands, and her hair primly arranged under her white cap, presented the picture of astonishment and apprehension, and the helpless way in which she looked from the visitors to Fanny and Lucy, and then to the superb Miss Eleanor enthroned in state in her arm-chair near the window, was comic in the extreme.

Miss Eleanor Talbot was far from exhibiting any similar emotion. On the contrary, she returned the admiring glances of bluff old Lord Ferrers and the keen gaze of Tarleton with perfect coolness; and was indeed—with her richly arranged hair, her red lips and roses—a personage calculated to excite the admiration of any one.

Lord Ferrers made the bow of the nobleman he was, and took the seat to which Miss Eleanor Talbot motioned him with a careless movement of her jeweled hand—Col. Tarleton taking another.

"I have the pleasure, I and Col. Tarleton, I believe," said Col. Ferrers, "of making the acquaintance of Mrs. Cartaret and her daughters?"

14

“N—n—o, sir,” faltered Mrs. Talbot; “we—are only —relations of the late Mr. Cartaret.”

“Ah! Well, madam, I have at least the satisfaction of visiting relatives of that excellent gentleman at his house of Chatsworth, the name of which I have frequently heard him mention. I knew Mr. Cartaret very well in England, both when he was a young man at Oxford, and later. I may even say that I believe there is a distant connection between our families—certainly the tie of friendship was strong; both my brother, Lord Ferrers, now dead, and myself, were intimate and cordial friends of Mr. Cartaret.”

“Y—es, sir,” said Mrs. Talbot, gradually recovering her equanimity in some degree.

“It is the unhappy result of war, madam,” continued Col. Ferrers, “to produce these apparent antagonisms, and bring a soldier often, as an enemy, to the house of his friend. I say apparent antagonisms, for I need scarcely assure you that it is not an enemy who enters the house of Henry Cartaret when George Ferrers enters it. You will, therefore, I beg, ladies, dismiss all apprehension of annoyance, and be at your ease. If so much as a twig is broken here by officer or man I will make him rue it, whatever be his rank.”

A sound resembling a suppressed growl issued from the lips of Col. Tarleton, who had listened to these elaborate assurances of the old *militaire* with ill-subdued disapprobation. Lord Ferrers half turned his head, but as at that moment Lieut. Tom Ferrers came in, he took no further notice of the young colonel.

Tom Ferrers entered and executed a low bow, the

feather of his cocked hat trailing on the floor. His glance embraced the whole group, but suddenly remained fixed on the superb Miss Eleanor, who returned his salute with an unmistakable smile of recognition.

" I have the great pleasure of renewing my acquaintance with Mrs. Talbot and the Misses Talbot," said Lieutenant Tom, not looking in the least at the aged lady or Fanny, but continuing to gaze with unbounded admiration at Eleanor.

"Take a seat, sir," said that young lady, with a fascinating glance, and she made an almost imperceptible movement of her hand toward a seat beside her, which Lieutenant Tom hastened to occupy.

A suppressed chuckle issued from the lips of Lord Ferrers, who was sitting with his sword between his knees, his left hand grasping the weapon, his right hand resting on his thigh.

" It seems to me, my good sir," he said, "that when I give a military order to an officer of my command I am entitled to a brief report from the officer in question, as to whether my orders are obeyed."

"Oh!—beg pardon, Colonel—the fact is—yes, sir! Your orders have been obeyed."

" Devilish quick!" grunted the old soldier, with his grim smile.

" I left Lieut. Jones in command, sir, with express orders."

"Have the goodness to repeat those orders for the satisfaction of the ladies."

"Your orders, sir, were that no depredations of any

description should be committed by officers or men on pain of severe punishment."

"Good, and I swear the punishment will follow, on the word of George Ferrers. War is war with me—it is not rapine."

Col. Tarleton had listened to this colloquy with obvious impatience. He seemed to be aware that the old *militaire* was not a person with whom he could venture far; but carried away now by his impatience, he said stiffly:

"It is a pity, sir, that the American officers in the Carolinas did not in the last campaign participate in your liberal views, and practice them in reference to the loyalists adhering to the cause of his Majesty."

"I have nothing to do with the American officers," was the indifferent reply. "I take my own precautions to prevent outrage."

"Rather an elaborate precaution in an enemy's country, if I am permitted to express an opinion, sir."

"That is your opinion, eh?" said Lord Ferrers, in a tone of mingled indifference and *hauteur*.

"Yes, sir, and if your lordship will allow me to say it, I am somewhat at a loss to comprehend this extreme solicitude in reference to persons in arms against his Majesty, or sympathizing with those in arms against him."

"I will reply to that," said Lord Ferrers, gruffly. "In the first place, this house is or was the property of Henry Cartaret, my friend, and a gentleman of the highest character. In the second place, it is at present occupied only by ladies."

"The rebel ladies are worse than the rebel gentlemen," said Col. Tarleton, laying ironical emphasis on the word gentlemen. "You will please, however, allow me to add, my Lord, that the fair rebels stand much higher in my estimation. The gentlemen are an illiterate set—those at least whom I have met."

"They are—eh?" grunted Lord Ferrers. "Who?"

"Well, my Lord, I give you as an instance Col. William Washington. He is so illiterate that he is hardly able to write his name!"

Lord Ferrers was looking at Fanny and saw her cheeks suddenly flush.

"What do you say to that, madam?" he said, with his grim smile. "Are you not disposed to say anything in defense of your countryman?"

"I could easily reply to Col. Tarleton," exclaimed Fanny, with her head proudly erect.

"Reply, then! Reply, madam," said Lord Ferrers, who seemed to scent some retort at Col. Tarleton's expense. "So Col. William Washington is able to write his name, eh?"

"Col. Tarleton should have at least discovered, sir, that Col. Washington knows how to make his mark!"

At this palpable allusion to the defeat of Tarleton by Col. Washington Lord Ferrers uttered a laugh.

"Madam!" exclaimed Tarleton, suddenly flushing with anger, "I should be happy to meet your friend Col. Washington!"

"I thought you had made his acquaintance, or, at least, had seen him," Fanny replied. "If you had

looked behind you at the battle of the Cowpens **you** would have enjoyed that pleasure, sir!"*

Lord Ferrers shook from head to foot with merriment at this answer, and, throwing back his head, uttered a louder laugh than before. **As to** Tarleton, he was so much enraged that by a movement evidently unconscious, his hand darted to his **sword-belt.**

Fanny did not shrink at this furious gesture, but with head erect, fixed her proud eyes on his scowling face. **It** was Lord Ferrers who broke the silence. The old soldier's mirth **had** disappeared in an instant at Tarleton's threatening gesture, and his eyes flashed.

" Miss Talbot! " he said, twisting his white mustache, **a** dangerous sign with him always.

The young lady turned her head.

" Say just what you please, Miss Talbot," added Lord Ferrers; " Col. Tarleton knows better than to insult a lady in my presence!"†

As he uttered these words he turned round and fixed his eyes upon Tarleton with **a** *hauteur* evidently galling in the extreme to the latter. With **his** dark face flushed, and his voice altered by the effort to suppress his anger, Tarleton replied:

" Lord Ferrers is good enough to read me a lesson —a somewhat unnecessary one, I must be permitted to add, as I have insulted no one. As my presence here, however, is obviously distasteful, I will not inflict it further."

He rose, saluted stiffly, and went out of the **room,**

---

* These retorts at Col. Tarleton's expense are historical.
† This speech is also historical.

Lord Ferrers returning his salute after the same fashion, but making no effort to detain him.

"Rather a fiery young **gentleman**," grunted **Lord Ferrers** as he disappeared. "**An** excellent **cavalry** officer, and not **a** bad fellow, **but** with a devil **of a** temper when anything excites him!"

As he spoke, Lord Ferrers **looked** carelessly around the apartment. **All at once** he started, and then fixed his eyes with an expression of the deepest astonishment upon one of **the portraits.**

"Who in **Heaven's name** is that, madam?" he exclaimed, addressing Fanny.

CHAPTER XII.

THE PORTRAIT.

The emotion of Col. Ferrers as he gazed at the portrait was so remarkable that for a moment a profound silence reigned in the apartment. The portrait represented a young gentleman, or rather a youth, of about seventeen, with dark hair curling at the temples, and an open, ingenuous, and even noble face.

The original of the picture was evidently either Canolles or Harry Cartaret, to judge from the likeness to them, and allowing for the greater roundness and freshness of youth, Lord Ferrers had exclaimed:

"Who in Heaven's name is that, madam?"

The question was addressed to Fanny, but a quick look of constraint, and an apparent conviction that caution was necessary in replying, made the young lady hesitate.

"Is my question disagreeable? Is there any objection to responding to it? Is there any reason why I should not be informed who is or was the original of that portrait, madam?" exclaimed Lord Ferrers.

Fanny hesitated still, when the worthy Mrs. Talbot came to the rescue.

"Oh, no! no, indeed, sir!" said the excellent and nervous lady. "That is a portrait of Hartley!"

"Hartley!" exclaimed Lord Ferrers, pushing back

his chair so suddenly that his scabbard clashed against the floor. "Who was Hartley?"

So completely paralyzed was good Mrs. Talbot by this abrupt exclamation that she began to tremble, and the frills of her cap nodded nervously. Before she could speak, Fanny interfered and said quietly:

"The portrait is that of—a friend of the family, sir. And now as you have been so courteous, may I beg you to grant me a single request?"

"Make it, madam," said Lord Ferrers in a voice of great emotion, and continued to gaze fixedly upon the picture, which as fixedly returned his gaze.

"My request is that you will not press for a reply to your question, sir, or seek to ascertain the original of this portrait. I can only explain this request so far as to say that there are reasons at present why the original does not desire to be identified with the picture."

Lord Ferrers looked at the speaker with an expression of utter bewilderment.

"I am sure," said Fanny, in her sweet, earnest voice, "that you will not insist upon a question which it would be painful to us to reply to further."

"I will not—certainly—you are at liberty, madam—but—good Heavens! what a likeness!"

"I have your word, then, sir?"

"Yes, madam—since you insist, I shall give it. But one other question—you say I must not seek to discover who the original of the portrait is. Then the original—is not dead."

Fanny hesitated; then said:

"He is not, sir."

Lord Ferrers listened to this reply with the deepest emotion.

"He is living?" he exclaimed.

"He is, sir."

"Is he in Virginia—in America?—is he—"

"I must recall to you your promise, sir," Fanny interposed. "You have given me your word that you would ask no further questions in reference to this picture."

Lord Ferrers sank back in his chair.

"If I have given my word I will keep it," he murmured in a voice which was scarcely recognizable. "So the portrait is that of a person still living—'of a friend of the family'—of this family!"

His eyes were again raised to the picture, and an expression of profound tenderness slowly came to his face—the white mustache on his lip shook slightly.

"That portrait is the picture of Hartley Ferrers!" he muttered, "or old George Ferrers is blind or losing his senses!"

A deep silence had settled on the apartment, and no word was uttered—either by Lucy, seated by Mrs. Talbot, or Eleanor and Lieut. Ferrers, who had been engaged in what seemed a most intimate and confidential colloquy, carried on in a low, nearly inaudible tone, the young lady listening or speaking with eyes cast down, a slight rose tint in her cheeks, and from time to time a quick, furtive glance at her ardent companion.

The evident emotion of Lord Ferrers had impressed

every one, however, so forcibly that all was stillness for the moment in the apartment.

Suddenly a rapid firing was heard in the direction of the bivouac of the British troopers, and Lord Ferrers started up, losing sight instantly of all but his duty as a soldier.

"Something is going on yonder which it behooves me to know, ladies!" he exclaimed gruffly. "I beg to bid you good evening."

A moment afterward he and Tom Ferrers had left the house, leaped on their horses, and were going at full speed in the direction of the firing.

CHAPTER XIII.

HOW COL. TARLETON ARRIVED TOO LATE.

Canolles, with about twenty-five men, had attacked the British detachment, dismounted and off their guard.

It is unnecessary to inform the reader that after turning his back on the advancing column on the night before, the partisan had hastened to get his men under arms, and that the mysterious noises in the Swamp accompanying the enemy's movements were made by Canolles and his Rough Riders.

There was for this man apparently, as for his followers, a singular attraction in partisan warfare—the tracking an enemy as a hunter tracks his game until the moment arrived for a sudden attack. It had for him all the charms of tiger hunting in the Indian jungle, and on this occasion Canolles took an unwonted interest in the prospect of an encounter, as one of his opponents was Colonel Tarleton, for whom he had conceived, as a Virginian, a great hatred. It was obvious that the expedition of the enemy had for its object either a reconnoissance or the collection of supplies, though what had induced Lord Ferrers and Tarleton both to take part in it Canolles could not imagine.

The plain course before the partisan, however, was to follow the manœuvre of the column until a favorable moment came for attacking it; and this he did all day

long, keeping entirely out of sight even of the British
flankers—a manœuvre easy of execution from his perfect
knowledge of every road and by-road in this singular
region of thicket and swamp land.

Reconnoitering in person at every favorable point,
Canolles observed every incident of the march; the
halts at farm houses, where, controlled by Lord Ferrers, the troopers were not permitted to leave their
horses or indulge in any outrages; the occasional hesi-
tations as to the course to pursue, and all the details of
the movements of cavalry in an enemy's country.

Evening came at last, and when Lord Ferrers and
Tarleton entered the Chatsworth grounds, Canolles,
who had halted his men a quarter of a mile off and
ridden forward alone, observed from a clump of trees
in rear of the house all the details of the interview between the British officers and the two young ladies—
the hand laid by Ferrers on Tarleton's bridle, the entrance of the two officers into the house, and the
march of the British troopers to the glade beyond,
where they were seen to dismount, tie their horses to
the boughs of the trees, and rest.

The moment for the attack had evidently arrived,
and Canolles returned to his men at a swift gallop, and
gave his orders. At the word the Rough Riders moved
rapidly, but in profound silence, through a narrow
road in the wood, just visible beneath its overhanging
boughs in the moonlight; and in fifteen minutes he
was in sight of the British detachment, scattered about
and, many of them, with their arms unbuckled.

Tarleton was not present. Chafing at the reproof

administered to him by Lord Ferrers, and disposed for the moment to nurse his wrath in solitude, he had walked down to the bank of the river, and reaching the vicinity of the Moss Rock, had leaned against a tree, and was indulging, *sotto voce*, in some muttered words, neither very elegant in themselves, nor very indicative of regard for his superior officer.

From this moody reverie he was startled by the firing from the British bivouac.

In fact, Canolles had made, as we have said, a sudden and determined attack upon the British troopers, and before Tarleton or Lord Ferrers could reach the spot, the struggle was substantially over. Taken completely by surprise, and having in young Lieut. Jones, left in charge by Tom Ferrers, a mere youth, wholly incompetent to contend with a soldier like Canolles, the men had made only a brief resistance, many of them—from their unarmed condition—no resistance at all; and when Tarleton and Lord Ferrers approached the spot the panic was general.

Lord Ferrers and his nephew were in front, followed close by Tarleton, who had caught his horse from his orderly in the grounds and came on at a headlong gallop.

Before Lord Ferrers reached the bivouac he was surrounded and captured.

The old nobleman was in a rage, but, even excited as he was, could not be blind to the fact that his captors were treating him with most scrupulous respect. In spite of the vigorous sweep of his broadsword, which cut more than one of the Rough Riders out of the saddle, no attempt was made to injure him—he was simply secured and his horse led off by the bridle, the old cavalier cursing and swearing in a manner violent enough to make the blood run cold.

Canolles, by whose orders, it is unnecessary to say, this respect had been paid to Lord Ferrers—now turned his attention to the opponent whom he wished to meet in person—Col. Tarleton.

Tarleton came on, his horse driven by the spur, and making long bounds. His face, seen clearly in the moonlight, was furious. In no mild mood before, in consequence of the scene in the Chatsworth drawing-room, the surprise of his men made his rage overflow. With drawn sword, and form bent forward in the short stirrups, drawing up his knees, he made straight at Canolles, who came to meet him, and whom he evidently recognized.

"It is you! I thought so!" he exclaimed.

"And you! I knew that!" was the answer of Canolles.

The two horsemen rushed together as they spoke, and their broadswords clashed.

It was easy to see that both were superb riders and swordsmen. A dozen cuts, right, left and front, were parried.

"Good!" cried Canolles, whose face glowed, "it really is a pleasure to engage a good strong wrist, like yours, Colonel."

"I will make your pleasure short, Mr. Marauder!" was the furious reply.

"If you can!" Canolles laughed; and, shortening

his sword, he was about to plunge it into Tarleton's breast, when one of the British fugitives, who had completely lost control of his frightened horse, ran violently against the animal on which Canolles was mounted.

The shock was so great that Canolles was hurled back and nearly unseated. Before he could recover, a panic-stricken rush of troopers in red coats completely separated him from Tarleton, who seemed to be borne away in the *melee*. Whether forced thus from the field against his will, or seeing that by flight alone he could escape capture—as he had seen at the Cowpens—Col. Tarleton certainly did not reappear. He and the remnants of the force, including Tom Ferrers, disappeared in headlong flight in the woods.

Canolles reined in his horse, dancing on all four feet, and turned to Walter Hayfield, who was near him.

He was laughing.

"I promised you I would lay my hand once more on the worthy Col. Tarleton!" he said.

"And you laid it rather heavy, Captain! The defeat is out and out."

"So it seems—and let them go. I could never catch up with them, and I want no prisoners. Order the recall to be sounded at once, and get the men in line."

Walter wheeled his horse.

"Wait a moment. My orders in reference to Lord Ferrers are obeyed?"

"Yes, sir. He was captured without injury to him, although some of the men suffered."

"Very well."

"He is under guard—and not under guard, as I ordered?"

"Yes, sir."

"He retains his arms?"

"Yes, sir."

"Well.   See that no one makes any attempt to deprive him of them or annoy him in any manner—it will be at their peril.   I repeat that he is to be treated with profound respect."

Walter saluted.

"When the men are in column you will take command and move back with them by the Malvern Hill road to the Swamp.   I am going before on the same road."

Walter saluted again.

"A last word," said Canolles.   "You will give orders that none of Lord Ferrers' questions are to be answered.   He will ride in front of the column, twenty paces in advance, wearing his arms, and unguarded; and you will ride with him."

15

CHAPTER XIV.

HOW COLONEL LORD FERRERS RODE IN AN UNEXPECTED DIRECTION, AND WITH WHOM HE SUPPED.

An hour afterwards the Rough Riders, accompanied by a few prisoners, were moving back in column through the devious bypaths of the pine thickets towards White Oak Swamp.

Canolles was not visible. Lord Ferrers rode in front of the column, very much as if he were in command; and this impression had to support it the fact that he still wore his sword, and his pistols were still in his holsters. There were no indications whatever that he was a prisoner—no guard rode near him, and Walter Hayfield moved respectfully several paces in rear, like an aide-de-camp following his general.

The column moved on through the moonlight, gradually approaching the White Oak Swamp. The silence was profound; the hoof strokes of the horses on the sandy road were so light as only to make it more striking.

Lord Ferrers moving alone, in advance, seemed at last to be oppressed by this mysterious nocturnal march, and turning his head, said to Walter gruffly:

" Ride up."

The boy obeyed.

" What the devil does all this mean?" growled the old *militaire.*

"Mean, Colonel?"

"So you know me, eh?"

"You rank, naturally from your uniform, as Colonel," returned Walter, correcting his slip of the tongue.

"Well, I repeat my question. What is the meaning of what has occurred to-night? Whose prisoner am I? Where is your commander? You are not too young, my friend, to command this troop, and I have known some devilish good soldiers and officers no taller than you who had six-footers under them, and deserved to—but you wear no evidence of rank. Who and what are you and your men, and where is your officer?"

Walter smiled and said respectfully:

"You ask me a great number of questions, Colonel —more than I can reply to in a breath."

"Reply to each singly, then!" growled Lord Ferrers.

"Will your Lordship first reply to one I shall myself ask you?"

"My Lordship!—humph! So it seems I am better known than you make out!"

Walter, conscious of another *lapsus linguæ*, was a little taken aback, but answered quickly:

"I heard one of the prisoners utter your name and title, my Lord."

"Very well; ride up close, and let's talk, my young friend, for this infernal swamp is enough to depress a man's spirits."

"It is rather melancholy, Colonel."

"But, thank Heaven! you can't make much out of old George Ferrers with your swamp and your night riders—damme! Ha! ha! I take things as they come, *mon garcon;* but I indulge a slight curiosity to know who the devil has captured me, and where we are going?"

"Your Lordship has not promised to reply to my question."

"Ask it."

"Has your Lordship been treated with respect and due consideration?"

"Yes; I'll say that for you—damme! I've been handled as gingerly as if I were a piece of porcelain. I made a good right and left cut in the fight yonder, but nobody took the trouble to cut at me in return. Then you leave me my arms; I ride in front without a guard, and I even have, ha! ha! an aide-de-camp!"

"Very much at your orders, my Lord; I am glad to find that you are disposed to look at things so philosophically."

Lord Ferrers smiled grimly.

"I like your lingo, my young friend. You talk like a book! Well, I've always been a little or a good deal of a philosopher. War is a game—you play, and win or lose; and why not make up your mind to take the chances of the cards? I am an English soldier making war on you Americans. I follow my flag and you follow yours; each takes his chance. I am captured—well, other people have been captured before— I don't care a button, as I'll soon be exchanged, no doubt. My only sentiment at present is one of slight curiosity to know what officer of the American army has caught me napping."

At the words, "What officer of the American army," Walter, remembering the orders of Canolles, was more than ever on his guard.

"Your Lordship must pardon my not replying," he said; "as you may soon rejoin your flag by exchange, it might be imprudent. It is a good rule not to answer the questions of an able opponent. Were I to tell you that Gen. Lafayette was present to-night you would know that his force was in this vicinity, would you not?"

Lord Ferrers uttered an absolute guffaw.

"Sharp!" he said, "infernally sharp, my young friend. I begin to think that I have the honor of conversing with the real commanding officer of these worthies moving in our rear."

Walter smiled.

"If you are not, who is?"

"That is, after all, the question, Colonel."

Lord Ferrers knit his brow and seemed to reflect.

"Do you know, Mr. Impromptu Aide-de-Camp," he said, "that if I did not know to the contrary I should suppose one thing?"

"What is that, Colonel?"

"That your commanding officer was a former friend of mine."

"A former friend, Colonel?"

"A certain Captain Canolles, chief of Rough Riders."

"Capt. Canolles?—Canolles?" returned Walter, with a puzzled air.

"You must certainly have heard of that gentleman —eh?"

"The name is not unfamiliar to me. He was a partisan, I believe?"

"Yes, and a devilish keen fellow, I can tell you, commanding a troop just like yours, and in this very region. The fact is, I begin to think that I have made the acquaintance to-night of the gentlemen Rough Riders in person—only, Canolles cannot be your commander for two excellent reasons."

"Two reasons, Colonel?"

"He left the country some time since. He told me at Petersburg that he would be off at once—and in the second place, he and I are old companions, and he would never have attacked or captured me."

"You are a friend of Captain Canolles, Colonel?"

"Yes, and no man better deserved friends than Canolles—a devilish brave, splendid, cool, magnificent fellow, or George Ferrers is no judge!"

Walter could not conceal his satisfaction at this speech.

"I really should have liked to know a person whom your Lordship esteemed so highly," he said; "and now, my Lord, as I find we are entering upon dangerous ground, you will allow me to precede you and show you the way."

"The devil!" grunted Col. Ferrers, with his short laugh; "we are in a drawing-room, it seems! Well, go on, my friend, but don't tumble me, man and horse, in a quagmire, if you can avoid it."

"Your Lordship need not fear—the road is practicable and I know it perfectly. You have only to ride directly in my rear."

Walter passed ahead, and the column entered the White Oak Swamp. The scene was similar to that described in earlier pages of this narrative. A vast expanse of thicket—water sleeping in the moonlight—a tangled undergrowth here and there, wholly impenetrable—the mournful cry of the whippoorwill, which was answered from time to time by the weird laughter of the owl from the remote depths of the pine and oak thicket. Such was the great White Oak Swamp on the night when Lord Ferrers entered it. The moonlight surrounded every object with a mysterious attraction with which the weird mingled, and the English officer gazed around him with curious interest.

The column, with Walter and Ferrers in front, moved on thus mile after mile, now on firm ground, now through large expanses of shallow, nearly covered by the long, lush swamp grass, and at last came to a considerable sheet of water, beyond which was a sort of island. Walter pushed on, the water reaching to the girth. Lord Ferrers and the column followed, and five minutes afterwards they gained the island, which seemed of considerable extent and was nearly covered with trees.

To the right a light glimmered, and in the direction of this light Walter, after giving an order to the men, led the way, followed by Col. Ferrers—the troop defiling to the left, where they soon disappeared in the thick foliage.

"As it is forbidden to ask questions, my young

friend," said Lord Ferrers, "I will not inflict the said questions. I content myself with the observation that I am devilish curious to know where we are going, and whether we are to have any supper?"

"I think I can promise you some supper, Colonel."

"Glad to hear it. I'm as hungry as a wolf, and as thirsty as a dozen fish."

"The Captain has some excellent rum, too, I believe."

"The Captain? There's a captain—eh?"

"Yes, my Lord."

"And he's here?"

"I think so."

"Introduce me without delay!—ha! ha! Excellent rum!—and what did you say was the *menu*, my friend?"

"I think there's an old ham—we have some excellent hams in Virginia, my Lord—and some fried chicken, which is also agreeable when one is hungry, and perhaps a few potatoes, peas, and such trifles."

Lord Ferrers drew rein, and, stopping, looked at Walter with solemnity.

"My young friend," he said, "it seems that questions are not to be asked, but I mean to ask one. Are you jesting with your miserable captive? Ham! chicken! potatoes! peas! and excellent rum! And this to a soldier—a wolf—who has eaten nothing for nearly twenty-four hours! My friend, are you wantonly trifling with the feelings of a fellow-creature?"

"By no means, my Lord. There is old black William preparing supper."

Indeed a sable figure was seen busily engaged at a fire beneath an oak near a rude cabin, through the window of which light shone.

"Good Heavens!" cried Lord Ferrers with an electric gesture, "'tis true! It is not an illusion of the brain!—ha! ha!"

"I would never deceive you on so serious a subject, Colonel!" laughed Walter.

"And my host awaits me?" exclaimed Lord Ferrers with beaming countenance.

"I think so, my Lord."

"Then *en evant!* my young friend; lead on."

We have arrived, my Lord.   Allow me to take your horse."

"Not at all.   Here is a bough."

And Lord Ferrers tied his own horse, Walter imitating him, and then leading the way toward the cabin about twenty paces distant.

It was a rustic affair, with a chimney of logs built up outside, and had a door and window on the side which Lord Ferrers now approached. As they drew near, a rich and savory odor invaded the atmosphere —an odor of broiled ham and eggs, broiled chicken and other edibles.   Lord Ferrers closed his eyes and drew a long breath through his nostrils.

"I no longer regret my capture," he said, "if this is a specimen of my rations during my captivity."

"We shall try to make them better, my Lord," Walter said, with a laugh. "Remember what short notice we had of the pleasure of your company to-night!"

"Yes—you say 'we,' I observe.   You are, then, a friend of his Excellency the Chief?"

"A very warm friend."

"And we are about to see him?"

"Yes."

"Delighted to know him; but I swear I regret one thing."

"What is that, my Lord?"

"That your captain is not Canolles! I would rather hobnob to-night in the Swamp with that lad of mettle than sup with the Premier Duke of England."

The door of the cabin had opened as he was speaking.

"You have your wish, my Lord," said Canolles, appearing in the doorway, "and I assure you I reciprocate your preference in reference to yourself."

CHAPTER XV.

THE SUPPER.

The sudden appearance of Canolles standing in the doorway of the cabin seemed to fill Col. Ferrers with the utmost astonishment. He stopped short, exclaiming:

"You!"

"In person, my dear Colonel," replied Canolles, whose face indicated unmistakable pleasure. "What surprises you?"

"Nothing surprises me in this curious world," grunted Lord Ferrers with affected indifference, though it was perfectly plain that his pleasure at the meeting was as great as that felt by his host; but here you are, and I don't mind saying I'm devilish glad to see you, Canolles!"

The partisan had advanced quickly to receive his guest, with his hand extended to bestow a cordial grasp. Lord Ferrers extended two fingers.

"So it's not your ghost, or *simulacrum?*" he said. "They didn't make a ghost of me, too, eh?—in the fight yonder, and we are not meeting in Hades?"

"The surroundings are rather prosaic for that classic region, Colonel," laughed Canolles, "and you may perceive an odor unknown probably to Achilles and Ulysses—that of a Virginia ham."

"I do!" was the old Colonel's emphatic response.

"Ambrosia never equaled it, and I catch a glimpse of bottles yonder which contain, I'll venture to swear, something a long way ahead of nectar!"

"You shall test the question, Colonel. But come in!—come in! I never hoped to have the good fortune to see you beneath my roof."

Canolles drew the Colonel in, and Walter, having repaired to the bivouac of the troop at the other extremity of the small swamp island to carry an order, the friends found themselves alone in the cabin. It was a rude affair, with one room only and unboarded rafters. A broad fire-place, a rough table, a camp couch and two or three rustic arm-chairs, evidently the handiwork of some member of the command—these objects were seen by the light of two tallow candles, burning in superbly chased silver candlesticks. On the camp couch lay the hat, gloves, and belt containing the broadsword of the partisan. Canolles hastened to receive the cocked hat and accoutrements of Lord Ferrers, which he deposited beside his own, and then drawing up the chair of honor—a broad-seated affair with sturdy arms—said:

"Sit down, Colonel, and let me say that no one could be more welcome here than yourself."

"Humph!—well, that's highly flattering to a prisoner, i' faith!"

"A prisoner! You do not seriously consider yourself a prisoner?"

"What else am I?"

"You are a guest—do not doubt that for a moment, my Lord."

Ferrers looked at Canolles with his grim-looking smile and said:

"So I'm in a cavern of the Arabian Nights, where all's unreal! I've dreamed all this, then! There was no fight to-night; I was not captured; we have not been marching through the most damnable roads that I ever laid eyes on, except that I could not see where I was riding, and I am free to depart from this abode of the genii whenever I choose—eh!"

"At this very moment, if you desire, Colonel, with an escort to conduct you; but you will not go before supper, I hope."

"If I do I'm—but let us not be profane!"

"No doubt you are hungry?"

"Hungry? No wolf ever approached me!"

"Then I will order supper."

Canolles called to the dusky figure at the fire, and a muttered response as of some high functionary disturbed in important business came back.

"I venture to assure you, my Lord," he said, "that you will not have long to wait."

"Glad of it; but while we are waiting, tell me were you not in command yonder to-night?"

"Yes."

"You laid a trap for us, eh?"

"Not for you—for another person."

"Col. Tarleton, eh?"

"Precisely."

"Hey! I begin to understand now. You do not indulge a very strong affection for that excellent young man!"

"I do not, naturally, since I am a Virginian. Col. Tarleton has carried the torch as well as the sword wherever he has moved."

"Fact! I have told him twenty times to stop that damnably disgraceful way of making war, but nothing came of it. Cornwallis don't know of it, or lets him do it, and though I rank Tarleton, he is not under me —except on occasions such as this to-night, when we went together on a reconnoissance."

"I saw you on the march and regretted your presence, but you are far too good a soldier to blame my attack on that account."

"Who could be so absurd?"

"I could only give the strictest orders that you should be treated with the utmost respect. Were my orders obeyed? If not—"

"To the letter! Not a finger touched me. I was lifted gently from the saddle like a delicate young female, most tenderly cared for and marched to this charming retreat at the head of the column, and apparently in command of my captors—"

"Whither I preceded you, Colonel, in order to have some supper ready for you. Here it is."

As Canolles spoke, an aged African, with snow-white hair and clad in a mass of rags, appeared at the door in the rear, and coming in saluted the company with respect and dignity. On one arm he bore a snowy cloth and napkins; in the other hand some plates of exquisitely delicate porcelain-like china, knives, forks and silver spoons. With the air of long practice, evidently in a gentleman's family, he covered the rude table with the cloth, placed the damask napkins neatly folded beneath the plates, arranged the knives, forks and spoons by a single movement, it seemed, of the hand, and then silently retired.

"Humph!" grunted Lord Ferrers; "do you know, my friend, there's not a major domo in the finest castle in England that could have done that better?"

"Old William is well trained, Colonel. An old family servant."

"Of yours?"

"Of my father before me. He wore a black suit and white gloves once, and stood behind some distinguished company. He is in rags now, as you see, and everything is changed, except the company."

Lord Ferrers turned his head and looked at the speaker.

"Canolles!" he grunted, "do you know that I'm more puzzled to-night than I ever was before to know one thing?"

"What is that, Colonel?"

"To understand what the devil ever made a man of your rank in society turn marauder!"

Canolles laughed.

"My rank in society? I'm a mere swamp rider, as you see."

"I see nothing of the sort—exactly the contrary. But all this can be put off until after supper. I never could talk when the center of my system was in the condition that it is at present."

"Very well, Colonel; here is something which I hope will revive you."

Old William had entered with a pile of dishes, all of the same exquisite china; and these contained an old Virginia ham, red and juicy, chickens fried and stewed, roast lamb, early peas, potatoes and other vegetables, and a Virginia hoe cake.

"To table, my guest," said Canolles; "but first try and adopt our Virginia habit of an appetizer."

He went to a corner and returned with two long-necked bottles with dusty labels.

"This is excellent Jamaica rum," he said, presenting one. "I know it to be ten years old—and this is old Madeira, or at least has attained its majority, as you may see from the year, '1759,' upon the label."

An expression of rapture passed over the face of Col. Ferrers.

"Rum ten years old! and Madeira twenty-two!" he cried. "Is this scene a dream, then? Or am I in the cave of the Arabian genii, where all will flit ere one can cry out 'Hold?'"

"Not in the least, my dear Colonel. You are in the White Oak Swamp in Virginia. This is simply a good bottle of wine from my father's cellar, and nothing before you will flit until that imp of darkness, William, clears the table."

Canolles drew up the chairs, and they took their seats, the face of Col. Ferrers glowing with the same profound expression of satisfaction. Old William had brought the glasses and fresh water, had opened the wine and Jamaica, and the supper began and went upon its way, evidently to the extreme enjoyment of Lord Ferrers.

CHAPTER XVI.

IN WHICH LORD FERRERS COMES TO THE POINT.

Lord Ferrers consumed his supper with the deliberate gusto of an epicure not the least in a hurry, and the perseverance of a hungry soldier. An hour afterward it had come to an end—the table was cleared, and host and guest were seated opposite each other in the light of the two candles in their silver candlesticks.

"Well, my dear Colonel, I hope you have supped to your satisfaction," said Canolles, "or at least, which is much with us soldiers, have ceased to be hungry."

"Supped to my satisfaction! Are you making fun of me, Canolles? Never in the finest Paris cafes have I supped as I have supped to night!"

"Delighted to hear it Colonel," laughed Canolles.

"Your 'old Virginia ham,' above all, is past the power of words. How are the animals fed which produce that wonder? What is the secret of the flavor it imparts? It is grand—it is imperial! It is the prince of edibles. Your lamb conciliates respect—but your ham, my friend, arouses in me an enthusiasm which I cannot express."

"You are good enough to make flattering observations, and I recognize your well-known courtesy, my Lord," said Canolles, with a smile.

"Humph!" grunted Col. Ferrers, "I am not at all

flattering, comrade—I am just. As well say that this old Madeira I am sipping is an ordinary vintage."

"I believe that to be good."

"It is superb. I have in my time quaffed many flagons, comrade; but I do not quaff a beverage like this. I taste it with the tip of the tongue and the edge of the lips, for fear that I shall feel it in my head and lose the flavor."

In fact the Colonel, who had only swallowed a single mouthful of the strong Jamaica rum, and then abandoned it, had tasted his Madeira with the air of a humming bird hovering over a flower, apparently with the apprehension that some of the delicate aroma would escape him. And the good wine had responded to this flattering treatment. Co-operating naturally and healthfully with the excellent supper—partaken of slowly by the old soldier with the wisdom of a true epicure—it had warmed his faculties, exhilarated without exciting his spirits, and he had evidently reached that stage of physical well-being when the body and the mind are in their most favorable condition. Mirth beamed in his eye—good-fellowship in the manner in which he hobnobbed with Canolles—and with his white mustache and ruddy face he was the model of a jolly old *militaire* and gentleman.

"Well, Colonel," said Canolles, "you must be aware that nothing pleases a host so much as to have his guest pleased with his entertainment Nothing now remains but to inform you that an escort will await you at daylight—if you desire to go so soon—back to

the English pickets; and to add that if you are sleepy,
your bed is ready."

"Sleepy?" said Lord Ferrers. "What an idea! I
was never more wide awake in all my life, and I mean
to cling to that bottle of Madeira, Canolles, until I see
the bottom."

"Well, I'll assist you."

"Like the jolly boy you are! And why not make
the 'winged hours' flit on with song? Come, give me
a song; you shake your head—then you shall hear the
favorite of the late Lord Ferrers."

And in a jovial, rollicking, and richly musical voice
the old soldier trolled forth the famous ditty beginning:

> "There was a jolly beggar,
>   And a begging he was bound,
> And he took up his quarters
>   All in a landart town.
>
> "And we'll go no more a-wooing,
>   A-wooing in the night;
> We'll go no more a-wooing, boys,
>   Though the moon shine ne'er so bright!"

Clear, sonorous, and full of the richest spirit of merriment, rang out the "loud, lilting chorus," and old
Lord Ferrers as he sang was a sight to see. He sat
with his shoulders thrown back, his stately old head
erect, his eyes laughing, his white mustache clearly
relieved against the ruddy cheeks, curling with the
mirth that shook his frame.

"Bravo!" cried Canolles as he ended, "what an admirable tenor you have, my lord!"

“Ho! ho! now you are flattering me, comrade! My song’s not equal to your Madeira by long odds!”

“It is admirable! You will sing me something more, I hope—a song of sentiment.”

“If you like. What shall it be? Stay! I’ll sing you something I’ve not sung for years—it was the favorite of a person whom you wondrously resemble.” The old nobleman uttered these words in a voice of deep sadness, and his head drooped. Silence reigned for some moments in the cabin, and Lord Ferrers seemed the prey of some sorrowful memory. Then slowly, in a deep, rich, nearly tremulous voice, he began the old Scottish song, “The Flowers of the Forest,” which seems in its long murmur full of sadness, like the sigh of the winds of autumn. As he proceeded his tones grew sweeter, sadder, more affecting, and penetrated to the heart of his listener. At last the song ended in a long sigh, as it were, and again there was silence. Each of the two men turned away his head to conceal the traces of tears; those in the eyes of Lord Ferrers seemed to spring from memories connected with the song, those of Canolles from the profound effect produced upon his feelings.

“Well, well,” said the old nobleman, arousing himself; “all that is buried in the grave, comrade. It is many a year since I sang that song. Your face made me sing it once more—looking at you I think of one who’s gone—a boy—whom I loved more dearly than all else on this earth save the mother that bore him. Enough—this unmans me—let us not speak further of it.”

Canolles bowed his head with deep respect, and for some moments the silence was unbroken. Then, with a deep sigh, Lord Ferrers rose erect in his chair and said to the partisan :

"Well, friend, I have endeavored to entertain you with my old cracked voice—in your turn entertain me or rather satisfy my curiosity. Do you remember when you were at Petersburg and condemned to death, you authorized me to read a paper in which you had related the story of your life? We are alone now—tell me that story."

CHAPTER XVII.

HENRY CARTARET, OF CHATSWORTH.

Canolles, leaning back in his chair, with one arm extended upon the table at his side, the fingers idly thrumming, for some moments remained silent. He was evidently reflecting. The dreamy eyes of the partisan were plainly looking upon other scenes, and his memory filled with figures belonging to the past.

He roused himself from the reverie at last, and seemed to think that some apology for it was due to his guest.

"A bad and very uncourteous habit this, dear Colonel," he said; "but you will pardon me my dream. Life, after all, is little better."

"I don't know," was Lord Ferrers' reply, in his habitual, short, gruff voice. "I've found it devilish real, and I thought you, the headlong partisan and Rough Rider, Canolles, would have little or nothing to do with dreams—reveries."

"A natural conclusion, but not correct. I am the dreamer of dreamers, and take refuge in hard riding and fighting to escape these dreams."

"They are not pleasant, then?"

"They are not."

"Humph! Well, that brings us back to the main point. Tell me your history—and observe, comrade, that I am not making the least apology for my blunt request. I liked you from the moment I laid eyes on you. I came near cursing Arnold to his face as a poltroon and scoundrel when he signed your death-warrant. You are a wondrous likeness, I've said, of one who—has left me—no more of that—who and what are you?"

Canolles looked at Lord Ferrers with his old grim, melancholy smile.

" Why not go for information to the first person you meet? " he said. " They will tell you that I am a freebooter, a bandit, a highwayman—that I rob both sides, and fight like a free lance of the middle ages, for money, and only for money—so much for the what I am ; and as to the who, is it not natural to adopt the obvious theory that I am sprung from the dregs of the social cauldron, that I am ' base, common, and popular '—and fitly associate myself with the rough fellows I command, my equals, save, perhaps, in will and brain ? "

" A single word, Canolles," said Lord Ferrers. " Stop all that talk. Don't expect to fool old George Ferrers. If you are a marauder you have left your social rank to become one. What I want to know without further parleying is who you are and what made you adopt this wild idea of fighting under no flag ? Will you tell me, or will you not ?"

" I will tell you everything," Canolles replied with his melancholy smile. " The story need not be long, which is fortunate, perhaps, as it will not be gay ; and I no longer object to speaking frankly. You recall the scene in Petersburg on the night before my expected execution, when, regarding myself already as a dead man, I authorized you to read the paper in which I had explained all that I now propose to explain *viva voce.* Well, it is a dead man in another sense who now speaks to you—a man whom after to-night you will probably never see again. Having attained the aim I had in view in becoming a commandant of partisans, I have no longer anything to induce me to remain in Virginia, I should before this time have disbanded my troops, but for the satisfaction of striking at Col. Tarleton for his many outrages. I shall now disband the men and leave Virginia forever—hence I may speak with candor, and even desire to speak. You have known me as a mere plunderer, apparently; why not let you know me as a gentleman? I must have seemed to you eaten up by a base greed for gold. Why not let you see that of all the treasure I have seized I retain not so much as a single penny? Why, in one word, my dear Lord Ferrers, should I not open my breast to you, a faithful and devoted friend, so that in going away never to return, I may not rest under these imputations, but carry with me at least the good opinion of a man whose good opinion I value?"

"You have that now, don't doubt it. The devil! I think you heard me say what I thought of you the very morning you were brought to poor Phillips' headquarters. Well, I've never wavered in that opinion. I know as well as I know I am in existence that there is some mystery in your past life—something other than the love of gold that has made a marauder of a gentleman. Tell me what it is—it is not necessary at all for securing or retaining my good opinion. I say you have that. My curiosity is the sentiment I want gratified, Canolles."

"It shall be gratified, Colonel," returned Canolles, "and you will probably be surprised to ascertain how very simply and briefly the apparent mystery of my career may be explained."

"I am the eldest son of Henry Cartaret, of Chatsworth, dead in poverty and exile. My name is Hartley Canolles Cartaret—the name Canolles being derived from my mother, who came of an old French Huguenot family, emigrants to Virginia for conscience sake, and the name Hartley from your brother, the late Lord Hartley Ferrers, to whom my father, as you may be aware, was bound by ties of most intimate, almost tender friendship."

"I know it well! Astonishing! So you are a son of Henry Cartaret! Humph! Is it possible? Well, he was not only my friend, he was a relation of ours; and no doubt that accounts for your remarkable likeness to my poor boy. These resemblances often come out strongest, at intervals, skipping a generation or generations. So you are a son of Henry Cartaret?"

"Yes, but to proceed with my story, Colonel. I was born at Chatsworth, at that time a grand manor, the abode of wealth and luxury—for my father's possessions were large—and here in this good old Virginia home I passed my childhood and youth—a happy Virginia boy, loving everybody, and they say beloved by all. My disposition was naturally mild and my affection very strong. I remember well what passionate grief

I experienced at the death of my dear mother soon
after the birth of my younger brother, Harry, and
going back in memory I now recall a thousand trifles
indicating to my mind, beyond all doubt, that by nature
I was intended for anything rather than to take part in
this dirty and bloody trade of war, to which, as you
will see, I was driven by outraged love and pride, which
I must confess have made me quite relentless.

"For my younger brother Harry, whom you have
seen, I think, at Petersburg, I cherished the warmest
affection, and this affection, thank Heaven, has never
changed, nor has his changed for me. Our likeness to
each other seemed to draw us more closely together,
and I have never known the time when my first instinct
was not to interpose myself between him and danger,
as I know it has been his first instinct when peril
threatened me, an evidence of which you had in his
night attack to rescue me when I was condemned to
death. But warm as my love was for Harry—and
never did brother love brother more than I loved him—
my devotion to my father very far exceeded it. Had
you known him, my father, you would easily have
understood this devotion, almost passionate in its
character and extent. Colonel Cartaret—as he was
called after the Virginia fashion—was indeed a remarkable person. I have encountered in my life, short as
it has been, many eminent individuals, but none quite
up to his moral and mental stature. He was the soul
of sweetness and benignity—tall, erect, courtly, with
the gentlest smile for every one around him, and a hand
as open as the day to any one in distress—and in a

circuit of twenty miles there was scarce a poor family who at some time had not been relieved by him in their hour of need. To enter his presence was like going into the sunshine, and from my earliest years I recall his exquisite and caressing smile. His politeness was princely, and bestowed upon the low equally with the high. The poorest was as welcome in his house as the richest; and he would rise from his wine and leave the most elegant company to go and listen to some poor person who came to him for relief."

"Yes, all that is true. I knew Henry Cartaret as well as you did," grunted Lord Ferrers.

"Then you know, my Lord," continued Canolles, "that my father possessed other traits, also, than those I have noticed. When I said just now, in referring to him, that he seemed to me to be in some respects the most remarkable person I have ever known, I referred to the singular union in him of the most apparently incompatible traits. Under this sweet and gentle exterior—this suavity and kindness which I have never seen surpassed—was not only an intellectual organization of the first order, but also a very powerful and obdurate will, and a temper which, once aroused, made him a dangerous adversary. I may sum up this account of my father by saying that he seemed to me to be a mixture of the lion and the lamb—up to a certain epoch in his life I saw only the lamb. The day came when the lion revealed himself."

Canolles paused.

"Continue, friend," the old nobleman gravely said, "and be assured that I take the deepest interest in all

that you tell me. I see with your eyes, and have before
me the widowed gentleman, loving and beloved by all
around him — you and your younger brother, simple,
affectionate country boys, like the boys of our dear old
England — the great house of Chatsworth, with its elegant company — all the places, the faces, the members
of your happy family group."

"There were other members of the group, my Lord,
whom I was about to mention — Mrs. Talbot and her
two nieces, distant relatives of the family. My father,
hearing some years after the death of my mother that
these ladies were reduced in fortune, invited Mrs. Talbot
and her nieces to make their home at Chatsworth.
They assented, became cherished members of the household, and they have remained at the old manor house
up to the present time, even after the alienation of the
property and my father's death—of which circumstance,
with others, you shall have, in a few moments, an explanation."

Again Canolles paused and his eyes assumed the old
dreamy look; but they slowly filled with blood, his
swarthy face was slightly tinted with color, and a latent
flush, as it were, came from beneath the dark eyelashes.

"I now come to the main substance of my narrative," he said, the tone of his voice growing stern,
almost harsh, as he proceeded. "The political agitation
heralding the present armed struggle began, and young
as I was at that time — the year 1765 — I well remember the general excitement. My father was a member
of the House of Burgesses, and as he had taken me
with him on a visit to Williamsburg, the capital, I was

a personal witness of the celebrated debate on the
Stamp Act. Mr. Henry offered some resolutions which
aroused a storm, since they distinctly declared that the
Virginia Burgesses alone had the right to tax Virginia.
This was regarded by many members as an open defiance of Parliament, and the resolutions were bitterly
opposed by some of the greatest patriots of the day,
as premature and injudicious. My father came to
Henry's support, and advocated the resolutions in a
speech of passionate eloquence. I still remember the
fire of his eyes, and the grandeur of his appearance,
as he drew himself to the full height of his tall stature,
exclaiming: 'Treason? Does the gentleman seriously
characterize these resolutions as treason? Treason
against whom or what? Against the King of England? It is not the King of England who taxes the
colonies! Against a body of country gentlemen calling themselves the House of Commons, or a body of
titled gentlemen calling themselves the House of
Lords? I have yet to learn that a subject can be guilty
of treason against a subject! The resolutions before
the House declare that the Burgesses of Virginia alone
have the right to tax Virginia, since in the House of Burgesses of Virginia alone are the people of Virginia represented. Is that true or false? If it be true, the
resolutions ought to pass. I am conservative in my
views, sir. I love England next to my own country,
but I would rather lay my head on the block, so help
me God, than shrink from asserting the just rights of
my native country—Virginia!'

. "I have given you nearly the exact words uttered by

Col. Cartaret. I cannot convey the proud accents of the loyal voice, pleading passionately for the assertion of right. The resolutions passed—largely, I am sure, from the effect of my father's speech—and he was re-garded from that time by Mr. Henry, and Mr. Jeffer-son afterwards, as an ardent revolutionist, bent on effecting a separation between the colonies and the mother country. Any such desire, however, was ut-terly absent from his breast. He loved England with all his heart—her ancient Church establishment, her social fabric of class, her ancestral glories—her poets, statesmen, law-givers were his—and with his far-seeing glance he saw that the new *regime* would overthrow all, from turret to foundation, inaugurating upon the ruins of the fabric toppled down an equalizing democracy which would sweep before it, like a torrent, all the *debris* of the old world of his affections. Of this he spoke to me often, pointing out the tendency of the moment toward separation. One day when Col. Washington, now the great leader of the colonies, was at Chatsworth—it was about the year 1774, I believe—they sat over their wine conversing upon political affairs, and I recall as distinctly as though it had been yesterday, that both gentlemen absolutely agreed with each other in reference to a separation from the mother country, Col. Washington expressing himself upon the subject in terms so strong and tones so animated that it was plain he regarded such a severance with abso-lute repugnance, and never dreamed that events could render it necessary.

"I grow tedious, perhaps, my Lord—but this preface

was essential to a just comprehension of the events which I am now about to relate. Col. Cartaret, after serving in the Burgesses, took no further part in public affairs until the opening of the present conflict, remaining at home and passing his time in what he loved better than all else, the supervision of his estate—for he was passionately devoted to country life. He entertained a great deal of company, and among this company were some of the first statesmen of the epoch— Mr. Edmund Pendleton, Mr. Edmund Randolph, Mr. George Mason, and others, who agreed with him in every particular, and looked with unconcealed regret upon the possibility of being forced to a separation and war with England. You knew Col. Cartaret, my Lord, and must be aware that his political opinions were not based upon personal considerations. He was quite superior, I need scarcely say, to any such weakness, and in advocating as he did moderate action instead of precipitation, was actuated by a very high sense of duty and a true love for his country—about to be plunged into a bloody and, as he thought, unnecessary conflict in pursuit of a fancied good which he firmly believed would turn out a deplorable evil. Do you say that he was mistaken—that America is about to gain her end? Very well, my Lord. To each his opinion. This continent will doubtless become the seat of a great democracy; a mighty empire of the people—success to it—but leave Col. Cartaret, who has sealed his opinions by poverty, exile and death, his attachment for England, the home of his family, the old constitutional monarchy, essentially a republic, which

has proved the sole bulwark against absolute government on the continent of Europe.

"Well, the year 1776 came. The fire, which had
been so long smouldering broke forth. The country
was convulsed from one end to the other, and the General Congress found itself called upon by the ardent
revolutionists to formally decree a separation between
England and the colonies. Of this Congress my father
was a member."

CHAPTER XVIII.

WHAT HAD TAKEN PLACE IN CONGRESS.

"Col. Cartaret had accepted the appointment of delegate to the General Congress with the greatest reluctance and only after long hesitation. He was well aware that his opinions were not in unison with those of the great men of the community, and that, instead of proving of any service, he would only embarrass the body in the action they were now plainly bent on taking.

"These opinions were fully stated to the gentlemen who brought the appointment. The reply was brief; the people of Virginia were willing to trust to the action of the man who had supported Henry in '65. Col. Cartaret then said that until the further development of events nothing should induce him to vote for a declaration of separation from England, and consequently formal war between the countries. The response was that the gentlemen of the Burgesses left Col. Cartaret and all her delegates wholly untrammeled. His action would be taken, unless he was distinctly instructed, in accordance with his own views of the interest of the colony: and overcome at last, Col. Cartaret accepted the appointment and repaired to Philadelphia, where in the summer of 1776, as you are aware, my Lord, the great, passionate, bitter struggle soon began on the question whether the colonies should or should not declare themselves independent states and make war on England formally to support their declaration.

"I come now to the vital portion of my narrative—to the incidents which drove my father from this country, to sink, eventually, a sorrow-stricken man, into his grave. He never wavered in his opinions to the last; but the bread of exile is bitter, and the chords of his great heart snapped under the strain.

"The sittings of Congress were often secret, and no record was made of many of the most passionate debates—the body indulging a natural apprehension that, in the event of failure, certain persons would be singled out by the British Government as ringleaders, and made to suffer for their action. This was notably so in the case of the resolutions offered by Mr. Lee, that the colonies should declare themselves independent—neither the name of the mover or seconder having been entered on the journals.

"I have scarce sufficient equanimity, my Lord, to enable me to protract my account of what now occurred in connection with Col. Cartaret. He remained obdurately unconvinced of the propriety of a declaration at the moment. That the necessity for such a proceeding might arise he acknowledged—it was even probable that the country would be driven by events to take that step. But a formal separation and declaration of war were not yet necessary, he urged; and if any possibility remained to avoid that course, it was, he said, incumbent on the Congress, as a body of statesmen and patriots, not to act under the influence of passion, but spare the country, if possible, the fearful effusion of blood which must ensue. These views he advanced with all the powers of his passionate eloquence, and for many days, during which the bitter conflict of opposing opinions went on night and day, Col. Cartaret found at his back a powerful party, which shared his views.

"In support of this statement, if it requires any support, take the expression used on his return to Virginia, by Mr. Jefferson, that this powerful opposition to the Declaration at that time resembled the ceaseless action of gravity, weighing upon us by night and by day. I give you his exact words, of which I am accurately informed; and they will serve to dissipate the fancy, widely prevalent at this time, that there was in the Congress no wide divergence of opinion. There was a bitter difference, on the contrary, and Col. Cartaret was the leader of the party for deferring action until the prospect before the country was clearer.

"Hour by hour, however, the sentiment of the body in favor of prompt action grew stronger, and Col. Cartaret, finding that any further struggle was useless, abandoned the contest, and, retiring to a seat in a remote part of the hall, listened in silence whilst the desultory debate yet continued. He was not permitted to retire in peace. Smarting under the lash which Col. Cartaret had more than once applied to him in debate, a delegate, as remarkable for his personal insignificance as for his flippant and reckless haranguing day after day, singled his now silent adversary out as the mark of his denunciation. I will not repeat the insulting expressions of this person, of which my father informed me afterwards. It is enough to say that every base motive was attributed to him—personal absence of nerve, apprehension that the cause would fail and that he would lose his estate, and the speaker even intimated that British gold was at the bottom of the action of the gentleman from Virginia. Can you imagine anything more insolent than that, my Lord," said Canolles, with knit brows and the old dangerous, latent flash of the eye, " to charge Henry Cartaret, of Chatsworth, with personal apprehension—to attribute to him the apprehension of pecuniary loss—and to hint that he had been bought? Well, there was something still worse behind, as you will discover. When his adversary had taken his seat, Col. Cartaret rose, and, beginning his reply with the words, ' Mr. Speaker, who is that person ?' proceeded to utter what has been described to me as the most bitter and powerful speech of the Congress. There can be little question that the tone of it was injudicious, and that Col. Cartaret regretted in calmer moments the phraseology employed, if not the sentiments uttered. The result was to enrage the more ardent revolutionists, and, to end my account of this painful scene, a resolution strongly denunciatory of the sentiments and expressions of one of the delegates from Virginia was offered, promptly seconded, and passed by the House, as indignant at the tone of my father's reply as he had been at the attack made upon him in the first instance.

" The result of this scene, which took place in secret session, was that Col. Cartaret at once resigned his seat in Congress; the resignation was accepted, and he returned to Chatsworth without having voted either for or against the Declaration of Independence.   He promptly reported to the Virginia Convention, then in session, the details of his course in Congress, and the Convention took no action upon the paper, laying it on the table.   This my father, in his indignant mood, at the moment profoundly resented—and although Mr. Pendleton and other eminent friends assured him that the gentlemen of the Convention retained unanimously the highest sense of his untarnished honor, and would not even investigate the subject, Col. Cartaret would not accept this non-action as just, and retired to Chatsworth, whence, a year or two afterwards, after mortgaging his estate, he went to England, where, worn out with the passionate conflict into which his conscientious opinions had placed him, he soon afterwards died.''

"After refusing," said Lord Ferrers, " the honor of Knighthood and the Governorship of Jamaica, with a salary of £20,000 a year."

" I thought it useless to recall that circumstance to your mind, my Lord, as my father's refusal to accept rank or emolument in his situation was natural. Indeed, all his sympathies were with the colonies, and he expressed them freely.   He refused to return to America—although urged incessantly to do so by friends in Virginia—from a sentiment most powerful with him, pride.   He had acted in Congress from the highest motives of public duty, with the good of the country and that alone at heart.   The result had been a public and official insult inflicted upon him by the Congress—and this he never forgave."

"And he was right," growled Lord Ferrers. "These civilians—curse 'em!—never tolerate a difference of opinion, and throw mud at people who won't think as they think! I'd like to have a regiment of 'em under my command; but they never get near enough to know the smell of gunpowder. Well, now, Canolles, tell me about yourself, and your own story."

CHAPTER XIX.

HOW COL. FERRERS PROPOSED A TOAST.

Canolles slowly passed from indignation to melancholy, and uttered a deep sigh.

"I need not consume much time in speaking of myself, my Lord," he said sorrowfully, "and there are some circumstances connected with my career since the death of my father which I regret not to be able to refer to even to so true a friend as yourself. With the exception of these I shall use no concealment, and tell you frankly my motives in entering upon a course of partisan warfare without the pale of the American flag.

"When these events occurred I was just entering upon manhood, and my father's exile embittered my whole life. My attachment to him had, as I have informed you, been the master sentiment of my being, and I could not forgive the American cause the wrong inflicted by the American Congress. Nothing would induce me to join the Continental forces, although Harry did so promptly under the effect of the war fever. I remained at Chatsworth moping and unhappy, and was fast settling down into a confirmed misanthrope. For this there were other reasons—I am unable to state them at this moment. I can only inform you that I fell into a deep melancholy, and shrunk from the sight of a human face even."

"But your cousins—those handsome young ladies—were still at Chatsworth, eh?" said Lord Ferrers.

"Yes," said Canolles, in a low tone.

"Faith! I think they are worth looking at."

Canolles made no reply and Lord Ferrers, looking keenly at him, suddenly felt, as by a species of instinct, that something in connection with one of the young ladies must have occasioned in part the melancholy alluded to by his companion. At once his high breeding came to his relief, and he said:

"But I am interrupting you, comrade. Go on with your story—telling me what you please and no more than you please."

Canolles inclined his head as though accepting this, and said:

"Well, my Lord, I was moping, as I said, at Chatsworth, and day by day grew more melancholy. All the good fortune of the Cartarets seemed to be reversed. My father was dead in exile, the estate of Chatsworth was hopelessly mortgaged, I was a waif, an estray, a poor sorrowful youth, prevented even from seeking in the career of arms some distraction from my melancholy, and the future had in it no ray of light or comfort. From this apathy I was at last aroused. Harry came home wounded, and for some months was confined to his bed, his poor, pale face full of suffering, as it was full of sweetness. I have said that next to my father he was the nearest to my heart. I loved him indeed with all my soul—and when he returned to the army, as he soon did, I had formed my resolution. I was, I said to myself, a poor useless creature, of no good to myself or others; why not change my whole life and make myself of some benefit—to Harry? I was the eldest son, and the Chatsworth estate, if ever relieved of the mortgage, would be my property. But why should I look forward to that, or care? I was utterly unhappy—cared naught indeed for my life—but there was my dear Harry, the very reverse in all things of myself. To explain—he was and is still engaged to the younger of my two cousins, Miss Fanny Talbot; and if I could only do something to redeem the property, give it to Harry, and then take my melancholy face out of sight, then Harry's future would be full of sunshine, and I should, after all, have done some good in the world."

"I understand!" grunted Lord Ferrers.

" How to effect the redemption of the estate was the question," continued Canolles. "The mortgage amounted to nearly twenty-five thousand pounds sterling in gold, and it was doubtful if that much coin could be found in all Virginia—certainly I had no means of procuring it, no security to offer for any such loan."

" Aha!" said Lord Ferrers. " I now begin to understand! You formed the project of effecting your loan from Gen. Phillips, eh?"

" Precisely, my Lord," replied Canolles, the grim smile replacing the melancholy, "and I set about the negotiation without delay. I have said that nothing could have induced me to fight for a cause whose authorities had insulted and outraged my father; but I was far from having any objection to making war on the British if they invaded Virginia, my native country, and after my father and my brother, my first and last love. In a word, the plan which I now formed, and soon carried out, was to raise a troop of partisans, inflict all the injury possible upon the invaders of Virginia soil, and, as an offset to these public services, appropriate to myself any captured property, to be converted into money—which money I designed promptly to pay to a Mr. Atwell, the holder of the mortgage on Chatsworth, and so redeem the estate. Not for myself, I repeat—for my brother, who I may inform you is at this moment the undisputed owner of the estate, wholly unincumbered."

"And a devilish fine property too?" laughed Lord Ferrers; "but go on, comrade."

"I had no difficulty," continued Canolles, "in carrying on my plan. I had a large acquaintance among a certain class along the river—hunters, fishermen and other rough but brave and trusty young fellows. In a word, Colonel, I raised my troop, established my head-quarters here in the White Oak Swamp, and dropping my full name to call myself simply Capt. Canolles, have been making war for some months on my private account under no flag but my own. Of course, this proceeding is irregular, and I have secured the repute of a marauder; am even reported, although it is the purest calumny, to make war on both sides—but I risk my person and fight man to man, often against odds, to free Virginia from the public enemy. Am I a bandit?"

Lord Ferrers burst into laughter.

"You are a soldier, and a devilish cool one, comrade—and, speaking for myself, I approve with all my heart of your motives and course—that is, old George Ferrers does. *Colonel* Ferrers, **of course,** regards **you,** officially, **as an** outlaw."

"Very well, Colonel," said Canolles, a ghost of a smile flitting across his face in response **to the broad merriment** on the ruddy countenance of Lord **Ferrers, "and** now I believe I have come to the end of my narrative. Thanks to the army **chest of Gen.** Phillips, which **I have had recourse to upon two occasions,** I **have dis-**charged the mortgage on Chatsworth; transferred **the title of the** entire estate **to Harry; and he now has the** paper in his possession. Thus my **work is done and I** disappear. I scarcely know whither **I** shall go, or what **career** is before me. I shall fall in some foreign war, **no doubt. I only know** that I am going to leave Vir-**ginia, never to return** to it. I shall at least **have** the **happiness of knowing** that my brother is **happy.** The **war is about to end, I** think; this seems **to be** the last campaign—Harry **will marry** his cousin **and** keep up the family at Chatsworth—and so all ends, you see, Colonel. **The sun will** shine **again on** our **good old** home—on a **bridegroom and bride bearing the** name **of** Cartaret—and **the poor** marauder Canolles **will have the** satisfaction **of knowing** that it is he **who has brought back the sunshine!"**

The partisan smiled, but the tones of his voice were **profoundly sad; and Lord** Ferrers, with his **keen ear and eye, had** little difficulty in understanding **that** his **companion was a** prey to the deepest melancholy.

"Well, well," the partisan added, "I have told you **a long and very sad story, have** I not, friend? But life is almost always sad.   Let us now rest.   You must be weary from remaining so long in the saddle.   There is your bed.   Old William, you see, has improvised one for me also." ·

"Not before I give you a toast, Canolles!" exclaimed Lord Ferrers, emptying into his glass the remnants of wine in the bottle which he had promised to cling to until he saw the bottom.

"A toast, my Lord?" said the partisan, sadly.

"The health of a friend I esteem as a soldier and gentleman!"

And raising his glass above his head, the white-mustached nobleman exclaimed:

"I drink health and long life to the marauder, Canolles!"

CHAPTER XX.

THE ROUGH RIDERS.

With the explanation given by Canolles of the motives actuating him in entering upon his eccentric career, and his resolution to disband his troop and leave Virginia, the drama aiming to set forth his fortunes might be supposed to terminate—or if not to terminate, to reach one of those convenient halting places where so many writers bid their personages farewell, leaving the sequel of the drama to the reader's imagination.

But the writer of these pages is unwilling to close so abruptly his narrative, and dismiss with so little ceremony the children of his fancy—the brave partisan, the bluff old English soldier, and Walter, Lucy, Fanny and the rest. These persons are not shadows merely to him, as perchance they may be to the reader; phantoms only, like the evanescent shapes, the flitting forms we see at twilight, when each bush is a figure, each rustle of the leaves the whisper of some living thing. They are rather real personages of flesh and blood, with their loves and hatred, their joys and sorrows, their tears and their laughter, living actual lives, and not mere dream lives in the fine domain of Fancyland!

So, may it please the friendly reader, we are not going to abandon Capt. Canolles and the stories of his fortunes. Other adventures remain to be related. All does not end with the explanation of his aversion to esposing the Continental cause, and the attraction exercised over **him by** British gold. The writer even ventures to vaguely intimate that in the **life of** the partisan there was still **a secret—a sentiment** which **he** guarded carefully, **even from his friend** Lord Ferrers, and this **will be set forth now in a few** concluding pages, which will aim also to narrate **some** additional scenes in **which** the chief persons of this drama **were** the actors.

In spite of their long conversation and late sitting up **in** the **hut in** White Oak Swamp, Lord Ferrers and Canolles awoke with the first gleam **of** daylight glimmering through the **tangled** thickets, and went out to **breathe the** morning **air—cool and** fresh from its passage over the surrounding water **and** under the dense **shade** of the intertangled foliage.

There was nothing longer to detain the **old soldier at** the quarters of Canolles, as he was not in **any sense a** prisoner; **and** learning from his guest **that he desired to return at** once to the British **army, camped on the** Chickahominy a few miles distant, **the partisan** left him **to** go **to the bivouac of** the **Rough** Riders and detail an escort.

He **was absent** for an hour nearly, and on his return exhibited unwonted **emotion. He had been** detained by the **necessity of making** arrangements for carrying **out, on** this day, **the resolutions** he had **formed** to terminate his connection **with** the brave fellows **whom he** had so long **commanded.** We shall **not** describe **the scene, or the** emotion of his old companions **at this announcement, which, in** spite of the fact **that all knew** of their captain's determination, filled them with the deepest sorrow.

Canolles retained with difficulty his own self-possession. He repressed his feelings, however; directed a division between the men of his command of all the camp contained, reserving nothing for himself; and, having informed the partisans that he would see them again and issue his last orders to them, tore himself away, with a flush in his cheeks and a moisture in his eyes which they had never before seen.

Old William had prepared breakfast, and Lord Ferrers proved himself as mighty a trencherman as on the night before. Canolles ate nothing, and hearing without the hut the tramp of horses, rose from table.

" There is your escort, my Lord," he said, "awaiting your good pleasure. I ordered ten men to report here under your young aide, Walter Hayfield, and conduct you as a guard of honor to the British picket line."

" And you——"

" I go with you, as a matter of course. Believe me, I should always regret and reproach myself for having lost this hour of your company."

" Devilish fine fellow !" grunted Lord Ferrers half inaudibly, " how can·a man help liking such a brave as this who talks so ?" ·

" You say, my Lord——"

" I say, I am ready."

They buckled on their arms, left the hut, and mounting their horses set out at the head of the roughly clad detachment, which Lord Ferrers had greeted with a curt nod of friendly recognition, for the English pickets.

The ride took place nearly in silence. Each seemed busy with his own thoughts, and a few words only were exchanged. At last they emerged from the swamp, entering upon a tract of open ground, beyond which a long line of lofty trees, festooned with wild honey-suckle and other forest creepers, indicated the course of the sluggish river. To their left, at the edge of a clump of trees, a figure on horseback, motionless in the morning light, was visible.

"There is your vidette, I think, my Lord," said Canolles, "and the picket is near."

"Yes."

"Then we must part here, as it is not my intention to charge your redcoats, and I do not wish them to charge me."

"Yes, we must say good-bye, and I repeat to you, Canolles, that I am devilish sorry to do so—on my honor?"

"And I, my Lord; but you know the adage, 'The best friends must part, as the longest day must end.'"

Lord Ferrers remained motionless, knitting his white mustache and looking at Canolles with a long, lingering regard, in which it was easy to read his emotion. The partisan, too, had fallen, it seemed, into one of his moods of dreamy reverie. Suddenly he aroused himself and said:

"Yes, yes, my Lord! this parting is sorrowful, very sorrowful to myself, since it is more than doubtful whether we shall ever meet again. It is my intention, as I informed you, to disband my troop at once and leave Virginia, which I now regard as virtually freed from occupation by the English forces, since Lord Cornwallis is retiring after declining battle, and is known to intend transferring his army to the North. So I shall have no solicitude as to my good old State, and go with an easy conscience. There are your friends yonder; you have only to wave your handkerchief on the point of your sword, and ride into your lines. Farewell, my Lord; health and happiness attend you."

"Thanks!" said Lord Ferrers, gruffly, "but do you know there is one thing I don't in the least believe, Canolles?"

"What's that, my Lord?"

"That we are not going to meet in future."

"It is improbable."

"I'll lay you a hundred to one we do! At least it depends on you. Come and see me in England. The war, I agree with you, is virtually over, and I'll not be sorry to go home again—not in the least. Come and see me, I say, comrade, at my home in Hertfordshire."

"Such a visit, I need not assure you, would be a happiness to me, but I shall not probably be in England."

"You are going to the Continent?"

"Yes."

"Give up this idea, Canolles, and stay at home at your house of Chatsworth."

"That is no longer my own."

"Marry, I say, and settle down, and abandon this wild project of exiling yourself. Exile is bitter, comrade."

“Bitter enough, I have little doubt—like life. But I do not wish to remain in Virginia. Something banishes me—let me keep my own counsel as to that—and now, my Lord, if you will not say farewell, let it be ‘ to our next meeting.’ ”

“ Good! That’s the way to talk ! ”

And exchanging with Canolles a close grasp of the hand, accompanied by a look which indicated the deepest interest in his companion, Lord Ferrers rode to the English picket, made himself known, and entered the British lines—the partisan returning with his detachment toward his bivouac in the Swamp.

On the way he gave Walter Hayfield, who rode beside him, his last instructions.

“ I shall disband the Rough Riders this evening, Walter,” he said, “ but they are one and all determined to join the regular American forces, and I wish them to become a part of Harry’s command, which they, too, desire. You must, therefore, ride to the American camp and inform Harry that I am about to transfer my troop to him, to have the men at once enrolled.”

“ And you, Captain ?”

“ I ?”

“ You are going ?”

“ Yes, I shall leave Virginia.”

The boy’s head sank.

“ Why not yourself enter the American army in command of your own troop ?”

Canolles slowly shook his head, and the youth seemed to feel that all argument was unavailing.

“ But, Captain !—think,” he faltered, “ you cannot

go off in this way at a moment's notice! You must have arrangements to make—persons to bid farewell, and your passage abroad to secure if you go by sea, as I understand you design."

"As to securing a passage, yes," said Canolles; "as to delaying to bid any one good-bye, no! There is nothing further to detain me, and I shall see no one."

"Not even ——"

Walter hesitated, with flushed cheeks and a sudden moisture in his eyes.

"Even—you would say?"

"Miss Fanny," said Walter; "it would break her heart for you to go without bidding her good-bye."

"Fanny!—break her heart!—your words are idle, Walter!" Canolles exclaimed with sudden emotion.

"Oh, no, Captain, they are not idle. I have told you once before, and tell you once again, that—shall I go on?"

"No," said Canolles in a low tone, "you are dreaming—and if what you say, absurd as it is, had the soundest reason in it, that would only be another obstacle in the way of an interview. No, I shall not see her, or any one. I shall go with old William to the Glen Lodge, where I shall remain for two or three days while making my few arrangements."

"The Glen Lodge? You mean the hunting lodge, near Chatsworth?"

"Yes, the small lodge built by my father for entertaining hunting parties of guests—a secluded spot, you know, sylvan and hidden—where I shall not be discovered by any one. After seeing Harry you will report to me here; if I am not here, then I shall be at the Glen Lodge. You will march the men to Harry's camp at once. That is plain, is it not, dear Walter?"

"Yes, Captain!" the boy murmured with a sob, "only too plain! Oh! why do you go?"

Canolles smiled sadly.

"'It is written,' as the Orientals say," he replied, "and now let us speak no further of this; I am heavy-hearted to-day."

They soon reached the Swamp island, and Walter set out on his mission to Harry Cartaret, to notify him that the troopers would immediately offer themselves for enrollment under the American flag. Canolles then gave his orders to old William, who quietly and in silence collected his master's personal effects, including the silver service brought from Chatsworth, and stowed them in bags on a pack-horse. Then, as the light of evening began to steal over the Swamp, Canolles assembled the men.

This intention, as we have seen, had been announced to them. His blow at Tarleton, he had informed them, would be the last that he would strike. Each and all had promptly assented to his proposal that they should become a part of the command of his brother; and having informed them that Walter would conduct them, after his departure, to the American camp, he went along the line, grasping the hand of every man of the troop in turn.

The scene was picturesque and full of emotion. The long shadows of approaching sunset ran through the Swamp, and the red light fell upon the rude faces of the Rough Riders, many of them bathed in tears, which had a strange look on the bearded cheeks. It was plain that this parting with their beloved leader sent a pang through the hearts of the rough fellows who had fought with him so often. Canolles himself was not exempt from agitation. The faces before him were associated in his memory with scenes of desperate combat, sword to sword, with night marches, forest bivouacs—with perils shared together and martial merriment and rejoicing by the camp fire in the Swamp. Every man was a close personal acquaintance, even a friend—for Canolles had been rather the chief of a hunting party than an officer in command of troops. The parting was thus painful to him, too; and it was not without a tremor in his firm voice that he bade them in a few soldierly words farewell.

The parting was one in which Canolles seemed to feel that he could not trust himself longer, and waving his hand, he mounted his horse, and followed by old William on his pack animal, was soon lost to sight.

As he disappeared the men burst forth into cheers which rang through the Swamp, and must have startled the pickets of the two armies posted near.

It was the farewell of the Rough Riders to their beloved commander.

CHAPTER XXI.

WHAT TOOK PLACE ON THE SAME NIGHT.

When this scene was taking place in the Swamp bivouac, Walter Hayfield was far on his way to the American camp.

Fortune favored him. A detachment of the Virginia Light Horse was stationed at the forks of the road which he approached, and hearing the challenge of the man on post, an officer, who had been lying under a tree fifty paces distant, rose and came forward. Walter recognized Harry Cartaret, who, recognizing the youth in turn, called out to the sentinel to pass him through the picket.

"I thought I knew you, Walter," said the gay young officer, as the youth rode up.

"And I was at first a little doubtful whether you were yourself or not, Lieutenant," was the reply.

"Oh, yes," said Harry, "in this old coat, you mean."

In fact the young man, who usually appeared in a fine full dress uniform, gaily decorated with gold braid, wore on this evening the shabbiest of old undress coats, entirely divested of any insignia of rank, faded, dingy, and covered with dirt. In this equipment the dazzling young Lieutenant Harry Cartaret was almost unrecognizable. He resembled rather a Rough Rider than an American officer, and Walter was struck suddenly by the exact resemblance he bore in dress as in face to Canolles.

Harry beckoned the youth toward the tree where he had been lying down, and said:

"Well, I am rather a shabby-looking fellow to-day, Walter; dress goes for a great deal in this world, I confess, and that is why I am in this old coat."

"Why, Lieutenant?"

"In order to keep my best uniform for fighting and —visiting the fair sex! You see a man ought to dress in his best when he goes into action, so that in case he is captured he will be treated with consideration, and not thrust into a dirty guard-house with the rank and file."

"Right, Lieutenant."

"And need I explain my motive in reserving my braided uniform for that other agreeable occupation—visiting young ladies? If it is well to be in full dress when you go to fight, is it not as rational to wear your very finest coat when you advance upon that other and more dangerous enemy in furbelows and flounces, ready to exterminate you with the flashing artillery of their eyes?"

"I understand, Lieutenant."

"So, to wind up this interesting explanation, Walter, I am here on a mere fatigue duty, looking out for stragglers, and I wear my shabbiest coat—so shabby that I might be taken for a follower of a certain worthy Capt. Canolles! But we have talked enough on this point. Sit down here by me and tell me what brought you?"

Walter threw his bridle over a bough, and taking a seat near Harry, said:

"I came to see you, Lieutenant."

"To see me?"

"Yes, Lieutenant."

Harry Cartaret for the first time observed the deep sadness in the face and voice of his companion, and said, anxiously:

"You came from Hartley? You bring bad news. Tell me what it is!"

"Good and bad news both, Lieutenant. You may think a part, at least, is good news—it is all bad to me. Capt. Canolles has by this time disbanded the Rough Riders, and is going to leave Virginia—never, as he says, to come back."

Walter then described the capture of Lord Ferrers, how he had been released and escorted back to the English lines, and how Canolles had then announced his resolution in the evening to terminate his connection with the partisan troop, who one and all would report to him (Harry Cartaret) for enrollment under the American flag.

At this intelligence the face of the young officer filled with pleasure, and he rose quickly to his feet.

"Thank Heaven!" he exclaimed. "This fighting without a flag has preyed on my spirits day and night! Now there will be no more of it! Hartley will no longer be in danger, if he is captured, of being shot as a marauder, as he nearly was at Petersburg! Thank Heaven that he has come to this resolution, and sends me his brave fellows! Oh! yes, I will enroll them—

they are a magnificent present! They will be a full
company, and I shall be commissioned captain, too!"

"I will bring them here to-night, Lieutenant."

"Oh, no! I will go and see Hartley and receive
them in person! This moment, Walter—this very
moment! There is nothing going on in this quarter;
I can easily leave a subordinate in my place for a few
hours."

As he spoke, Harry Cartaret went quickly to his
horse, which was tied to a bough, rode to where the
men of his detachment were lying beside their horses,
a little in rear, and having given his orders, returned
to Walter, when they both set out at full gallop in the
direction of the island in the Swamp.

On the way the young lieutenant asked a hundred
questions, particularly inquiring in reference to the
intended movements of Canolles after leaving the
Rough Riders. Walter could only inform him that the
partisan had stated his intention of leaving Virginia in
a few days, perhaps in two or three; and that meanwhile he designed taking up his lodging in the small
deserted hunting lodge on the Chatsworth estate.
Harry listened with earnest attention and some sadness
to this account, making no comment until Walter had
finished speaking. He then said:

"Well, the main thing is that this irregular and
dangerous fighting without a flag has come to an end.
As to Hartley's leaving Virginia, we will see about
that. Time enough for me to see him before he takes
ship. The Rough Riders first! How far is it to the
camp, Walter?"

" Less than a mile, Lieutenant.   Here we are at the Swamp."

They penetrated the thicket just as the twilight was deepening into night; but the moon was shining, and they had no difficulty in threading their way through the devious paths, all of which were well known to the young lieutenant's companion.   At last the moat-like circuit of water surrounding the Swamp fastness appeared; they plunged through, and Harry Cartaret, accompanied by Walter, found himself in the midst of the Rough Riders.   They were nearly one and all personally known to him, as they had been recruited in the neighborhood of Chatsworth, and the young man had in old days been a favorite with them from his gay and cordial disposition and his fondness for their own occupation of hunting and fishing.   At his appearance, therefore, they received their future commander with a shout of welcome, and in ten minutes Harry had made them a speech, they had expressed their desire to serve under him, and preparations were made for a prompt march to the American camp.

Harry Cartaret had looked around for Canolles as soon as he reached the island.   He was nowhere to be seen, and he was soon informed that the partisan had left them more than an hour before, going no one knew whither.   Harry rode with Walter to the hut which had been the headquarters of his brother.   It was open, melancholy and deserted.   The moonlight falling through the window lit up the rude table at which Lord Ferrers and Canolles had supped.

" A body without the soul!" muttered the young

man, "but, thank Heaven! Hartley will hide himself here no more!"

Returning to the bivouac they found the partisans ready to march, every man with his sword buckled around his waist and his rude wrappings behind his saddle, and at the word of command they fell into column, and Harry, with Walter beside him, gave the word, " Forward!"

At the word the column began to move slowly, and descended into the water, through which they defiled in a long line—dusky phantoms in the dim moonlight.

Walter had advised that the troop should proceed to the American camp by another and better road than that which he and Harry had followed in coming. This led in a direction somewhat nearer to the British lines than was desirable; but confiding in their perfect knowledge of the locality, and their good broadswords, the Rough Riders moved on without solicitude, and soon emerged from the thicket on a broad flat space covered with broom-sedge, waving now in the gentle night wind.

Suddenly Walter laid his hand on Harry Cartaret's arm, and whispered:

" Hist!——who are those yonder, Lieutenant?"

" Those dark figures coming out of the woods? "

He pointed quickly to a dusky mass moving toward them with muffled hoof strokes.

" Yes," said Walter.

" The enemy!" exclaimed Harry Cartaret. " They are after us!"

And turning to the Rough Riders he shouted:

" Form fours!   Draw broadswords!   Charge?"

A loud voice from the dusky mass was heard giving nearly the same order, and the two columns rushed together—that of the British evidently far outnumbering the body of Rough Riders.

Cartaret crossed swords with the leader of the English, a short, thick-set officer, riding a powerful horse, who, dropping his rein as they came together, drew a pistol and fired almost in Harry Cartaret's face.

The flash lit up like a quick lurid glare the entire person of the young American, and Tarleton—for the leader of the English was that officer—uttered a sudden shout of joy.

" Canolles!" he cried, "I am in luck to-night! I came to hunt you, my dear Captain Canolles! to pay you my respects in return for hunting me! I have you, my good Canolles, my worthy freebooter without a flag! and at sunrise, if I do not kill you, you will swing from the gallows with a hempen cravat around your neck!"

These words were shouted between every clash of the broadswords.   Colonel Tarleton was evidently convinced that Harry Cartaret, in his plain, rough dress, and commanding the Rough Riders, was no less a personage than Canolles.

CHAPTER XXII.

AT GLEN LODGE.

It was the evening succeeding these scenes. The sun was just setting, and his last beams full upon the sylvan building called Glen Lodge, which stood in a picturesque hollow in the hills less than a mile from Chatsworth. This house, as the reader has been informed, had been built by Mr. Henry Cartaret for the convenience of hunting parties and for woodland festivities. Many a youth and maiden had wandered through the grassy grounds, or seated themselves on the rustic chairs beneath the great oaks; and under the roof many an excellent repast—presided over by old William in respectful silence—had been partaken of by the bright beauties and the gay gallants of the years preceding the war; beauties whose golden hair was dashed with silver now from long and cruel anxiety; gallants who had exchanged their lace, embroidery and ruffles for rude home-spun coats, to shoulder the musket or buckle on the broadsword and follow Washington.

The sunset fell lovingly on the little *chalet*—it was scarcely rude—which, lost under overhanging boughs, seemed dreaming still of the merry *fetes champetres* it had looked on in the past. The windows of its three or four small apartments were closed by shutters, with the exception of the main room on the ground floor, opening on the graceful verandah, with its slender, airy-looking pillars — and into this apartment now plunged the last rays of sunset, lighting up the dilapidated furniture, which had never been removed—a table, some chairs, and a wicker work lounge comprising the whole.

The spot was utterly deserted. A little stream ran rippling at the foot of a knoll near by, disturbing with its murmurs the sweet silence of evening. This sound and the " cheef-cheef" of some Swamp sparrows settling to their rest in the foliage, was all that gave life to the quiet scene, which otherwise might have been taken for some painting, full of the charm of rustic silence, loneliness and beauty.

The sun had just descended to the summit of the western woods, and was poised on the verdant fringe like a golden shield, when the loneliness of the scene was dissipated by the appearance of a figure at the extremity of the grounds, coming on slowly toward the sylvan *chalet*.

Fanny—for it was our little heroine—had strolled out from Chatsworth, with no object but to find in solitude an opportunity to indulge undisturbed in reverie; and more by chance than from design had found herself in the vicinity of Glen Lodge, which she was quite familiar with. The spot she supposed to be entirely deserted, as it had been for years, and there were indeed no traces whatever of the presence of any human being. Canolles, who had reached the lodge on the preceding evening, had ridden away to make arrangements for his voyage to Europe; and old

William, his henchman, was either asleep in a small
outbuilding, or had gone to see his friends at houses in
the neighborhood.

The spot was then as lonely and deserted as if Canolles
had never returned to it. Fanny, coming on slowly,
with her fair face drooping toward her bosom, her eyes
half closed, and veiled by the long silken lashes, a wild
flower in her hand and one in her hair, resembled some
fairy genius of the spot, as beneficent and kind as she
was beautiful.

For a long time now Fanny had fallen into low spirits. What was the origin of this depression? Youth
should bring happiness, but Fanny, although young,
was evidently not happy. The roses in her cheeks had
turned to snowdrops, and the mobile lips, though red
still, had about them that downward curve which indi-
cates the presence of some weight upon the heart.
But the beauty of the girl was even more exquisite
than before, and as she entered the small hunting lodge
and stood in the mild light of evening, gazing around
her with dreamy eyes, nothing more fascinating could
be imagined than her face and figure.

Unconsciously, and as though slightly fatigued, she
looked around for a seat, and saw the wicker lounge.
She seated herself, placed her elbow upon the curved
arm, rested her bent head on the palm of the hand,
and closing her eyes gave herself up evidently to
musing.

The beautiful eyes had closed by the will of their
owner; but very soon it was plain that they remained
shut without further exercise of volition. Weary in-

deed from her long walk, and yielding to the languid summer evening, with its drowsy influences, Fanny had fallen gently, or rather glided, into slight slumber, as easily and unconsciously as a dove that folds its wings at twilight.

Light as her sleep was, she did not hear the hoof strokes of a horse on the grass without, or a step on the portico. The step drew nearer, crossed the threshold, resounded on the bare floor—and then Fanny woke with a start. Canolles was standing before her in the light of sunset, looking at her.

His face was sad and quite pale under the bronze produced by sun and wind. His head drooped, and his eyes were fixed upon her with an expression of such melancholy that her own eyes filled with tears.

"You, Fanny!" he said in a low tone; "you here!"

"And you!"—she murmured; "how do I find you at Glen Lodge, Hartley? I thought you were in the Swamp with your Rough Riders."

Canolles shook his head slowly, in the manner habitual with him.

"I have left the Rough Riders. They are disbanded, and my life as a soldier has ended."

"Ended! Oh! how glad I am! And now—now— you are coming home!"

The partisan repeated the movement of his head.

"I am going away. In three days I shall leave Virginia, Fanny."

"Leave Virginia! Why do you leave Virginia, all your friends—your dear old home—all you love, and— those who love you?"

"I must. Let me not speak of it, Fanny. It is sad enough to give up all, but I shall have the consolation of knowing that I leave happiness behind me."

Fanny could not suppress her tears. The accent of the speaker's voice was so unutterably sad that as she listened to it her head drooped, her cheeks were bathed in tears, and her bosom heaved with an agitation which she was plainly unable to control.

"Happiness?" she murmured in a voice, faltering and stopping as it were at every syllable; "happiness? Do you think—that I am happy?"

"Why should you not be?" was the response of Canolles in a voice nearly as low as her own. "You are young, beloved, the war is nearly ended, and—shall I go on?"

She made no reply.

"You are the affianced of one of the noblest young fellows that ever lived—my dear Harry, who loves you with all his heart."

The head bent lower—the pale face grew a little paler.

"He will soon come back to you now," Canolles went on; "you and he will be Lord and Lady of Chatsworth, Fanny"—he attempted to smile—"and will represent the Cartarets in our old home. Is it possible that he did not tell you that we had so arranged our family affairs? We have succeeded in relieving the estate from all debts and incumbrances, and as I am called away, my dear Harry naturally takes my place, and supports the family name—with you to aid him."

19

Still the head drooped lower, the face grew paler.

"You do not speak, Fanny," he went on, "indeed —you seem unwell. Have I said anything to wound you?—to hurt your feelings? I would not do so for all the world. You know that! You know—how much —how much I love you! I am going now. Let us part loving each other; that at least I have the right to ask, as I am leaving you, never, perhaps, to see you again!"

His voice trembled, and his very frame shook. His lips opened, and he was about to speak again, but only a quick exclamation came from them. The slender form of the girl swayed like a lily beaten by the wind, her eyes closed, and she fell forward, fainting, into the arms of Canolles.

*   *   *   *   *   *   *

Half an hour afterward they were seated side by side, and the tears and smiles and blushes of the girl, with the happy light in her companion's eyes, told clearly that the two hearts had spoken.

Suddenly, in a moment, all the old misunderstanding had disappeared. Canolles knew now that Fanny had loved him "long and dearly," and she knew, too, that he had been about to leave Virginia forever in consequence of a hopeless passion for her.

"Then I need not go now!" he said, looking with a proud smile and eyes full of profound tenderness at the beautiful, shy face, "I may stay in Virginia?"

"Oh, yes—why should you not?" she whispered, in her innocent, true voice. "And so you thought that Harry and I were still engaged? But I forgot that you could not have known we only yesterday had an explanation. I discovered long since that I had quite mistaken my feelings, and was very wretched. I was about to write and tell him so, when he came, and I found that he too was not happy—did not wish to marry me; and, do you know why?"

She laughed through her tears—it was the hearty laugh, full of sunshine.

"Because Miss Lucy Maurice had taken my place—my friend whom he met at Petersburg."

Canolles listened with an expression of joy and wonder which made his face radiant.

"Miss Maurice!" he exclaimed, "the young friend you stayed with when you came to save me! Who would have dreamed of such a result, Fanny? Oh, yes! you saved me twice, not once only, by your brave ride! You saved my life and—my love!"

She turned away her head.

"You loved me first! that paper told me everything—how noble you were in giving up all to Harry! —me with the rest, because you thought he loved me! Now I know all—and—and—how could I keep from—"

The sentence ended in a murmur.

*   *   *   *   *   *   *

Thus these two faithful hearts had spoken at last, and all was cleared up. A portion only of the happy colloquy has been here recorded. Such scenes are not for the garish day and the eyes of readers who would perhaps laugh if we were to set down all this man and woman said to each other, agitated, wondering, trembling almost, under the weight of their new and unexpected happiness. It had taken only a little time to explain all—now, not the least shadow of misunderstanding remained—Canolles was not going, he would remain in Virginia, and Fanny would be his own.

*   *   *   *   *   *   *

When they parted in the grounds of Chatsworth, with a long embrace, and Canolles returned to Glen Lodge, a new world seemed to have dawned for them both. Fanny went along with steps almost bounding; the face of the gracious creature was full of child-like joy; and the countenance of Canolles had undergone a transformation even more remarkable. The haunting sorrow of brow and lips had been swept away, as the shadow of a cloud is swept from the landscape by the winds of August; and the partisan went on with a rapid step, his head erect, his cheeks glowing, his whole frame instinct as it were with a new life.

He had just reached and entered Glen Lodge, on which the shadows of night were descending, when his ear caught the swift gallop of a horse.

The gallop drew nearer; a horseman appeared at the edge of the opening in front of the lodge; reached the grass plat, threw himself to the ground, and Canolles recognized Walter Hayfield.

The boy was pale, agitated, and so faint that he tottered as his feet reached the ground.

" Walter!" exclaimed Canolles, " you are ill! You bring bad news! What has happened ?"

" Oh! Captain! Lieut. Harry is captured—by Tarleton—who swears he is no other than yourself, Captain Canolles! He will hear no denial—he was tried by drum-head court-martial to-day, and condemned to death as a marauder, fighting without a flag! I escaped—they shot me in the arm, you see, as I got off—but it is nothing!"

Canolles had listened without a word, but his face had grown extremely pale.

"He is condemned, you say?" came now in low tones from his lips.

"To be shot at sunrise."

"Where is Tarleton's camp?"

"Near Spencer's Ordinary, below the Chickahominy."

"At sunrise, did you say?"

"Yes, Captain."

Canolles went into the house and buckled on the belt containing his broadsword. Then he slowly unbuckled it again, and laid down the weapon. Then he went to where his horse was still standing and mounted.

"You will remain here," he said, in his old brief accent of command. "William will see to your wound. I can find Tarleton's camp. There is time between this and sunrise."

CHAPTER XXIII.

TEN MINUTES BEFORE SUNRISE.

The first red flush of sunrise had begun to appear on the fringe of pine hemming in a glade near Spencer's Ordinary, below the Chickahominy, where the cavalry of Col. Tarleton were encamped.

The camp was already astir. The British and American forces were dangerously near to each other—the former having rapidly retreated to this locality, and the latter having as rapidly followed. They were now face to face, though separated from each other by an intervening body of woods which concealed both commands; and under these circumstances Col. Banastre Tarleton, who was an excellent cavalry commander, was all eyes and ears, and had his men ready to mount at a moment's notice.

There was evidently, however, an additional source of interest, not to say excitement, in the camp. In front of Tarleton's tent a file of men were drawn up, each grasping his carbine, and two or three staff officers were standing at the opening of the tent, looking at and listening apparently to something which was going on there.

The scene which absorbed their attention was a singular one. Lolling on a camp couch, and moving his spurred boot backward and forward so that at each movement the rowel tore a fresh hole in the cavalry blanket spread on the couch, Col. Tarleton, swarthy, thick-set, stern and forbidding, was looking with ill-dissembled anger at another person standing erect before him.

This person was Harry Cartaret, who after a desperate resistance, had been overpowered and captured in the fight near White Oak Swamp, together with a few of his men. The result of this capture we have heard stated by Walter Hayfield. Deceived by the remarkable likeness of the young man to Canolles, by his fatigue uniform without insignia, and by the fact that he was in command of the Rough Riders, Tarleton had remained obstinately convinced that he had captured the veritable Canolles, his personal foe, who had struck him so heavily near Chatsworth ; and in spite of the young man's statement that he was not Canolles, but Lieutenant Cartaret, of the American army, had hastily tried him, the improvised Court had found him guilty of marauding without a flag, and he had been condemned to be shot at sunrise on this morning.

Harry Cartaret's attitude was erect, calm and proud. There was no trace of apprehension at his approaching fate in eye or lip. The constitutional courage of the Cartarets evidently defied the idea of death to shake it, and the brief colloquy which now ensued clearly indicated that the young American did not mean to plead for his life.

"You requested to see me ?" said Tarleton, curtly.

"Yes," said Cartaret.

"Well, I have little time to give to interviews; the enemy are within half a mile."

"What I have to say will not consume ten minutes," was the calm reply of the young officer, "an amount of time which I presume may be allowed a man who is about to be shot, sir."

"Yes, I allow you ten minutes."

He took out his timepiece and looked at it.

"You are entitled to as much as that," he added, grimly, "as it is just ten minutes to sunrise."

"When I am to be shot. Well, sir, so be it. A soldier ought not to shrink before bullets for the pain of death they inflict—he takes that risk on the field and everywhere; and you may see I do not myself shrink."

"You do not—you are brave enough. That is not where your fault lies. It lies in fighting for money, and robbing—"

"Not in attacking and defeating Col. Tarleton, since I am Capt. Canolles, you say."

At the slight disdain of the young man's tone Tarleton's brow darkened more than ever.

"You are in a position which gives you the right to say what you please," he said; "I cannot bandy words with a man who will be dead in an hour."

"In ten minutes, probably, or less," was the calm reply, "and I have no desire to bandy words. I have assured you that I am not Capt. Canolles, and you do not believe me. You assemble a drum-head court, which goes through the form of a trial, and condemns me well-nigh without a hearing. I am to be shot, though I am Lieutenant Henry Cartaret, of the American cavalry. Well, sir, nothing is left me but to bear my fate like a soldier, leaving you to discover some day, and I trust, sir, to lament my fate—my murder you will then call it. I requested this interview not to beg for my life, but to ask what I have the right to ask, even if I were a marauder, as you style me."

"What? I decline further discussion of the question of identity. No sane human being can doubt that you are Capt. Canolles. Every man in the troop you attacked near Chatsworth swears to your identity. When captured you were in command of your Rough Riders. You deny your own identity, but the thing is absurd. Your career has been such that it is necessary to make an example of you, as Gen. Phillips attempted to do at Petersburg, from which you escaped. You were fairly tried, you are justly condemned. The time has passed to discuss that further. What is your request?"

"That you will sent into the American lines these letters."

The young officer took from his breast two letters, both unsealed.

"For whom are these letters?" said Tarleton.

"One is addressed to a young lady who at the present time is on a visit to Miss Talbot, of Chatsworth. If I am not mistaken, you have seen her."

"I have seen the ladies at the place you mention, and remember that one of them exhibited very little breeding."

"Is it possible? They belong to what people sometimes laugh at us for calling our Virginia aristocracy, and I had supposed that even Col. Tarleton would not mistake their position in society."

"I said nothing about their position in society," was the gruff reply of the English officer. "I said that I was treated discourteously. But we are losing time. If your letters are unsealed I will send them. To whom is the second?"

"To Capt. Canolles."

"To Canolles!"

"Yes."

"This is a farce, sir," said Tarleton, frowning, "and you show singular bad taste in spending your last moments of life in enacting a comedy, since you yourself are Canolles!"

"So be it; but you have promised to forward my letter, which you may see is directed to 'Capt. Canolles, Glen Lodge, near Chatsworth.'"

"I will read both and send them."

"You will not forego the reading, then—even that to Miss Maurice? I confess I should like to have that remain unread."

"Impossible. War is a risky business, sir. A sealed letter might give the enemy a full diagram of the English position and amount of force."

Cartaret sighed.

"I must yield, then—and I prefer to have the letter sent open than not sent at all."

He laid both on the table, and added:

"I am now at your service, sir. I have already said my prayers, and I am ready."

Tarleton looked with a singular expression at Cartaret.

"You have given me reason to personally hate you,"

he said, with a keen flash of the eye, "since you have twice surprised me, and the last time defeated me in open fight; but you are a brave man and I am glad the court did not condemn you to be hanged as a spy."

Tarleton rose and called the officer of the guard.

"The prisoner Canolles will be taken," he said "to the place assigned, bandaged, and shot."

A stir was visible in the group without.

"A moment!" said a voice at the opening of the tent.

"Who is that?" said Tarleton.

"Captain Canolles," was the reply.

And the partisan came into the tent.

CHAPTER XXIV.

THE BROTHERS.

The first rays of sunrise fell upon the figure of Canolles, standing unarmed and perfectly quiet in the opening of the tent. Tarleton, looking at him, gave an unmistakable start. The extraordinary resemblance which the partisan bore to Cartaret evidently aroused in him the greatest astonishment.

"Canolles!" he exclaimed; "so I was about to shoot the wrong person."

"Yes," said Canolles, calmly; "and I will do you the justice, sir, to say that I think you would have regretted it. You have the reputation of cruelty and an unscrupulous mode of warfare, but it is hard to regard an English officer and gentleman as a cold-blooded barbarian."

"You are right, sir," said Tarleton, scarcely recovered from his astonishment; "so you are the real Capt. Canolles? May I ask how you came to be here?"

"I came to save the life of my brother, who was about to be shot from his likeness to myself."

"Your brother?"

"Yes; this gentleman is my brother, Lieutenant Henry Cartaret, of the American army."

"And you—"

"Capt. Canolles, at your service," was the calm reply.

The appearance, expression, attitude of the partisan were all perfectly cool and composed. Natures like that of the man whom we have essayed to delineate under the name of Canolles have this predominant trait—that when impelled by the dictates of feeling or duty to adopt any course, however perilous—nay, fatal—they banish, from that moment, all nervous emotion, face the fate before them calmly, and die, if they are forced to die, like brave men.

Tarleton looked for some moments fixedly at the speaker; then he said:

"How happens it that you are here? Were you captured?"

"I was not. I surrendered myself. I had information of the capture of my brother, of his trial and the fate before him, owing to his resemblance to myself, and I came to take his place. Is that so astonishing, sir? I do not know how it is in your country, but in Virginia we keep our faith of gentlemen, and do not allow innocent blood to be shed when it is our own that is forfeited—certainly not the blood of a brother."

"You are right, sir," was Tarleton's reply, with a flash of the eye at Canolles not devoid of stern admiration; "you are a soldier and a brave man."

He turned to an officer and said:

"The execution is suspended. March the men to quarters and keep Lieut. Cartaret under guard. You will then summon a court to examine into the case of Capt. Canolles."

Harry Cartaret was standing near the opening of the tent, trembling from head to foot. All the coolness with which he had faced impending death had deserted him. His face was pale, his eyes swollen by tears, and his breath came in gasps. As the order was given that he should be conducted away, he suddenly turned as though under a passionate impulse, and threw his arms around Canolles."

" Oh ! brother ! brother ! why did you come here?" he cried; " why not let them shoot me ?—I am worth nothing !—and you are the head of the house !"

He sobbed like a child, burying his face in the breast of Canolles. The partisan seemed to share his emotion ; when he spoke, his voice was brief and husky.

" I came because I bear the name you bear, Harry, and because it is my blood, not yours, that these people want; and I do not wish my brother to die for me ?"

He held the young man close in his arms, and, bending down, placed his lips as tenderly as a father might have done, on his brother's forehead. A moment afterward Harry Cartaret, shaking from head to foot, and uttering sobs, was conducted away.

" Now for our business, Colonel," said Canolles to Tarleton.

CHAPTER XXV.

THE SENTENCE.

Col. Tarleton, leaning back upon his camp couch, looked at Canolles with the same expression of stern admiration. Compelled by the exigencies of our narrative to exhibit only the harsher traits of this well-known personage, we have not dwelt upon certain phases of his character redeeming it from entire condemnation. Col. Banastre Tarleton, who had proved himself the scourge of the Carolinas, burning and laying waste the whole land, was popular at his home in England, a gentleman by birth and breeding, if curt and brusque in manners, and had a soldier's admiration for, and sympathy with, the cool courage which faces death unmoved. Looking now, as we have said, at the calm figure of the partisan, this sympathy was obvious in the expression of his countenance, and he said slowly:

"So you have come to die in place of your brother?"

"Yes," said Canolles.

"I repeat that your act is that of a brave man; that you were a true soldier I knew—for I have felt the weight of your hand. You followed me step by step, did you not, before that fight near the Chatsworth House?"

"Yes."

"The thing was excellently managed, sir. Pity that

a genius for war such as you possess should not have a fair field, and that you persist in this discreditable—excuse the word—I will say injudicious habit of fighting without a flag or commission."

"I have both."

"Ah! Exhibit them!" said Tarleton, starting up. "You have a flag—a commission! Glad of it—I ask nothing better than to have some warrant for not treating you as a common freebooter, as you are aware under other circumstances I must."

"Yes, sir."

"Your commission first."

Canolles drew from his breast the commission sent to him by Gov. Nelson. As Tarleton unfolded it, a small silken flag on which was painted the Virginian coat of arms—a virgin trampling upon a tyrant—fell from it.

"You have there my commission and my flag," Canolles said coolly. Tarleton ran his eye over the commission, let the hand holding it fall at his side, and looked for some moments with knit brow upon the ground.

"I am afraid," he at length said, "this paper will avail you nothing with the Court who will examine your case. The question is a nice one, doubtless, but the letter of military law is against you, since the offenses you are charged with were committed prior to the date of this commission—even conceding that it be a valid commission."

"I am aware that I have little or nothing to expect from it," returned Canolles, "and only exhibited it at your request."

He took the paper from Tarleton, picked up the flag, and returned both to his breast.

"I will die with these on my person," he said.

Again Tarleton knit his brows.

"I swear I regret this whole business," he said, "and if I had known you were the man you are, I would never have attacked you with a view to your capture. Even now—but the wish is idle! The Court is summoned—there is my officer of the day coming, paper in hand, to report that they are assembled."

Canolles inclined his head, making no reply.

Tarleton was correct in his supposition. An officer entered and reported that the Court to examine into the case of Capt. Canolles was waiting.

Tarleton rose and said with the same expression of stern sympathy on his swarthy face:

"Make your defense as able as possible. I leave all to the Court."

Canolles made the same movement of the head, and said calmly:

"I shall do so. To be frank, I have a desire to live at present."

He was then conducted from the tent under guard.

* * * * * * *

Two hours afterward Col. Tarleton, who seemed to be laboring under unwonted emotion, and sat with his brows knit and his eyes fixed upon the ground, was aroused from his moody abstraction by the entrance of the officer of the day.

"The finding of the Court in the case of Capt. Canolles, Colonel," said the officer.

20

Tarleton snatched the paper so abruptly from the officer's hand that he nearly tore it asunder. It contained these words:

"The Court assembled to examine into the charges against Capt. Canolles find as follows: That Capt. Canolles having made war on his Majesty without warrant or commission, except a paper of recent date, purporting to be signed by a Mr. Nelson, calling himself Governor of Virginia; and the said Capt. Canolles having been shown to have robbed the convoys of his Majesty in the night time without a flag, the Court is unanimously of the opinion that he ought to suffer death."

Tarleton allowed his hand to fall.

"Fools!" he muttered; "the man is a soldier, and made war like a soldier, for his birthplace!"

CHAPTER XXVI.

THE END OF ALL.

Tarleton had scarcely uttered these words when the long roll of cannon was heard near at hand, and he started to his feet, dropping the paper, upon which, either by accident or intention, he placed his heel, grinding it into the earth.

"Sound the bugle to horse!" he shouted.

And rushing from the tent he threw himself on horseback, nearly overturning as he did so the orderly who held the animal by the bridle.

"To horse! to horse!" he shouted, passing at a furious gallop through the camp; and at the same moment the ringing bugles sounded the same order.

Tarleton did not wait for his men, who were seen on all sides running to their horses. He went at the same headlong gallop in the direction of the ominous roll of the cannon. As he passed a tent larger than the rest, apparently a guard tent, he saw Canolles and Harry Cartaret in the midst of a group of officers at the opening. Passing like some warlike meteor, Tarleton had only time to salute Canolles and send these words behind him:

"Who knows? We may cross swords yet, Captain!"

And to the Court:

"Suspend action in this case till further orders!"

As he spoke, a cannon shot, skimming the low foliage surrounding the camp, struck the tent pole fair and square, hurled it to the ground, and passing on disemboweled a horse which one of the cavalrymen had just mounted. Man and horse were overthrown, and when two additional shots whizzed through the camp the greatest confusion ensued. On all sides the men hastened to fall into line, and still nearer and nearer came that ominous roar, with which suddenly mingled now the sharp rattle of musketry and the round of ringing cheers.

*　　*　　*　　*　　*　　*

The battle of Spencer's Ordinary was one of those combats which decide absolutely nothing, but are full of the glare and glory of war.

Following Cornwallis step by step as he retreated toward the Chesapeake, Lafayette, now reinforced by "Mad Anthony" Wayne and Baron Steuben, had come up with the English commander just as he was retiring from Portsmouth.

The brief and hot engagement at Spencer's Ordinary ensued, and nothing but the impetuous courage, almost the audacity, of Wayne saved the Americans from the consequences of an attack planned by the enemy, so to say, and meant by them to result in Lafayette's destruction.

Lord Cornwallis had taken up a strong position, covered by a morass in front and on his flanks, through which a narrow causeway was the only means of passage. Then, throwing into the way of the Americans a dragoon and a negro, who were to pretend they were deserters, and give the requisite false information, the English commander waited.

The design had full success. Lafayette believed that his opponent's main force had crossed the James River, leaving behind a detachment only; and this detachment Wayne was ordered, with eight hundred men and three cannon, to attack.

The reader has made the personal acquaintance of this gay and headlong Pennsylvanian with the mercurial mirth of a boy and the nerve of a veteran. "Mad Anthony" moved at the word, Lafayette followed across the causeway of the morass, and suddenly the long thunder of artillery began—that thunder which had aroused Tarleton in his tent on the British left.

Lafayette had meant to crush the enemy, amounting, as he supposed, to a detachment only. He soon found that their entire army was in his front, and that retreat or destruction were the alternatives before him. The whole British army rose suddenly from the waters of the morass, as it were, and at a glance "Mad Anthony" saw the trap. To retreat was the only hope; but to retreat he must attack first, and he threw his eight hundred men with impetuous courage on the English front.

The very audacity of the charge imposed upon the enemy. They moved with caution, thinking the force before them large. This gave time for the withdrawal of the troops. They retired rapidly across the morass, abandoning their guns, and Lord Cornwallis, thinking the retreat a feint to draw him into an ambush, halted.

Thus ended the battle, the British army soon continuing to retreat. It only connects itself with the fortunes of our personages from the fact that both

Canolles and Harry Cartaret made their escape during the confusion.

This escape had been effected with far more ease than might have been supposed possible. The two prisoners were mounted on spare horses to move with the cavalry, as the camp was instantly broken up; and watching their opportunity, they broke away from their guards, dashed into the morass pursued by shots, and reached the American lines just as they were retiring.

Getting a superb horse in front of his line, drawn up to cover the retreat of Wayne, the young Marquis Lafayette, wearing his brilliant Major-General's uniform, with the decoration on the breast, awaited with glowing face the expected counter attack of the British.

Wayne's war-thinned battalions slowly fell back, emerging from the morass, and their commander galloped up to Lafayette.

"A real trap, my dear General!" cried the gay and impetuous Pennsylvanian, saluting gallantly with his broadsword, and laughing as he spoke.

"A *guet-a-pens*, indeed, my dear *M. L'Insense!*—my brave Mad Anthony! But you emerge—you were not caught! And listen to this—they are not about to attack. You make them afraid."

"Yes! There is one thing only I regret—the loss of my guns! Give me the order and I'll go back and recapture them!"

"No, I will not do that! You would not retake them—shall I tell you what you would do, *mon ami?*"

"Tell me."

"You would die at the head of your column, as you wished to do at Stony Point."

And with these words, which sent a thrill of soldierly joy through the heart of Wayne, Lafayette wheeled his horse, when suddenly he found himself face to face with Cartaret and Canolles.

"You!" he exclaimed. "You, my brave Cartaret —escaped and safe!"

"Myself, General," replied the young officer, "and this is my brother, whom you know as Capt. Canolles."

"Canolles!" exclaimed Lafayette, spurring forward and grasping the hand of the partisan. "The brave of braves! the hard rider and fighter of the Swamps!"

"At your service, General," was the partisan's reply.

"*Au! mon cher.Capitaine,* my brave Cartaret has told me of you—it was not so necessary. It goes without saying I knew you were *un brave!*"

And raising his plumed hat with all the grace of his nation, the Marquis Lafayette saluted Canolles before the eyes of the whole army.

EPILOGUE.

Need we lengthen out our chronicle? You can see, can you not, good reader, that everybody was married; that the war brought peace and happiness, and the land reposed—that repose came to the hearts and lives, too, of our personages tried by so many strange vicissitudes?

A few words only are necessary in terminating our narrative.

Miss Lucy Maurice was married to Lieut. Harry Cartaret, and Miss Eleanor Talbot, soon after the war, to Lieut. Tom Ferrers. It is, we trust, unnecessary to add that Miss Fanny Talbot espoused a certain Capt. Canolles, ex-bandit and marauder.

The partisan, now the most peaceful of citizens, refused to take back Chatsworth from his dear Harry, declaring that the management of so large an estate would prove a weariness to him; and he and Fanny went to live at the little *chalet* of Glen Lodge, where they were regularly visited by Walter Hayfield and his young wife.

And one day in the month of April, 1782, there appeared at the gate of the sylvan lodge a familiar face— a tall, white-mustached individual, accompanied by a French nobleman and servants, on a tour to the mountains.

"Who lives here?" the white mustache demanded in a gruff voice, from his post on horseback. Then as he saw a figure appear at the door of the woodland lodge, he burst forth into laughter, profanity and delight.

That night, Lord Ferrers, the Marquis de Chastellux and Canolles sat up late. The long hours passed like moments, and Lord Ferrers seemed to revel in gay recollections.

"What was better than all, Canolles, was that night in the Swamp!" he exclaimed. "What wine! what wit—and to think that I have just been supping again with you, old boy!"

He raised his glass.

"Do you remember a toast I drank that night in the Swamp?"

"Tell me what it was, my dear Colonel," said his host, laughing.

"It is useless to tell you, as I mean to drink it again!"

And, with glass raised high above his head, and ruddy, martial, beaming face, the brave old *militaire* exclaimed:

"A health to the robber and marauder of the Swamp —CANOLLES!"